"You've got the wrong man," Hagen told him. He pushed the offending hand away and wiped his own on his jeans. "My name is Charlie, Charlie Hagen. If I happen to look like someone you know, there isn't a hell of a lot I can do about that."

Frowning, Farrel shook his head. "Bill . . . Bill." He repeated the name softly. "If you're still concerned about that business over in Bisbee, put it out of your mind. It's all done with. Forgotten." He grinned. "So there's no need to be calling yourself by any other name."

"I'm not your damned friend," Hagen said in a low, hard voice. "So just leave me to drink in peace."

Farrel's face was mottled with dark color. "Think you're too good for me now," he said. "Don't want to remember who your real friends are." He lurched forward, his thin fingers closing around Hagen's arm again.

"Damn it. I told you to keep away." He shoved Farrel, who went staggering back, while Hagen, in a single, smooth motion, swept the Colt from its holster, raised it, aimed and . . .

NEW FRONTIERS
VOLUME I

Edited by Martin H. Greenberg & Bill Pronzini

TOR

A TOM DOHERTY ASSOCIATES BOOK
NEW YORK

NEW FRONTIERS I

Copyright © 1990 by Bill Pronzini and Martin H. Greenberg

A Tor Book
Published by Tom Doherty Associates, Inc.
49 West 24th Street
New York, N.Y. 10010

Cover art by Company

ISBN: 0-812-58329-9   Can. ISBN: 0-812-58330-2

First edition: January 1990

Printed in the United States of America

0 9 8 7 6 5 4 3 2 1

Acknowledgments

Table of Contents

BILLY THE KID: DOG KILLER,
by Arthur Winfield Knight

Arthur Winfield Knight is an acclaimed poet and playwright whose work deals with many different subjects and eras, including prominent Western historical figures. He has authored two plays about the Old West: Blue Earth, *about Jim and Cole Younger; and* Burning Daylight, *about Jesse James's relationship with his sister. A collection of his Western poems,* Wanted, *was published by Trout Creek Press in 1988.*

• BILLY THE KID: DOG KILLER •
by Arthur Winfield Knight

Killing men is easy
because most people
deserve what they get.
Animals are different,
though. Innocent.

When I was working
at the Rio Feliz Ranch
I had a collie.
Lady was the only dog
I ever had.
More than a dog, a friend.
Lady. Lady Luck.

One night she came home
with blood on her jowls.
She'd gone bad,
killing chickens,
the way some people say
I have. Mr. Tunstall asked
what I was going to do
and I said,
"I'll take care of it."

When I called Lady
she must have known
her luck had run out
because she slunk
under the porch.
All I could see was her eyes
staring at me
from the darkness, ·
and I thought
I could hear her whining.

I stuck the muzzle of my .45
into her face,
but I didn't look at her
when I pulled the trigger.
(I never look away
when I kill a man.)
Mr. Tunstall told me
it was the right thing to do
and I said, "Sure, sure,"
walking away.

I never cried
when I gunned a man down.

LITTLE PHIL AND THE DAUGHTER OF JOY,
by John Lee Gray

John Lee Gray is a pseudonym of a long-time writer of Western fiction. In recent years he has authored a succession of meticulously researched best-sellers dealing with American history, including a Civil War trilogy. "Little Phil and the Daughter of Joy" is his first Western short story in many years—a delightfully wry and good-humored tale of a "soiled dove" named Jimmy, her determined plan to do away with Major General Philip Sheridan, and the heroic efforts of cavalry scout Rolf Greencastle to deter her.

• LITTLE PHIL AND
THE DAUGHTER OF JOY •
by John Lee Gray

"Whoa, that's new," Rolf Greencastle said. He couldn't help sounding alarmed.

"Yes, it is," Jimmy said. She slid an old cloth along the short squat barrel of the .44-caliber Deringer she'd taken from the drawer of her writing desk. It was an old piece. Rolf always thought of it as the Gold Rush gun because his talkative uncle Wallace, one of the failed argonauts, had often mentioned the large number of .44 Deringers carried by men in the diggings. It was an outmoded weapon, but a murderous one.

Spring sunshine through the lace curtains ignited a little white fire at one spot on the metal. Jimmy rubbed and rubbed at the barrel, though it was spotless. Sunshine falling on her flexing wrist illuminated the white scars there. Rolf was silent and a little bug-eyed over the unexpected sight of the piece.

He considered the awkwardness of another remark. Her three-word reply had shut the door on easy continuation of the conversation. After several moments of combing his fingers through his shoulder-length hair, he decided that this was serious enough for him to bull right ahead:

"What is it?"

Jimmy gazed at him with those wide eyes that reminded him of a beautiful gray he'd ridden as a boy in Ohio. Jimmy's eyes were her beautiful feature; she was otherwise a plain young woman, with wrinkles already laid into her face by the ferocious Kansas weather and no doubt by her trade, which required her to deal with all sorts of rough types, from customers to her pimp (she had none at the moment). He had known her a little more than a year, both socially and in the biblical sense, and in that time he'd learned that she had a history of violent behavior, sometimes directed against herself.

"Why, it's a genuine Henry Deringer. I bought it in Dodge last Saturday."

"I mean what's it for, Jimmy? Is somebody bothering you or making threats?"

"Why no, I'm going to use it when General Phil Sheridan arrives next month to inspect the fort. I'm going to kill him with it."

Rolf Greencastle almost fell off his chair in the process of removing his bare feet from the edge of her table. He crashed them down on top of his fancy boots with the pointed toes and mule ears; Rolf was of the opinion that a cavalry scout had to project a special aura—one so strong and awe-inspiring that the officers who signed his pay authorization would think he knew exactly what he was doing even when he didn't.

"I beg your pardon?"

"You heard me," Jimmy said. She kept her eyes on him. It was a disconcerting habit. She kept them open even when she was bare naked on her back, taking care of him.

"That's a pretty damn strange thing to admit to me or anybody, Jemima Taylor."

"I wish you wouldn't use that name. My daddy gave it to me and it's the only thing he ever did that I hate."

"Let's get back to the subject of Little Phil Sheridan. I believe you said you figure on killing him."

"I do." Jimmy saw he wanted further explanation. She shrugged. "Once a Virginian, always a Virginian."

"What does that mean?"

"That foul-talking Yankee rooster and his murdering hordes of mounted shopkeepers and factory hands just completely tore up my daddy's farm in Shenandoah County in September of eighteen and sixty-four."

"You never told me that."

"Hadn't any occasion," she answered with another shrug. She polished some more.

"Jimmy, come on. What's the rest?"

"Simple enough. The day after Sheridan's brutes drove General Jubal Early off Fisher's Hill and sent him scooting down around Masanutten Mountain to hide and lick his wounds, the Yankees came south along the Valley Turnpike, where my daddy's farm was situated. They were chasing stragglers but they ripped up everything belonging to the local people. They trampled our vegetables and torched our fruit trees . . ." She closed her eyes briefly. Her voice grew much quieter. "Just terrible." A moment passed. "Next thing, Phil Sheridan himself showed up, with a lot of his officers. My daddy was mad and het up and he took a shot at Sheridan. Sheridan's men wrestled him down and carried him off and beat him. Then they sent him to prison in Detroit, Michigan. As if he was an enemy soldier. He was sixty-two years old! It ruined his health and gave him the glooms. Same ones that devil me sometimes. But his never left, and they ground him away to nothing. He died two years after they let him out."

"You saw your pa fire off a round at Phil Sheridan?"

Her eyes drifted to the windblown lace. A bugle pealed somewhere on the prairie. Out past the fence that neatly circumscribed her little house, called the Overton Place after a former owner, a troop of shiny-brown Negro cavalrymen cantered by.

"No, I never laid eyes on the little fiend. I was in the smokehouse with some of his men who ripped my dress and—took liberties."

Rolf Greencastle whistled. All of a sudden he was chilly in the spring air. He'd had a perfectly fine time with Jimmy, as per usual when he paid his weekly visit, but this new twist was disturbing; terrifying. Rolf reached for his fringed deerhide shirt. He pulled it on and smoothed it, then reached beneath to free the necklace of big bear claws he never removed. Rolf was a tall, skinny young man with eight knife and bullet scars at various points on his body.

"You absolutely sure it was Little Phil?"

"Yes, it was him. People described him later. Black horse . . . that funny flat black hat he always wore. It was him, and I'm going to kill him."

"Jimmy, I don't think I'm making myself too clear. Don't you see that what you said is pretty—well—unusual? You don't just go tell somebody that you're going to do a murder."

She didn't say a word; apparently she didn't agree.

"Why did you do that, Jimmy?"

She was tight-lipped and silent a while. Then it kind of erupted in a burst. "Because you're my friend. You're not just a customer. After I kill General Sheridan they're going to lock me up—hang me, probably. I'm going to need a friend to straighten things out. Sell this house and send the money to my sisters in Front Royal."

"Well, I appreciate your confidence," Rolf admitted, touched by her unexpected words. "What I'd rather do, though, is talk you out of it."

"You can't. Sheridan's villains raped and pillaged the whole Shenandoah, and they wrecked my daddy's health by throwing him in that Yankee prison, and a Virginian never forgets."

"I think I ought to remind you that the war's been over for three years now."

"Not mine, Mr. Greencastle. Mine isn't over by a damn sight. One more battle to go."

And she snapped the cloth so that it popped. Then she wrapped it around the .44-caliber Deringer. He tried to undermine her determination with scorn:

"If you're going to kill Sheridan, you bought the wrong gun. That little toy only gives you one shot."

She slid out the drawer. "That's why I bought a pair." The drawer clicked shut, hiding both Deringers.

She rose and smoothed her old black bombazine skirt. Rolf Greencastle fleetingly wished that he was just a customer again, not a friend, and didn't have to concern himself with Jimmy's mad pronouncement. Which he knew wasn't so mad. She was a determined thing. Whores had to be to survive.

"You'll have to excuse me, Rolf. Lieutenant Peebles is due any minute."

"All right, but I wish you'd think it over." In the door he turned back to gaze at her in a pleading fashion. "Please."

She gave a little shake of her head.

"Once a Virginian, always a Virginian."

Rolf Greencastle put on his cream-colored Texas hat with its decorative star and red band and left. If General Phil Sheridan did arrive at Fort Dodge as part of his scheduled inspection of the Arkansas River posts now under his command, he was certainly a dead man unless the scout did something about it. But what?

Rolf lay in his bunk in his underwear with a copy of the *Police Gazette* in front of his nose. One of those inscrutable turns of fate seemingly designed to torment a man had brought this tattered copy of the paper into the barber shop in Dodge where he went for a semimonthly trim of his luxuriant hair and mustachios. Who should be pictured in an heroic pose on the front page? None other than Jimmy's announced victim.

It was four days after his visit to the Overton Place, which Jimmy's husband and pimp, Nimrod Taylor, had bought and occupied for about three years before he up and disappeared. Jimmy once explained with a sad, resigned look that Nimrod had warned her on their wedding day that he was a restless man. He was also something else, because that day Jimmy had a large yellowing bruise around her left eye. She refused to talk about it. After Nimrod Taylor left, he never came back. At least Jimmy got the Overton Place.

In the bunk, Major General Philip Sheridan stared at Rolf from within the engraving as if he were infuriated with the scout. The man had a reputation for a temper, and for peppering almost every sentence he spoke with some kind of obscenity, plain or invented. To Rolf, the new commander of the Department of the Missouri looked like an Irish bartender from New York City (Rolf had never seen any of that species, but he had a fair imagination). With his fierce black eyes and squat, bull-like build, and the somehow sinister soap-lock hanging down in the center of his forehead, Phil Sheridan looked like one hard son of a bitch. Rolf Greencastle had seen a few other pictures of the general, and none was any friendlier.

He tossed the paper aside, hiding the face. "She'll never do it," he said.

Then he considered what he knew about Jimmy.

Suppose she really did murder Phil Sheridan; did she have much to lose thereby? No. Mrs. Jemima Sturdevant Taylor had apparently lived a pretty wretched life till now. She'd inherited the same dark moods, the glooms, that she said contributed to her father's death. Officers on the post had informed Rolf that on at least two occasions after her husband left, Jimmy had tried to commit suicide. Those scars on her left wrist were the evidence. When she was up, she was bright as a sunbeam, but at other times, there was no telling what dark, tormented thoughts roiled around in the depths of her soul.

In Dodge they said she had once grabbed a kitchen knife and mortally injured a teamster who had asked for more than he'd paid for and then began to abuse her when she refused. Evidently she thought a wife had to suffer beatings, but not an independent working girl. According to the story, the teamster was not well liked; he died and Jimmy was released after one night in jail and no more was said.

The image of a gleaming knife sliding into some hairy back, with a consequent gout of blood, caused Rolf to cover his eyes there in the bunk, and change his tune.

"She'll do it."

He fidgeted for half an hour, trying to think of some scheme to forestall the assassination. He was not a bright fellow, and he knew it, so he didn't have much confidence in the scheme he finally concocted. But he could come up with no other right then. He found a tack and slipped it in the pocket of his buckskin coat, together with the engraving of Sheridan ripped from the *Gazette*.

He saddled Kid, his swift-running little piebald, and set out from his cabin at the edge of town to ride the five miles along the Arkansas to the fort. It was a mean, gusty late-winter day, but you could smell April primping just around the corner. General Sheridan was scheduled to arrive at Fort Dodge the first week in April.

On the post, he nonchalantly tied Kid outside the adobe barracks that housed B Troop, waited until no one was paying attention, then stole inside. Luckily the dayroom was empty. He tacked Sheridan's picture to the notice board, slipped his sheath knife from under his jacket and proceeded to stab holes all over Little Phil's face.

"To what do I owe the pleasure of this visit?" asked Captain Tipton.

"Oh, I was just in the neighborhood," Rolf said.

Captain Tipton's face proclaimed his skepticism. "I never knew you to be so social, Rolf." The captain, whose behind-the-back nickname was Moon Face, was a pale, pudgy young man with a flaxen mustache and small oval spectacles. He'd once been a professor of geography at a young ladies' academy in Kentucky, a land of divided loyalties during the war. Rolf didn't know which flag Moon Face Tipton had followed, and Moon Face didn't say. That he was wearing Army blue meant nothing.

"Well, the fact is, Captain, I'm worried about this here visit of Phil Sheridan's next month."

"It's just a routine inspection of all the posts in the department. Hancock before him made the same tour. Every new commander does it."

"Yes, but it might be dangerous for him to stop at Fort Dodge."

Now he had Moon Face Tipton's full attention. "What the devil are you talking about?"

"Well, sir, I was just in the dayroom of B Troop, looking for a fellow that owes me a ten spot. On the notice board I saw this newspaper picture of Sheridan. Somebody cut it up pretty bad with a knife."

"You're jesting."

"Sir, I am not."

"But that's ridiculous. Why—?"

"Captain, there aren't more'n one or two other generals hated more than Phil Sheridan. Uncle Billy Sherman, for sure, and maybe that cavalry commander of his, Kil-what's-his-name."

"Patrick. Kilpatrick."

"Yes, sure. Sir, you know as well as I do, this Plains army contains a lot of men who enlisted under different names than their real ones. A lot of former *Rebs*," he added with breathy melodrama, in case Tipton didn't get it the first time.

"I'll grant you that's true," Moon Face said. "What am I supposed to do about it?"

"Well, sir, I thought you might go up the line to your boss, the adjutant, and have him tell

General Sheridan that he ought to stay away. Tell him that he ought to bypass this fort."

"*Tell* him not to visit a post he commands? *Tell* one of the toughest, most determined soldiers who ever served in the United States Army that he shouldn't come here because someone cut up his picture?" Rolf sank into his rickety chair. Of course he'd failed; he just wasn't a smart enough fellow. "I think you might as well try to stop one of Mr. Shakespeare's hurricanoes." It was all Tipton could do to keep from sounding supercilious. "Now, if you'll excuse me, I've been studying Pliny again, and I'd like to return to him."

"Yes, sir. Thank you, sir."

Rolf slouched out, humiliated.

Humiliated but not whipped.

He wasn't going to let the murder take place. He must use force on Jimmy. Restrain her physically from going anywhere near Fort Dodge while Sheridan was there inspecting it. He knew he wasn't glib enough to talk Jimmy out of her plan, so physical force was the only answer. He needn't hurt her—wouldn't ever do that—but he could lock her up and sit with her. For days, if necessary.

He stole into the B Troop dayroom again, to remove the picture of Phil Sheridan. Since his last visit, someone had penciled obscene words on the general's cheeks and forehead. It made him look all the madder.

During the next few days he blew around and around like a weathervane. "She'll never do it." "She'll do it." The two sentences became his litany.

He had never thought about Jimmy much when he wasn't with her, but now that she was endangered he thought about her a lot. He was surprised by the constancy and the urgency of these new feelings.

Riding past the Overton Place one showery afternoon, he saw her out in back, where the chicken yard sloped away toward the river. Three bottles of different size and color reposed on a log. Ten feet away, Jimmy extended her right hand. He saw a little squirt of smoke, then heard the crack as the amber bottle on the left exploded.

She heard Kid passing. Turned. Recognized him and raised her hand with the .44-caliber murder weapon over her head and waved. He snatched off his hat and waved back. "She'll do it," he said in a strangled voice. "By God she will."

Another blast from the other Deringer seemed to verify it.

On the night before General Sheridan's scheduled arrival, a dismal night of rain that made the Arkansas rush and roar, Rolf slanted his hat brim over his forehead to drip water and rode Kid to the Overton Place. He carried no weapons, but his saddlebags bulged with groceries bought in Dodge that afternoon. He was prepared for a long siege.

As he approached through the rain, opened the gate in front of the farmhouse, rode in, he heard a horse nicker. Then he saw the animal tied out in front. Regulation Army saddle. Did Jimmy have a customer from the fort?

He picketed Kid to the fence by the gate and walked to the porch. If she was entertaining someone, he'd just have to huddle out by the hen house till the man left. He'd just check to make sure; Jimmy never locked her front door even during business hours.

Sheltered by the porch roof, he eased the door open. Lamplight and the smell of dust drifted out. Beyond the closed door of the bedroom, bedsprings squeaked and groaned, and a bullish voice exclaimed, "Oh, that's mighty fucking good, oh my Lord yes . . ."

Rolf Greencastle would have lit out immediately for the hen house but for the intrusion of that obscenity into the unseen customer's declaration of pleasure. That word set his hair to crawling under his hat. An unbelievable premonition gripped him. Held him rigid on the porch a good five minutes, while similar professions of pleasure, similarly punctuated with all sorts of bad language, convinced him that his suspicion was correct and that, somehow, he was caught in one of those inexplicable apocalyptic disasters that left total carnage and sorrow in their wake.

Blood rushed to his head. His eyes felt bulgy as he flung the door wide and cannoned across the parlor, nearly knocking over a flickering lamp with a pearly globe. He took a deep, hurtful breath—this was worse than the time he'd ridden carelessly over a rise and come upon half a dozen young men of the Southern Cheyenne tribe, each and every one in a bad mood—and prayed for God and Jimmy to forgive him. But he had to know.

He opened the bedroom door.

A fat-bottomed little man rolled over on his back and shouted, "Who the profanity are you? What the obscenity is going on here?"

"Rolf, oh Rolf," Jimmy said, trying to cover herself with the bedding. She sounded more grief-stricken than angry. As for Rolf, his aching eyeballs were fixed on the soap-lock of the enraged chap leaping from the bed and seizing his yellow-striped trousers while throwing all sorts of obscene invective at the stunned intruder trembling in the doorway.

"Will you get the shit out of here, you bug-eyed intrusive little son of a bitch?" screamed General Philip Henry Sheridan; for it was the very same.

"General Sheridan, please calm down," Jimmy said. Rolf could not see her just then, the general was in the way. But he distinctly heard the cocking of the Deringer. Sheridan heard it too, and it arrested his angry rush to dress and depart. His little white corporation quivered above the waist of the regulation trousers he was hastily buttoning. Rolf reckoned him to be in his middle thirties, with careworn lines around his black eyes.

"I have a gun pointed at your back, General," Jimmy added.

"You have what?"

The barefoot Sheridan spun around and his disbelief quickly evaporated. Jimmy was sitting up in bed, one hand clasping the sheet over her bosom, the other pointing the hideout pistol at Sheridan's chest, which was white as a bottle of milk.

"General, how did this happen?" Rolf gasped.

"Who the double profanity wants to know? Who the repeated obscenity are you?"

"Just someone who wants to save your life if possible, General."

"Rolf," Jimmy said, "I don't want to shoot you too. My mind's made up. He's going to die. Don't make more bloodshed."

Water dripped from Rolf's chin. At first he thought it was rain but then he realized he was indoors, and it was sweat. The low-trimmed lamp at the bedside, the heavy draperies closed and securely tied that way, gave the room a confined, sultry air. The air of a tomb, he thought, wishing he hadn't.

Sheridan was struggling into his shirt, one moment looking miffed, the next letting his anxiety flicker through; the man was clearly no fool. "General, how the devil did you get over here?" Rolf exclaimed. "You're not supposed to arrive till tomorrow."

"Arrived early," Sheridan barked. "And I found this letter—this charming letter—" He indicated a paper sticking from the pocket of his blouse, which lay over the back of a chair half hidden by his rain-dampened caped overcoat. "From someone who signed herself Daughter of Joy. It was a very fetching missive." He sounded outraged. "It was a special invitation to one of our, ahem, country's heroes to enjoy an hour in the grove of Venus—free of charge." By now Rolf's mind had begun to edit out all of the simple and compound obscenities with which Sheridan filled these and all his other sentences.

"And you fell for it?" Rolf asked. In other circumstances, you might have heard the crash of an idol coming off its pedestal.

"Well, sir, God damn it, I am a bachelor—a man like any other. A man with appetites! A man with feelings!"

"You didn't have any feelings when you burned my daddy's farm on the Valley Pike in Shenandoah County, Virginia, and sent him off to Detroit, Michigan, to catch the glooms and die."

"Shenandoah County?" Sheridan muttered. He turned to the bed. "I remember that place of course, but not your father. What was his name?"

Jimmy whipped her other hand onto the hideout pistol's grip, and the sheet fell, baring her breast. She took no notice. Her beautiful eyes burned. Rolf knew the end was at hand.

"Cosgrove Sturdevant was his name. He took a shot at you because your damned brute soldiers had ruined our farm and carried me off to rape me. For punishment you sent him to prison up north. A poor helpless middle-aged farmer!"

General Phil Sheridan gathered himself and hooked his thumbs in the waist of his trousers, further revealing his potbelly, of which he took no notice. In a hard, strong voice, he said, "I do remember that incident. And you are wrong about it." He stepped toward the bed. "What happened was—"

"Stand back or I'll blow your head off," Jimmy whispered. Both hands, and the Deringer, trembled, and Sheridan's black eyes darted from the gun to Jimmy's face and back again. He clearly saw his death but a finger's twitch away. He didn't advance but he stood fast, and even a little taller. Rolf almost whistled; the man had testicles of steel.

"I ask you not to pull that trigger until I tell you what happened."

"Your men savaged me in the smokehouse, for one."

"I am deeply grieved," Sheridan said, without a single profanity. "I never intentionally made war on women. I do know such things happened."

Jimmy blinked and sat back, expecting, perhaps, something other than this soldier's calm and measured determination in the face of impending death. "I remember your father, and your farm, now that I put my mind to it, because it was there that we lost a young soldier named Birdage, the day after the battle at Fisher's Hill. A white-haired farmer came rushing from his house as we rode into his dooryard, and he fired a shot."

"Did you expect a man like Daddy wouldn't defend his property from filthy Yankee scum invaders?"

"No, I expect that would be any man's natural reaction," Sheridan said, his voice still level. Rolf swayed in the doorway, dizzy, hearing the beat of rain and what sounded in his ear like the rushing winds of black hell and judgment in the sky. Very soon, he expected to see fountains of blood all over the room's rose-pattern wallpaper. "I can understand why I was a target. Unfortunately your father's shot struck a soldier named Asa Birdage."

"Who cares, who cares?" Jimmy screamed. "He was sixty-two years old!"

"Asa Birdage was eleven years old. Asa Birdage was our headquarters drummer boy."

Jimmy's face was curtained by horror. She flung back against the headboard, wanting to deny Sheridan's statement. He simply stood there with his hands hanging easily at his sides—maybe he wasn't so easy inside, but you couldn't tell except for the rise and fall of his potbelly—and Jimmy began to shake her head from side to side. "No, no," she said, and then she burst out crying. "Liar. You're lying to save your hide."

"Young woman, I am an honorable man. I have been accused of many things, but never of deceit. Your father slew one of my soldiers. Who was scarcely more than a child. I felt prison was fair punishment. Perhaps I erred.

Perhaps I was unjust. I acted to prevent another death. Others in my command that day wanted to shoot your father on the spot."

"No, oh no," Jimmy wept. Sheridan's eyes took on a pitying look. Rolf leaped by him, giving him a fist in the shoulder—how many times did you get to land a blow on a hero? on a legend?—and with one quick decisive grab, he removed the Deringer from Jimmy's hand.

"I am thankful that you believe me, miss," Phil Sheridan said in a voice oddly humbled.

"I'm not, I'm not," she cried, covering her tearful face. Rolf knelt beside the bed and with both hands delicately lifted the hem of the sheet so as to hide her breasts. His cheeks were scarlet.

General Sheridan quickly donned his singlet and then his blouse. He was once more sounding stern when he said, "If anyone mentions these events, I will deny my presence. I will lie till the throne of Hell freezes."

Rolf Greencastle was trembling inside. But he tried not to let it show when he turned his eyes on the national hero and scorched him. "I think you'd better light out of here, Phil."

Phil lit out.

After about three hours, Jimmy's sobbing wore itself out and she fell asleep. Rolf pulled up a cane-bottomed chair and sat beside the bed, keeping a vigil. The rain fell harder. About four in the morning, Jimmy woke up.

She quickly covered her left breast, which had been peeping over the hem of the sheet as she slept; Rolf had been admiring it for the better part of twenty minutes. Although he knew her body intimately, his admiration was of a different nature than the simple lust he'd satisfied at the Overton Place before.

"Why did you do that?" she said. "Why did you stop me?" She sounded deathly sad. He feared the glooms were coming again. The terrible glooms.

"You tell me something first. How could you take him into your bed, hating him that way?"

"Oh—" A little sniffle. "Part of the trade, that's all. You learn to shut out everything. How bad the customer stinks. How mean he is. With him it was harder. For a while I thought it wouldn't work, I'd go to pieces. Then I remembered my daddy and I made it work. Got him right where I wanted him."

"It was a mighty good trick," he agreed. "You could have blown his head off any time you wanted to."

"Why did you stop me?"

"I didn't want anything to happen to you. I didn't want you to keep on having the glooms the rest of your life."

"Why, why?"

"I don't know, I guess because I love you."

They stared at each other. He was fully as surprised as she was.

The next day he helped her put the Overton Place up for sale and they rode away together and neither one ever saw General Phil Sheridan again.

GREYWOLF'S HOSS,
by Jane Coleman

Jane Coleman lives on an Arizona ranch, has taught at both the University of Arizona and Cochise College, does research and work in oral history, and writes fiction, nonfiction, and poetry. Her short stories have appeared in The Pennsylvania Review, The Antietam Review, and Plainswoman, *among other publications; and in a 1988 collection,* The Voices of Doves. *She is also the author of two other books,* No Roof But Sky *(poetry about the Western frontier, nominated for a Western States Book Award) and* Shadows in My Hands *(essays on the Southwest).* "Greywolf's Hoss" *is a fine example of her fictive talents—a story about a modern Arizona village where nothing much happens, and an impromptu horse race, and a great deal more.*

• GREYWOLF'S HOSS •
by Jane Coleman

By eleven that Saturday morning the bar was about as crowded as it was going to get. I mean you could go clear to California and not find a place as dead as the Hodil Bar and Grill. The most that ever happens is that a carload of tourists will pull in for lunch, or a beer, or a trip to the john, and once in a while Hodie and Tibbs will come in and we'll get to dancing. Or John Greywolf will get drunk on a Saturday night and come in and beat up on Becky, his wife, who's the waitress here.

Some waitress she is. Mostly she sits in the corner reading the newspaper, her lips moving after her finger that stops and goes, stops and goes, until I yell at her to give me a hand. Then she'll ease up—she's heavy and slow—and shuffle around sweeping or taking orders, her big boobs swaying under her T-shirt that says, "I lost it at New Mexico Tech." She has two of those T-shirts, one red and one bright blue, and she wears them in rotation, week in and week out. Becky, just like the rest of us, feels she's missing something, but doesn't know what it is, or even where to start looking.

It's easy to feel that way here. One day's the same as the next. Faces never change except to get older, and the road through town doesn't go anywhere except out into the sagebrush until it reaches the mountains. They never change, either, though I've heard strangers say the mountains never look the same twice. As far as I can see, they're just there, cutting us off, sealing us up like bugs in a kid's bottle so we act sort of slow like bugs do, holding on and staring through the glass without seeing anything.

Anyway, that morning started out like all mornings; dead quiet. The widow Price come in at nine and ordered her beer, and Mr. Duffy and Mr. Motherall, the two widowers, come in right after for ham and eggs. They always sit by the window so they can see who's doing what or how many cars are on the road, and then they speculate on whatever they see for the rest of the day.

The widow Price sits right at the bar beside the post that holds up the ceiling. After three beers she leans on it with her eyes closed and finds her mouth with a kind of radar. One of those long hands of hers will come up out of her lap and feel around, easy, for the glass. Then one by one her fingers'll close round it and lift it slowly past her chin till it hits her bottom lip. Then her top teeth come down over the rim and she swallows long and hard as if she's dry as a wash. Matter of fact, that's what she resembles; an empty riverbed, cracked, hard, good for nothing but the rain that never comes.

Now you'd think that being as she's a widow, Mr. Duffy and Mr. Motherall would strike up a friendship, or that she'd say a word to them now and again. But she's not made that way. My guess is she wants to die and have it over with, and there's not much she finds amusing or worth any effort. She and her husband moved here to retire, and then he up and died, and she's just shriveled a little more each year, keeping company with her own self and her bottle as if that was good enough, or better than folks.

Well, about eleven, a car pulled up and a man and a woman got out, she kind of lean and rangy, and him round as an egg, and they came in and ordered lunch from Becky who passed the slip to me over the bar. Then Hodie and Tibbs came and ordered beers and started the jukebox playing. They were arguing over by the pinball machine when old Mr. Motherall said, "Look here! Ain't that John Greywolf on that hoss?"

And we all swiveled to look, all except the widow who was chunking on her glass and taking a swallow.

"Goddamn Indian," said Becky. "He took my tomato money and got a hoss." She shuffled to the door, opened it, and stood there looking up at her husband who was sitting tall on a long-legged brown gelding.

"Goddamn Indian," said Becky again. "That money was for new curtains and those pink slippers."

I knew about those slippers. Becky kept a picture of them in her jeans pocket. They were slip-ons; flat and fuzzy and dyed bright pink like some kind of Easter egg.

The horse rolled his eyes at her till the whites showed.

"Go ahead," she said. "You roll your eyes. You do it."

The horse nosed those boobs of hers, and she swatted him away as if he were an insect. She looked up at John who was quiet-faced but with a gleam in his eye that said he'd like to nuzzle in there, too.

"Why'd you do it?" she said. "Why? That was

my money. I grew those tomatoes. An' those chilis. Next time I don't trust you. Next time it's me goes to the market."

"Shut up," John said. "You don't know a race hoss when you see one."

"I know this ain't a race hoss," she said, giving a flounce and putting her hands on her hips. "Who says he is?"

"I do," said John. "This hoss can outrun any hoss at two miles or over."

"Hoooo!" Hodie set down his beer can and came toward the door, belly first. "Hoooo!" He walked around the big critter that had ribs sticking out like rakes and hip bones that reared up back of the blanket John sat on. Finally he grinned. "This hoss couldn't take my Appaloosa," he said. "Not in two miles. Not in four."

"Huh," said John.

"Hell, my bay can outrun both of 'em," said Tibbs, hitching his thumbs in his belt and rocking back on his heels.

"You want to bet?" says John.

"Damnfool Indian," Becky screamed. "Don't you go making no bets."

"I got fifty says he can take 'em both," said John. He looked at Becky's breasts. "You go wait on your people. This here's a man's business."

"Shoot," said Becky, whose vocabulary has its limits. "Whose money is it, you're so ready to throw it down?"

"You goin' to get it sure, woman," he says, sitting up straight as an arrow.

About then the widow woke up and looked at me with those blue and watery eyes of hers. Her old hands skittered across the bar like leaves.

"Are they going to race?" she asked in her papery voice. "Are they?"

I shrugged. "Probably. Ain't much else to do today."

"Where?" She was kind of breathless. She hadn't put so many words together since I'd been tending bar.

I shrugged again. "Maybe out on the plains," I said. "There's plenty room there."

She scrabbled in her purse with her leafy fingers, pulled out her wallet, dropped the change all over. She had to go crawl for it, and I helped. While we were scrambling around under the stools and tables, she said, "I want to go. I want to see the race. I want to bet."

"Why, sure," I said. "You go. We'll get Mr. Motherall to take you." I thought that was a good idea, kind of bringing the two old folks together in a common cause, so to speak.

"Who's running?" she says. "Whose horses?"

"Let's go see," I said.

Just then, though, the egg-shaped man pounded on the table. He was cross and I couldn't blame him. "Are we going to get those hamburgers or not?" he said. He was real ugly when he frowned, his eyebrows running together down his nose like two caterpillars.

"Why sure," I said. "I'll get right to it. Soon's I find out about this hoss race."

"Race!" he yelled. "Is this a restaurant or a book joint?"

I thought that was a pretty clever thing to say, so I grinned at him and at his wife who was leaning back in her chair like she was enjoying it all.

"Well," I said, "you could've come in here pret' near any day in the last five years and this would've been a restaurant. Today's different." I waved my hands at him to calm him down. "I'll get your lunch soon's I find out where this race is going to be. You might consider coming along if you ain't pressed for time. Tibb's big bay is some hoss."

"Let's go, Sam," the wife said. "Let's go see a real race. Cowboys, Indians, and all."

I figured that as soon as Hodie and Tibbs realized they were on stage, they'd put on a real Wild West show for this lady and her husband. Keep them so interested they'd never know the hamburgers were slow in coming.

"Hey, Hodie," I yelled. "This here lady's never seen a real Western hoss race. Where's it going to be?"

Hodie turned, beaming. He snatched off his old black hat and sat down beside the round man. "Why, ma'am," he said. "This here race is going to be the best you ever saw. We'll start on the other side of the valley pass and race to Martin's corrals. Three and a half miles. And my hoss, my Scat'll be there ahead come the finish."

I could see the pair of them getting excited over the idea. Something to tell about back home. I was headed for the grill when I heard the widow. She has the kind of voice that, while it's not loud, sort of undercuts the rest, coming out thin and clattery like a twig covered with ice. "I wouldn't ever bet on an Appaloosa," she said. She stood there waiting.

"Why, ma'am!" said Hodie.

"Why not?" asked the round man, looking the widow up and down as if trying to assess what she knew and how sober she was.

"Appaloosa's not a breed," she said, kind of jerky like she wasn't used to hearing her own voice. "It's just a mixed-up spotted horse. Never knew one didn't have something wrong. Some fault. Some crazy trick."

"My Gawd," said Hodie.

"Who'd you bet on, then?" the round man asked.

"That Indian horse. Long-legged. Deep chest. Skinny but good muscles. Thoroughbred. Used to distance."

"Jeesuz," said Hodie.

"Prayers won't help," said the widow. "Give me a bourbon."

I tell you, I near fell over my feet I was so surprised by it all. I poured her a shot, and she drank it, quick, all in one motion like a man. "Miz Price," I said. "Where'd you learn about hosses?"

"Born and raised on a horse farm," she said. "Lost it and came out here. Haven't seen a good horse since." She tucked her purse under her arm. "I'll take the bottle," she said. "Might need it."

I handed it across the bar to her, and she frowned at me. "In a bag," she said. "In a bag. People will get the wrong idea."

I was about to say that there weren't any people out on those plains and wouldn't be any except us, but I thought better of it. I wrapped the bottle.

"Gentlemen," she said, turning toward Mr. Duffy and Mr. Motherall. It would have been a real elegant move except she was drunk. She slammed into a stool and stood there blinking. "Oh dear," she said.

I hated to see it. I surely did. She'd been so perky there for a minute. So sure of herself. I scooted under the bar. "You ever rode in a jeep?" I said to distract her.

"What?" she said. "What?"

I said, "If you're going out with these two,

you're going in that jeep, so you hold on now to your purse and that bottle, hear?"

Her face was scrunched up like she was going to cry. "It's no fun anymore," she said. "None of it. Nothing."

"Sure it is," I said, though I didn't believe it. I could see myself in fifty years, all shriveled up and empty and fearful of dying. I could see it plain as anything. I stood there wishing I'd never seen the widow, or this town that's two houses and a filling station, and a restaurant, all swallowed up by grasslands and mountains and the plains, and that god-awful blue sky day after day.

Nothing's fair in this world, I remember thinking. Nothing at all.

Mr. Motherall and Mr. Duffy got her settled in the front seat; belted her in so she wouldn't go out the side, and they gave her the bottle and the paper bag for the bet money to hold in her lap. The three of them rode off leaving a cloud of dry dust that blew in and lay over the tables.

I served up two hamburgers, burned, but I disguised that with some onions and green chilis on top, and I plunked down a fresh pot of coffee at Sam's elbow.

"Best pay now," I said. "So we can go when you're done."

He pulled out a fat wallet. "Who're you betting on?"

I thought about it; stood there remembering what I knew about those hosses. Tibb's big bay was part Arab and tough. John's gelding had caught the eye of the widow for all it looked like a hay rake. And Hodie's little Scat, as pretty a horse as I ever saw, wouldn't cross water. I grinned. Maybe the widow was right. That hoss could move quick as a jackrabbit but wouldn't get his feet wet. And I knew another Appaloosa that'd spook at the white line down the road. Dumped plenty on the concrete, that hoss did.

"It'll be between the bay and the Indian if they come to water. More'n that, I can't say."

I took the twenty, counted out change from the register. "I got to get my truck and get my sister to fill in for me," I said. "You can follow me up there or you can go on. Ain't but one road."

"We'll wait for you," the round man said. He counted his change carefully, debating on the size of the tip. I knew his type. All bluff and bluster till it comes down to it.

"Nothin' to be scared of if you want to go ahead," I said. He looked at me, quick-like, and subtracted a sum from what he'd decided to leave.

I grinned. You get to know folks after a while.

"You coming?" I said to Becky. She was picking up plates, slopping what was left all over.

"Naw," she said. "You think I want to see my money throwed away?"

"If he wins, you can buy two pairs of them slippers."

"Huh," she said. "Win? That bag of bones?"

"Suit yourself." I went out back to find Lou. She was sitting on the wooden bench by the door reading confession stories and pulling strings of that god-awful sweet grape gum out of her mouth.

"Spit out that gum and come mind the kitchen for me," I said. "I'm going to a hoss race on the plains."

"You're crazy," she said. "In this heat."

Lou is bone-lazy, and slower even than Becky. I'm surrounded by drunks and fools. By this land with nothing on it but cattle and coyotes.

I wanted to scream. "Nothing's fun," the widow had said. She didn't know the half of it.

I picked up Sam and his wife whose name was Eleanor, and we headed west through the creek bottom and the bare foothills.

Somewhere on that road, I turned wild. I mean, the devil was purely into me. There I was in my pickup leading Sam and Eleanor in their shiny Continental on the way to a hoss race. The road stretched out clear as a string. Sam, sure of himself, mean and full of bluster, sat on my tail. I stepped on the gas, watched the speedometer move up to 65, then 70, then 90, and in the mirror I watched old Sam, his round head a bump behind the steering wheel, fall back and disappear.

That truck flew over the dips in the road, took the hills like a good horse, clean and straight, the grass and the flowers in the ditches leaning away like fire. I left Sam standing still, passed Hodie and Tibbs in a two-horse trailer, and, away off to my right, a dark shape that might have been John easing the gelding toward the plains.

If nothing was fun, I thought, I'd have a time anyway. I'd make my own fun, even if it was only this, racing the road with the wind in my face. Leaving the hawks behind, and the dudes, and the sound of me hollering, urging myself on.

I passed the jeep, too, the old folks setting straight and stiff and choking on a curl of my dust. I went through the pass and on down to the plains without stopping to look. I pulled off where the shoulder was wide. Down below the yellow grass moved. The daisies and the white poppies fluttered. Out at Martin's corrals, a windmill swung round, caught the wind, flashed bright as a silver dollar in the sun. A few cattle hung around the base of the tank, heads down, legs planted square. A few more scattered out along the wash looking for shade.

I sat there for a spell just looking. There was something about that view; fifty miles of yellow grass, no trees but a few mesquite by the washes, nothing but grass and cattle and a streambed. And all around, in the distance, the mountains, blue and purple and changing color under the shadows of the clouds. It was a sight.

I thought maybe it was possible that nothing happens anywhere unless we make it. That the widow was copping out, and Becky, too, and Hodie and Tibb, and even me. Maybe it was only John who had the right idea, spending his wife's money on a dream just for the sake of trying for it.

Hodie and Tibbs pulled up behind me. "Hoooo," said Hodie. "You can drive some. Where'd you leave the dudes?"

"Coming," I said. "Sam's holding on to the wheel like the front end's going off without him."

They both laughed, then turned serious. "Let's get these hosses out 'n walk 'em a bit. Scat hates trailin'." Scat swung his spotted rear and hauled back on his halter.

Pretty soon everybody come up and parked and got out and stood around looking over the course. John rode up then, and the widow spent a long time talking to the brown hoss. I could hear her voice though I couldn't make out the words. The animal listened, pricking up his long ears.

When she come back she said, "Huh!" just like John did.

"Well?" said Sam. "Well?"

"Well, what?" the widow said.

"Which one?"

She looked at him. "Told you before," she said. She went over to the jeep, reached in, took a drink. "Place your bets and let's get started. I want to see that brown horse run."

They did. Eleanor was so taken by Scat (he is a picture, round-rumped and slick), that she put fifty dollars on him in spite of Sam's frown. He stuck with John, while I put ten on Tibb's bay and so did the two old gentlemen.

The widow shook her head at me and kept on drinking. Only when the three hosses and riders were lined up on the rise did she stop. "I'll drop my handkerchief," she said. "That's the signal." She rummaged in her purse, pulled out a piece of cloth that looked like she'd had it fifty years. She stretched out her arm, her eyes, for once, bright and focused. The handkerchief spun in the wind, hesitated, dropped.

"Go," she said, in what for her was a shout.

And they did, with Scat moving ahead like a jackrabbit on those black legs. Tibbs held down the middle, and John and the tall gelding were back in the rear sort of holding back like they weren't running at all. John wasn't using a saddle. He was riding Indian style, high up on the hoss's shoulders. I began wishing I'd bet on him instead.

"Smart," the widow said. "Should have had him riding for me in the old days."

The horses went down the rise and onto the flat, strung out one-two-three, the Appaloosa's rump twinkling in the sun, his black tail fanned out behind.

"Isn't he pretty?" said Eleanor.

"Pretty is as pretty does," said the widow.

"Whooop! Whooop!" I could hear Hodie yelling like he was driving cattle. He was happy out there, ahead of them all, telling the world.

We're all having fun, I thought. This here is fun, no matter what.

"What's that Indian doing?" Sam asked. "I thought you told me his horse could run." His eyebrows were far down on his nose, wriggling.

"Watch," the widow said. She took a drink.

"You could pass the bottle." Sam wiped his hand across his mouth.

"I could," she said, but she put it back into the bag and held on.

"My God," Eleanor wailed. "The bay! Look at the bay!"

Sure enough, Tibbs was making his move on the flat. The bay stretched out his neck. Gobs of dirt, sprays of grass flew out from under his hooves.

Behind them I saw John rise higher on the gelding's shoulders. The length of that hoss's stride grew. With those long legs he covered as much ground with one stride as the others did in two. He ate up distance without thinking about it, like it was easy. Like what he was and was able to do were the same thing so he didn't have to worry or fret or fight the man up there on his neck.

"Shoot," I said. "There goes my money."

"And mine," said Eleanor.

Then the thing happened that made sense out of all the widow had said.

Little Scat still had the lead when they hit the cattle grazing by the wash. The bay was close, but Scat was holding on. The cattle scattered, and the horses went over the edge, and then the bay come up the other side and kept on going. There wasn't any sign of Scat at all. What we could see was Hodie's black hat, just the top of it, rising and falling like he was being tossed in the air. He was.

There was six inches of water down there among the stones. Six inches of water that wasn't even running but was just setting there in the shade, green and still and harmless. But it was water, and Scat took one look, reared, sunfished, and left Hodie in it cursing for all he was worth.

Scat came up our side, shook himself, twitched his ears, and went to grazing like he knew a joke no one else had heard yet.

"Appaloosas," said the widow. "All crazy."

John and the gelding rose up out of the ditch in one leap, moving faster now, fast as a twister come out of the sky. They ran down the bay and kept on going, passed the windmill, Martin's corrals, and went another half mile before they even slowed down.

"Whoopee!" said Sam. Then we all stood there quiet like we'd seen something we knew was going to happen but didn't believe.

The widow emptied the bottle, threw it into the weeds, then retrieved it.

"The only thing I ever knew about was horses," she said. "The only thing."

"You sure know them, though," I said.

She looked at me. Her eyes were glazed over again. "It's done now," she said. "Finished. Now we'll all go back there and sit and sit . . ." Her face shook. All the little lines and creases on her skin stood out plain like roads on a map. "What'll I do?" she asked. "What'll I do?"

I stepped back. I'd been happy running alongside that hoss. Now here she was bringing back the emptiness. "I don't know," I said. "I sure can't tell you how to spend your time."

It was mean to say that, but I was feeling

mean. I didn't want to hear about her problems when I had enough of my own. I didn't want to think about Becky and her pink slippers, or Lou and her confession stories, or Hodie, come up now all muddy and saying, "Hoooo," between curses. I plain didn't want to think at all except about how John and that hoss had gone and done something beautiful, and that maybe, when I got old, I'd remember it: the yellow plains and the mountains, and the way that crazy Indian's dream brought us all to some kind of life for a day.

"Shoot," I said to her. "I'm sorry."

She shook her head. "I had my time. Wasted it. Didn't believe hard enough. You've got to believe. Take chances. Try, like Greywolf there. Like that old horse."

"Believin's hard," I said.

She screwed off the bottle cap, looked in, shrugged her shoulders, bony as that brown hoss's, and threw the bottle back into the weeds. "It's all we've got," she said.

SISTERS,
by Marcia Muller

Best known for her popular and celebrated mysteries, in particular her series about San Francisco private investigator Sharon McCone, Marcia Muller has published seventeen novels, one nonfiction book, and many short stories, articles, and book reviews. Her Western stories have appeared in Boys' Life and such anthologies as Westeryear and The Arbor House Treasury of Great Western Stories; though they number few, each one is as finely crafted as "Sisters"—a sensitive and moving tale of the curious friendship between a white pioneer woman and a Kaw Indian squaw on the plains of central Kansas.

· SISTERS ·
by Marcia Muller

The first time Lydia Whitesides saw Curious Cat looking through her kitchen window, she was more startled than frightened. She was sifting flour preparatory to making the day's bread, and had turned to see where she'd set her big wooden spoon when a face appeared above the sill. It was deeply tanned, framed by shiny black braids. The dark eyes regarded Lydia solemnly for a moment, and then the face disappeared.

Well, that's quite something, she thought. The Indians in this part of central Kansas were well known for their curiosity about the white man's ways, and Lydia had heard tell of squaws and braves who would enter settlers' homes unbidden and snoop about, but none had ever paid the Whitesides a visit. Until now.

"Thank the Lord it was a timid squaw," she murmured, and went on with her baking.

Lydia was not unfamiliar with Indians. She and her husband, Ben, operated a general store on the main street of Salina, and when she clerked there in the afternoons she traded bolts of cloth, sacks of flour and sugar, and dried fruit (but never firearms or whiskey; the Whitesides stood firm on that point) for the pelts and furs that the Kaw tribesmen brought in. The members of this friendly tribe spent hours examining the many wares, and the women in particular displayed a fascination with white babies. Their demeanor, however, was restrained, and previously Lydia had seen no evidence of the Indians' legendary boldness.

In the remaining few days of that month of April, 1866, the squaw's face appeared frequently at the kitchen window. At first she would merely stare at Lydia; then her gaze became more lively, moving about the room, stopping here and there at objects of interest. Lydia watched and waited, in much the same way she would were she attempting to tame a bird or squirrel. Finally, a week after her initial visit, the woman climbed up on the sill and dropped lightly to the kitchen floor. Lydia smiled, but made no move that would frighten her.

The squaw returned the smile tentatively and glanced about. Then she went to the nearby stove and put out a hand to touch it. Its black iron was hot, since Lydia had just finished her baking, and the woman quickly drew back her hand. She regarded the stove for a moment, then went on to the dish cupboard, drawing aside its curtain and examining the crockery. As she proceeded through the room, looking into drawers and cupboards, she barely acknowledged Lydia's presence. After some ten minutes of this, she climbed through the window and was gone.

Curious, Lydia thought, like a cat. And at that moment, in her mind, Curious Cat was named.

The next day Curious Cat returned and reexamined the kitchen. The day after that she moved boldly through the rest of the house. Lydia followed, not attempting to stop her. She had heard from other settlers that an Indian intent on snooping could not be reasoned with; to them, their behavior was not rude and intrusive, but merely friendly. Besides, Lydia was as interested in the squaw as the squaw was in the house.

Curious Cat seemed fascinated by the mantel clock; she stood before it, her head swaying, as if mesmerized by its ticking. The spinning wheel likewise enchanted her; she touched the wheel and, when it moved, pulled her hand away in surprise. She gazed for a long moment at the bed with its patchwork quilt and lace pillow covers. When she turned her eyes to Lydia, they were clouded by bewilderment. Lydia placed her hands together and tilted her head against them, eyes closed. Curious Cat nodded, the universal symbol for sleep having explained all. Before she left that morning she placed her hand on Lydia's stomach, rounded in her fourth month of pregnancy.

"You papoose?" she asked.

"Yes. Papoose in five moons."

Curious Cat beamed with pleasure and departed her usual way.

Thus began the friendship between the two women—so different that they could barely converse. Lydia did not mention Curious Cat's morning visits to her husband. Ben had spent a year in Dodge City before he had met Lydia and settled in Salina. He had arrived there in 1864, shortly after the government massacre of the Cheyenne at Sand Creek, Colorado, and had seen the dreadful Indian retaliation against the plains settlers. Murder, plundering, and destruction had been the fruits of the white man's arrogance, and on the frontier no settler was safe.

Although Ben was fully aware of the differences between the peaceable Kaw and the hostile Comanche, Cheyenne, Arapaho, and Kiowa, he had been badly scarred by his frontier experiences—so much so that he preferred Lydia or his hired clerk to wait on the Indians who came to the store. He would have been most alarmed had he known that a Kaw woman regularly visited his pregnant wife at home. Although Lydia was not afraid of her husband's anger, she held her tongue about the squaw. After all, she did not wish Ben to be troubled, nor did she intend to bar the door—or in this case, the window—to Curious Cat.

During her afternoons at the store, Lydia made discreet inquiries about Curious Cat among the squaws whose English she knew to be better than average. The woman was easy to describe because of an odd buffalo horn necklace she habitually wore. When Lydia did so, the women exchanged glances that she could only interpret as disapproving.

Finally a tall, rawboned woman who seemed to be leader of the group spoke scornfully. "That one. Cheyenne squaw of White Tail."

That explained the disapproving looks. White Tail was a local chieftain who at times in the past had allied himself with the hostile tribes to the west. That he had taken a Cheyenne wife had further proven his renegade leanings to his people. Curious Cat undoubtedly lived a lonely existence among the Kaw—as lonely, for sure, as that which Lydia herself lived among the ladies of Salina.

It was not that the townswomen shunned her. If anything, they were exceptionally polite in their dealings, particularly when they came to trade at the Whitesides' store. But between them and Lydia there was a distance as tangible as the pane of glass that would stand between her and Curious Cat should she close the window to her. The townswomen did not mean to ostracize or hurt Lydia; they simply had no way of engaging in social intercourse with one of her background.

She had been born nearly eighteen years before to parents who traveled with a medicine show—one of the first small ragtag bands to roam the frontier, hawking their nostrums to the settlers. Her parents had performed a magic act—The Sultan and Princess Fatima—and Lydia's earliest recollections were of the swaying motion of the wagons as they moved from outpost to outpost. Even now she could close her eyes and easily conjure up the creak of their wheels, the murmur and roar of the crowds. She could see the flickering of torchlight on the canvas tent. And she could smell the sweat and greasepaint and kerosene and—after her mother died when she was only five—the whiskey.

After his wife's death, her father had taken to drink, and to gambling. After the shows he went to the saloons in the strange towns, looking for a game of faro. Often he took his young daughter with him. Lydia learned to sleep on his lap, under poker tables, anywhere—oblivious to the talk and occasional shouts and tinny piano music that went on around her. When she was nine he put her to work as Princess Fatima. She hated the whistles and catcalls and often-evil attention from the men in the crowd. Many was the time that she stumbled with weariness. But in her world one did what one had to, even a nine-year-old. And she was effective as Princess Fatima. She knew that.

Ben Whitesides had realized it, too, the first time he saw her in Wichita, where he had drifted after leaving Dodge City. But, as he confided to her later, he had seen more than her prettiness and easy charm, had seen the goodness she hid deep inside her. In spite of the unwholesome reputation of the show people, he had courted her: for three weeks he had followed the caravan as it made its way from Wichita to Montgomery County; at night his clean, shining face would be the first she would spy in the crowd. Lydia had her doubts about this gentle, soft-spoken young man: his fascination with her, she thought, bespoke a lack of good sense. And much as she hated her nomadic existence, it was all she had known. Much as her increasingly besotted father angered her, she loved him. But Ben persisted, and in one month more he made her his wife.

Ben Whitesides had given her a home, a respectable livelihood, the promise of a child. But he could not eradicate the loneliness of her life here in Salina. No one had been able to do that. Until now. Now there were the eagerly awaited visits from the Indian woman she had named Curious Cat.

At first the two could converse very little. Curious Cat knew some English—as most of the members of the local tribe did—but she seemed reluctant to speak it. Lydia knew a few Indian words, so one day she gave Curious Cat a piece of fresh-baked cornbread and said the word for it in Kaw. She was rewarded by an immediate softening in the other woman's eyes. The next day Curious Cat pointed questioningly at the stove. Lydia named it in English. Curious Cat repeated the word. Their mutual language lessons had begun.

In the weeks that followed, Curious Cat

learned the English for every object in the house. Lydia learned words, too—whether they were Kaw or Cheyenne she wasn't certain. Curious Cat told her her name—Silent Bird—and Lydia called her by it, but since the woman was neither birdlike nor silent, she remained Curious Cat in Lydia's mind. In a short time she and her Indian friend were able to communicate simple thoughts and stories, to give one another some idea of their lives before the day Curious Cat had decided to look into the white woman's world through Lydia's kitchen window.

The first of these exchanges came about on the day after Lydia's birthday, when she wore for the first time a soapstone brooch etched with the shape of a graceful, leafless tree—her gift from Ben. The tree, her husband said, reminded him of those he had seen on the far western plains, before fortune had brought him to her.

Curious Cat noticed the brooch immediately upon her arrival. She approached Lydia and fingered it hesitantly. The intensity of emotion in her liquid brown eyes startled Lydia; the squaw seldom betrayed her feelings. Now she seemed in pain, as if the brooch called forth some unwanted memory.

After a moment she moved away and went to see what Lydia was baking—her ritual upon arriving. Her movements were listless, however, her curiosity about what was in the oven obviously forced. Lydia motioned for her to come into the parlor and sit beside her on the settee. Curious Cat did so, placing her hands together in the lap of her faded calico skirt.

Lydia touched the brooch with her forefinger. "What is it? What is wrong?"

Curious Cat looked away, feigning interest in the spinning wheel.

"No, you must tell me."

The anguished brown eyes returned to Lydia's. "The tree . . . my home. . . ."

"The tree reminds you of where you were born, on the plains?"

Hesitation. Then a nod.

"Tell me about it."

Curious Cat's face became a battleground where emotions warred: sadness, yearning, and anger. For a moment Lydia feared that what she wanted to say would be too much for their shared rudimentary language, but then Curious Cat began to tell her story in a patchwork of broken phrases, gestures, and facial expressions that conveyed far more than the most eloquent speech.

She had been born on the far western reaches of the Great Plains, to a chieftain of one of the Cheyenne's most powerful clans. When she reached womanhood, a match had been arranged with the son of another powerful chieftain—a union that would ally the two great clans. The young man, Curious Cat indicated, was more than agreeable. She had watched him from afar, and found him brave as well as handsome.

But then came the massacre of the Cheyenne at Sand Creek. Curious Cat's father was killed, and her brother disappeared after subsequent hostilities near Wichita. It was said among his tribesmen that he had fled, a coward. Now Curious Cat and her mother found themselves ostracized as family of a traitor, with no man to protect and provide for them. The young brave to whom Curious Cat had been promised would no longer look upon her face.

Within months Curious Cat's mother had died, broken and weakened by the struggle to survive. Curious Cat lived off the meager kindnesses people showed her. When White Tail of the Kaw traveled west hoping to strike an alliance between his tribe and the warlike Cheyenne, his eye was caught by the ragged outcast; he spoke of his interest to the chief of her clan, and it was deemed suitable that she leave as White Tail's squaw. With her departure, a shameful reminder would be removed.

Now, Curious Cat told Lydia, she lived among the Kaw much as she had among her own people. True, she had White Tail to protect her, and life was not such a struggle. But his warlike ways had made him and his family suspect, and the women kept their distance from his squaw. She was to be forever a stranger in the Kaw village.

So this, Lydia thought when Curious Cat was still, was the root of the bond she had sensed between them. They were both strangers condemned to loneliness. After a moment she told her own story to the Cheyenne woman, and when she was finished they sat silent yet at ease. The bond between them was welded strong.

The trouble began when customers at the store told Ben they had seen a squaw entering and leaving his property on a number of occasions. Ben was concerned and questioned Lydia about it. She readily admitted as much.

"The Kaw are a curious people, Ben. The squaw comes to spy. But she is harmless."

"She may very well be, but what of her tribesmen?"

"No one has come here but her."

"Still . . . they say she is a strange one. An outcast."

"And how do they know this is the woman of whom they speak?"

"The buffalo horn necklace she wears makes her recognizable. It is Cheyenne, and they *are* warlike."

Lydia pictured the necklace, which Curious Cat fingered often, as if to preserve her last link to the people who had sent her into exile. "But if she is with the Kaw, she is Cheyenne no longer."

"You cannot be sure of that. The Indians are a peculiar race; who knows what they may be thinking, or where their loyalties lie?"

Lydia was quite sure that Curious Cat's loyalties lay with no tribe, but she knew she could not explain that to Ben. She fell silent, seeking a way out of the dilemma.

Ben said, "I am only thinking of you and our child. The next time this squaw comes around, you must bar her the door."

The way out was in his words. "That I will," she agreed. Ben was unaware that Curious Cat entered and left by the window. By saying she would bar her the door, she was not actually lying to her husband.

As spring turned to summer Lydia continued to enjoy the Indian woman's companionship. Curious Cat came most mornings, cautiously so as not to come to the further attention of the townspeople. Together they baked bread, and Lydia demonstrated the uses of the spinning wheel, which was still an object of fascination for the squaw. They conversed with greater ease, and sometimes Curious Cat would sing— songs with strange words and odd melodies that

somehow conveyed their meaning. Lydia recip-
rocated with the lullabies that she would soon
sing to her child. The child quickened within
her, and the days passed swiftly.

The weather turned hot and arid. No breeze
cooled the flat land. From the west the news
was bad: prairie fires swept out of control near
Wilson and Lincoln; a sudden fierce gale had
caused fire to jump the Saline River and destroy the tiny settlement of Greenport. The Indians were on the rampage again, too. Enraged
by the wholesale slaughter of buffalo, the Cheyenne and Comanche attacked railroad crews
and frontier settlements, plundering and murdering. Nearby Mitchell County was in a constant state of siege, and the people of Salina
began to fear that the raids would soon extend
east to their own territory. Of the prairie fires
Lydia and Curious Cat spoke often. About the
Indian raids they remained silent.

As the news from the beleaguered settlements worsened, the populace of Salina grew
fearful. The Kaw, always welcomed before,
were looked at askance when they came to trade
at the Whitesides' store. Peaceable merchants
such as Ben, who seldom handled guns, armed
themselves. Women kept doors locked and rifles close to hand. The heat intensified the un-
dercurrent of panic. Tempers grew raw; brawls
and shootings in the saloons increased. During
the first week in August the distant glow of
prairie fire intruded on slumber.

Ben Whitesides took to returning home for
his midday meal, to reassure himself of Lydia's
safety now that the days of her confinement approached and she was no longer able to come
to the store. She was agreeable to the arrange-
ment, but it meant taking care that Curious Cat

departed before the time Ben customarily arrived. On a stifling day in mid-August, however, she let awareness of the hour slip away from her. She and Curious Cat were taking cornbread from the oven when Ben came through the kitchen door.

Ben saw the squaw immediately. He stopped, suddenly pale, his hand on the doorknob. Curious Cat seemed frozen. Lydia herself could not move or breathe. The sweat that beaded her forehead and upper lip felt oddly cold. The hush was so great that she could hear the mantel clock ticking in the parlor.

Ben's eyes were jumpy, wild. Lydia knew he did not comprehend that he had walked in on a peaceable scene. She put out a hand to him, opened her mouth to explain.

The motion freed Curious Cat; she slipped over toward the window. Ben's glazed eyes jerked after her, and his hand moved under his coat, to where he had taken to carrying his pistol.

Curious Cat gave a guttural cry and began scrambling onto the sill. Lydia's gaze was transfixed as Ben took out the gun. Then she heard a tearing sound and whirled. Curious Cat's skirt has caught on a nail, and she was struggling to free it. Lydia swung back toward Ben. He was leveling the pistol at the squaw.

"No, Ben!" she cried.

He paid her no mind.

"No!" Lydia flung herself at him.

Ben jerked the gun up. A shot boomed, deafeningly. The room seemed to shake, and plaster showered down from the ceiling.

Lydia crumpled to the floor and cowered there, her ears ringing. The plaster continued to rain down, stinging the skin of her arms and face. When she looked up, she saw Ben standing over her. He was staring at the gun, his whole body shaking.

"Dear God," he said in a choked voice. "Dear God, what I might have done!"

Lydia turned her head toward the window. It was empty. Curious Cat had gone.

After that day Curious Cat came no more, and a silence descended upon the Whitesides' home. A familiar but unaccustomed silence during the days as Lydia went about her household tasks alone. An unnatural silence at night, between herself and Ben.

Once his shock had abated, Ben had become angry and remained angry for days. When the anger faded, he was left with a deep sense of betrayal at Lydia's months-long deception, a hurt that shone in his eyes every time he looked at her. Lydia's pain was twofold: by lying to Ben she had put distance between them just before the birth of their child, when they should have been drawing closer than ever. And she had exposed Curious Cat, her only friend, to danger and humiliation.

During the stifling late-summer nights she lay huge and restless in the double bed, listening to Ben's deep breathing and thinking of how she had wronged him. Then her thoughts would turn to Curious Cat, and she would wonder how her friend was faring. She feared that, like Ben, the squaw thought she had betrayed her, somehow held her responsible for the near-shooting. But mostly she pictured Curious Cat as lonely, exiled once again to her life among the unaccepting Kaw.

Even the now-strong movements of her unborn child failed to cheer Lydia. She felt incapable of facing the momentous event ahead. Not the birth itself; that was painful and dangerous, but physical ordeals had never daunted her. What she feared was that she might not be wise enough to guide the small and helpless life that would soon be placed in her hands. After all, if she had so wronged her husband and her only friend, how could she expect to do the right things for her child?

On a brilliant September morning Curious Cat came again. She slipped through the kitchen window and dropped to the floor as Lydia was shelling a bushel of peas. When she saw her Indian friend, Lydia felt her face flush with delight. But Curious Cat did not smile. She did not check the baking bread or peer into the larder. Instead she stared at Lydia, her face intense.

"What is it?" Lydia asked, starting to rise.

Curious Cat came to her, placed her hands on her shoulders, and pushed her gently into the chair. She squatted on the floor in front of her, eyes burning with determination.

"You help," she said.

"Help? Yes. of course. What . . . ?"

"You tell. Save people."

"Tell what? Who?"

Curious Cat's gaze wavered. For a moment Lydia thought she might run off. Then she said, "Cheyenne. Many. Come White Tail, talk war."

"War? Where?"

"Now near Shady Bend. Be here two sleeps."

Shady Bend was in Lincoln County, on the other side of the Saline River. Two sleeps—two days—was what it would take a war party, traveling fast, to reach Salina. "They plan to attack *here*?"

Curious Cat nodded.

"Will White Tail join them?"

She shook her head in the negative. "White Tail grows old. Tired of war. I come tell you make ready. Save people."

"Why are you telling me? The Cheyenne are *your* people. They will be slaughtered."

Curious Cat fingered her buffalo horn necklace. Then she rose and was gone through the window.

At first Ben was skeptical of what Lydia told him.

"Why would this squaw betray her people in order to save our town?" he asked. "I fear this is a false story—some sort of retaliation for my nearly shooting her."

"I think not. Curious Cat was badly used by the Cheyenne; her loyalty is no longer with them. She is Kaw now, and her husband White Tail wants no part of this war."

Ben was watching Lydia's face, frowning. "How do you know so much about the squaw?"

"She told me."

"How could she tell you? Indians can barely speak English. And surely you cannot speak Kaw or Cheyenne."

"Curious Cat speaks English well, and I know a fair amount of her language as well. We taught one another, and we used to talk often."

Ben's face darkened. He did not like to be reminded of how the squaw had visited his house. "Perhaps you talked, but not of such important things as those. Of baking and spinning, yes. But of the squaw's loyalty to her people, or White Tail's feelings about a Cheyenne war? I think not."

Lydia felt her anger rise at his patronizing

dismissal. "One does not need important-sounding words to discuss important things, Ben."

"I am only saying that it seems improbable—"

"Curious Cat and I may share a limited language, but we talked about anything we wished. And we did not hide our feelings within a cloak of silence."

Her husband looked as if he were about to make a sharp retort. Then he bit his lip, obviously understanding her reference to his recent silence. After a moment he said, "Do you really believe the squaw is telling the truth?"

"I do."

"And you are certain her loyalty no longer lies with the Cheyenne?"

"Nor with the Kaw. She feels alone in the world."

Lydia could see that Ben did not want to believe her, did not want to give up his conviction that all Indians were devious and sly. But he was a reasonable man, and after thinking for a moment he shook his head, looking ashamed. "I have placed little value on your friendship with the squaw, merely because she is of another race. Now I see what it means to you—and to her. Your Curious Cat does have loyalties, but they lie not with her people, but with you." He reached out to stroke her cheek—something he had not done since he had found Curious Cat in their kitchen.

Lydia touched his hand, knowing all was mended between them.

Of course the men of Salina were equally skeptical of the threat of Indian attack. But Ben Whitesides had the forceful qualities of a leader, and once he had assembled them, his newfound conviction in the truth of Curious Cat's story gave strength to his words. When the attack came, the town was prepared, and the Cheyenne were driven off.

In the days that followed, many of the townswomen paid stiff formal calls on Lydia, to thank her for her part in the victory. The awkwardness was dispelled, however, when talk turned to her expected child, and several of the women returned bearing small gifts for the baby. Lydia knew Salina had finally taken her in on the day when Mrs. Ellerbee, wife of the bank president, hesitantly asked if she would consider joining a new musical society the ladies were thinking of forming. And while she realized she would never take as much pleasure in the ladies' refined company as she had in the mornings she'd spent with Curious Cat, she assented readily.

Curious Cat came one last time, on a day when wintry clouds lowered overhead. Lydia was tending to her newborn son in his cradle next to the stove, and she had to raise the window, which had been shut against the chill, to admit her friend.

The squaw went immediately to the cradle. She stared at Ben Junior for a long moment, then said, "Fine papoose. Strong." Quickly she moved on to the stove and inspected the bread that was browning there.

Lydia said, "I'm so glad you've come. I've wanted to thank you—"

Curious Cat cut her short with a gesture of dismissal. She looked around the kitchen, as if to fix it in her mind. Then she said, "Come for goodbye."

"But there's no need! You are welcome here anytime."

The Indian woman shook her head sorrowfully. "White Tail go north. I go with. One sleep, then go."

Lydia was overcome with a sharp sense of loss. She moved forward, taking the other woman's hands. "But there is so much I must say to you—"

Curious Cat shook her head again. "One sleep, then go. Come for goodbye." Gently she disentwined her fingers from Lydia's. Lydia knew Curious Cat was not one for touching, so she let her go.

The Indian woman glanced at the cradle once more. "Fine papoose. You raise him strong. Brave."

"Yes, I promise I will."

Curious Cat nodded in satisfaction. Then she put her hands to the buffalo horn necklace she still wore and lifted it over her head. She lowered it over Lydia's curls and placed it around her neck, smoothing the collar of her dress over it.

"White sister," she said.

Tears rose to Lydia's eyes. She blinked them away, unable to speak. She had no parting gift, nothing so fine. . . . And then she looked down at her bodice, secured by the soapstone brooch etched with the tree of the prairie, Ben's birthday gift to her. He would approve, think it fitting, too.

With fumbling fingers Lydia undid the brooch and pinned it to the faded calico at Curious Cat's throat. "Not white sister," she said. "True sister."

The Querencia,
by Lee Somerville

Lieutenant Colonel Henry Lee Somerville, USAF Retired, sold his first short story in 1929, at the age of fourteen, and has been writing off and on ever since. He has published hundreds of nonfiction pieces and more than 150 short stories in such diverse publications as True, Frontier Times, Field and Stream, American Legion Magazine, True Detective, Alfred Hitchcock's Mystery Magazine, and Western pulps in the thirties. His only novel, Charge of the Model T's, an hilarious tale based on fact, was made into a film in 1977 starring Louis Nye and Arte Johnson. "The Querencia" is his good-humored account of an 1869 cattle drive from Texas to Kansas, and of the fortunes and misfortunes of a young man named Win McCoy, a young woman named Betty Sue, and a pet steer named Sancho.

• THE QUERENCIA •
by Lee Somerville

Win Macoy always paid his debts and hated to be beholden to anybody or anything. When he got his uncle Sheb's letter, he didn't hesitate. He quit his job as ranch foreman of the Double Six and rode to Calamity County, Texas, eager to repay the favors of the folks there had done his family years ago.

This was in 1869, with cattle drives to Kansas not yet common in Texas. Win Macoy had gone up the new trail with Jesse Driskill in 1867. In 1868, he'd gone with the Slaughter herd along the same route.

Now the ranchers in Calamity County called for him to come home and take their steers to market. Folks in New York City were half-starved for beef, which was scarce up North following the Civil War. Calamity County had thousands of wild and half-wild longhorns on prairie and in thickets and no way to sell them. Most ranchers had worthless Confederate money but very little U.S. currency or Mexican gold or silver. And this new banker, Gage Ruddels, had mortgages and he would certainly foreclose unless the ranchers could get money from somewhere.

Some Texans in an adjoining county had made earlier drives to Kansas and had been beset by Jayhawkers and Kansas lawmen who were murderers. But on this new trail, the one that would later be called Chisholm, you were in unsettled country. It wasn't beset with farmers and lawmen trying to keep you out like the trail to St. Louis had been. Places like this new town called Abilene promised to protect the herds from Jayhawkers and Kansas free-soil farmers who had carpetbaggered in from back East and up North, hunting free land.

Knowing that Win Macoy had made two drives on this new trail, Sheb Tucker sent for him.

On his way to the ST, Win stopped at several homes in Calamity County. Preacher Jones and his family took on over Win like long-lost kinfolk. Mrs. Jones insisted on feeding him. She told him how sorry she was that his parents had both died of the Sickness in East Texas. She asked if he'd been to see the Logans yet. That didn't make sense, since Tanner Logan lived on the other side of Uncle Sheb's ST.

Later, still on the way to the ST, he saw the McKinsey boys, Hammer and Floyd, chousing cattle out of thickets. They wanted to talk about what he did in the war, but he didn't want to talk about that. He kept seeing people he knew. When he did reach the ST and saw how old and thin his uncle Sheb looked, he was doubly glad he'd come. Win and his parents had lived on the ST for several years, then they'd moved to Nacogdoches about six years ago.

He felt good about the proposed cattle drive until Pete Lopez told him about the Logans' pet steer, Sancho.

It was Betty Sue's fault, of course. Win remembered her as a freckle-faced, curly-haired blond tomboy who had a loving heart and who adopted baby animals from coyotes to armadillos. According to Pete Lopez, she had felt sorry for this orphan calf and had saved his life by feeding him milk. She had even fed him tamales and hot peppers when he was older. Now Sancho was fifteen hundred pounds of brown and white longhorn steer, five years old. Last week, while the Logans were gone, he had come through the rail fence and had pushed open the kitchen door to the Logan house. He hadn't found tamales or cookies, but he had found cold cornbread on the kitchen table and had broken a gallon jug of molasses. He was happily licking molasses off the floor when Mrs. Logan and Betty Sue came home.

Mrs. Logan grabbed the shotgun off the wall. Betty Sue wrestled the gun from her mother and yelled for Sancho to run. He did. He took the door frame and the door with him.

"One does not make a pet of a longhorn steer," Pete Lopez philosophized. "Tanner Logan decreed that Sancho must go to market with us."

Win Macoy stiffened. One of Win's peculiarities was that in moments of stress, he remained silent until he thought a while. He and Pete were both on the ground, standing in late afternoon in the shade of the covered lead wagon. He leaned his tall frame against a wagon bow and mentally counted to fifty.

Then he let go. "I know about pet steers! We had one on the Jesse Driskill drive! You get a pet steer in a group of longhorns, and he'll stampede at night and try to take the whole herd back home. I'll tell Logan we won't take him. If Tanner insists, I'll buy the son of a bitch and shoot him and let the buzzards eat him!"

Pete Lopez laughed. Then he looked startled and somewhat distressed and motioned toward two riders coming. Pete had ninety steers in the drive, and he was going along as cook. "You haven't seen this new banker who took over when old Lennox supposedly committed suicide over money troubles, have you?"

"I don't want to see him. Some talk that Lennox didn't really kill himself, isn't there?"

"Ruddels came in with money and was in the bank when Lennox supposedly shot himself. Ruddels had papers saying he owned everything. Mrs. Lennox went to Galveston to live with her sister. Well, here comes the new banker, Gage Ruddels, and one of his hired drunks."

Gage Ruddels looked as out of place atop his expensive Spanish saddle and Tennessee walking horse as a Gila monster would look sitting on a china chamber pot. He was short, fat, bloated. His face was blotched with broken veins under gray-red skin. His little pig eyes were almost hidden under sandy-gray eyebrows and the smoke from his black cigar. He wore a checkered Baltimore frock coat and fawn trousers. A brown derby sat atop his balding head. He had small feet encased in polished boots.

He spoke to the sullen lout riding with him. The lout nodded.

"Mr. Macoy." He brought his horse to a halt almost atop of Win. "Mr. Macoy. My pleasure, Macoy. My pleasure. We have not met, but I am the banker here now. I am Gage Ruddels, and we have business, we have business."

He blew smoke, chewed on the cigar, short of breath and puffing as he spoke. He stared, unblinking, his small eyes colorless as ice.

Win stared back. "If you want to talk to me, get your fat rump off that horse and stand here man to man instead of trying to gain advantage."

Ruddels's blotched face blushed crimson. The hired hand's fingers moved around his pistol as if to draw. The banker waved him down with a dainty hand. Pete Lopez, unarmed, put his hand inside the wagon cover as if to fondle a gun there. Win stood firm. At this point, he sensed, the banker would want talk and not gunplay from his hireling.

Ruddels slid off the saddle, puffing at the effort, and landed heavily. He extended his hand. Win took it, though the handshake felt like holding a wet dishrag.

"We have business, sir, we have business." The banker wiped his sweaty hand on his fawn-colored trousers. "Here are papers showing the bank foreclosed at noon today against John Preston. Preston had eighty steers in this drive. Those steers belong to the bank now, belong to the bank."

Win's jaw hardened. "Preston's place and his cattle are worth ten times what he owed the bank. If you had let him take those steers to Kansas, he could have paid his note."

The fat banker sucked wind. "Foreclosure is bank business, Mr. Macoy, bank business. Preston will not go with you on this drive as he planned. Therefore the bank will protect its investment, protect its investment, by sending Mr. Chum Wade here in Preston's place. This is Mr. Wade, Macoy."

Seated on his horse, leaning in threatening position, the hired hand, Chum Wade, scowled. He was stocky, medium height, beer-bellied but heavy shouldered like a man who has once been a wrestler. He had wild black hair under his filthy, broad-brimmed sombrero. His chin was bare except for a two-day growth, but his handlebar mustache and black sideburns almost covered his ugly face.

Win Macoy followed his procedure, made himself stand rock-still while he mentally counted to fifty. Then he said, "I don't like you, you hydrophobia'd son of a foreclosing skunk! And I don't like the looks of your hired scum here, either. If you have papers for the Preston steers, get them out of the herd. And this derelict is not going with me!"

Chum Wade's hand shook, but Pete Lopez kept his own hand under the wagon sheet, pretending he had a gun that wasn't there. Win had shifted to a tense stance, ready, though he was sure this was not the time for the banker to force gunplay.

Banker Ruddels puffed cigar smoke and smiled a cold smile. "I am afraid we have a misunderstanding, Mr. Macoy, a misunderstanding. According to your written agreement with the ranchers, and since the bank takes Preston's place, the steers will go with you and Chum Wade will go as the bank representative."

Win stood firm, but he knew the banker was right about the written agreement. Finally he spoke. "All right. You win this skirmish, banker. I'll take the steers and I'll take your flunky. By terms of my contract, I have authority to fire Chum Wade at any time he gives cause. Understand?"

He waited until they left, then turned to face Lopez. "Thanks for bluffing about the gun you didn't have, Pete. I don't trust Ruddels, but he wants us alive for the time being."

"Next time I'll have a gun with me," Lopez promised.

Mounting his chestnut, Win touched spurs to the horse and headed to the Rolling L, the Logan ranch. The sun was full in his eyes long before he reached the spread, even with hat brim pulled low.

Mrs. Logan stood on the porch, fat and forty, a motherly smile on her pleasant face. "Win Macoy! We saw you when you topped yonder hill, and I just knew it was you. You're still tall and slender and good-looking. You must be in your middle twenties now."

"Twenty-five."

"Tanner will be here soon. Soon as he comes in, we'll eat."

"Mrs. Logan, I can't stay. I just wanted to tell Tanner there's no way I'll take this pet steer on the drive."

"Nonsense! That steer goes! Now, that's settled, and I won't hear another word about it."

Win gulped. "Let me buy the steer, then I'll be free to shoot—"

Mrs. Logan shook her head and waved her hands. "Absolutely not! That would hurt Betty Sue more than you taking him on the drive. Sell him in Kansas. Don't shoot him here." She cocked her head as if listening. Win had already heard muffled sounds of water splashing in the back room. As though someone was hastily washing, maybe even in cold water if there had been no time to heat water.

Mrs. Logan listened and smiled. "Win, you do remember our little girl, don't you?"

"The tomboy. She used to spend lots of time with us when we lived on the ST. I never did get a chance to thank her for those gloves she sent me during the war. I'll bet you knitted them for her. She's such a tomboy she'd never learn to knit."

Mrs. Logan raised her voice. "Betty!"

A young woman dressed in a pink ruffled party gown came out on the porch, dimpling and blushing so much her suntan and freckles didn't show. The dress made her pert breasts stick out in front and emphasized her compact tail sticking out in back, as was the fashion. Betty Sue's blond curls were long now and freshly brushed. She stood five feet five inches in contrast to Win's six feet four inches, and she moved close to him, paused so he could smell the New Orleans perfume bought from a peddler, then threw both arms around his neck.

She had been eleven years old when Win had last seen her.

Mrs. Logan headed for the kitchen. Betty Sue hung on as Win tried to peel her away. Her breasts rubbed against his chest; her lips kissed and insisted.

He pushed her partly away. "You're just a kid, Betty Sue!"

"I'm seventeen. I'm an old maid." She moved even closer. "I knew you'd come back. I kept asking your uncle Sheb to write and ask you to come back. I prayed every night, and I promised God that when you came back, I'd tell you what I wanted to say when I was ten and eleven years old. I love you, Win Macoy!"

Win jumped as if wasp-stung. "No!" He started for his horse, but Tanner Logan arrived just then and made him stay for supper.

Afterward, on the porch again and with night breezes blowing, Win Macoy made himself leave after only a few dozen more kisses. He told Betty Sue she was crazy, but nice, and he lay awake most of the night trying not to think silly thoughts.

His uncle Sheb noted that he ate only four

sausages and three fried eggs for breakfast. "Don't get wrong ideas about that sweet little innocent girl, Nephew, or I'll thrash you myself. She hasn't dated any of the fellows, though Lord knows she's had opportunities. Everybody knows she waited for you. She's in heat for you and you only, but don't you take advantage of her."

"She's just a sweet kid."

"Your mama was fifteen when she married. Betty Sue is seventeen, and she's ready, but don't you take advantage of her innocence."

Later, when Tanner Logan and Betty Sue brought Sancho and staked him near the chuck wagon, Win tried to explain to the girl that he was not the marrying kind. She maneuvered him around to the other side of the covered wagon, and he lost that skirmish. He realized later that she hadn't heard a word he said.

When the ranchers and ranch boys started the herd on its way to Kansas, the steers wanted to go in ten directions. They had no group loyalty, no sense of anything except the desire to go back to their accustomed graze. There was too much trouble for Win to worry about Sancho. He had 1536 longhorns wanting to go in 1536 directions. He put ranch boys on drag, swing, and flank, had them pop their long whips and start the herd moving in a fast trot toward Waco and the Brazos.

He needn't have worried about Sancho. Pete Lopez had volunteered to cook and had put his yeast in the sun at the side of the chuck wagon. Sancho smelled the yeast and trotted as close to the chuck wagon as Pete and his long whip would allow.

At one point as they passed the SM spread,

four SM longhorns broke from the group and headed for a willow-flanked creek. Win yelled at cowboys not to follow, to let them go. At this point you couldn't spend too much time on small numbers—you tried to keep the bulk of the herd moving.

Later, Sancho slowed to the drag part of the herd and looked slyly around as if to make a break for a clump of trees in the distance. Lanny and Tom Hogan popped their whips at him, and he moved back near the chuck wagon. The chuck wagon, of course, was in the lead away from dust and animal hairs and smells.

Chum Wade rode slouchily at no particular position, reaching in his shirt pocket now and then for leaf tobacco to chew. Ranchers and their sons rode back and forth, wearing out horses, but Chum just slouched along, fingering his short, heavy quirt and not using it.

Preacher Jones had come with the group. Win had protested, saying the others could look after the preacher's forty steers. He said the preacher should stay with his church. Jones had replied that if the drive didn't bring in some cash money, there wouldn't be a congregation and there wouldn't be a church. Now Jones asked if Win couldn't get some work from Chum Wade.

"I'm too busy to pay much attention to him now," Win explained. "I'll ream him tonight."

Preacher Jones shook his head. "Ruddels carpetbaggered here from up North after the war. Lennox had tried to get outside money, and somebody sent him Ruddels. After Lennox shot himself, Ruddels showed papers saying he owned everything. Nobody could prove different. And Texas was and is, a defeated state, occupied by Yankee troops and run by a carpetbagger government."

By nightfall of that first day, Win had worn out three horses. At semidark, with the herd tired and bedding down except for a few that still grazed, Lopez brought out a sledgehammer and an iron stake. He threw a rope around Sancho's white horns and tied the rope to the stake driven deep near the chuck wagon.

"I was hoping the son of a bitch would break loose and go home," Win grumbled.

"Señor, he looks at my chuck wagon," Lopez explained. "I look in his big brown eyes, and I know what he plans. Later, of course, he will try to return to his *querencia*. Every animal has a *querencia*, a loved spot, to which even the mountain lion or the wildest animal returns. Every man himself has a *querencia*—"

"Popcorn!"

"You laugh? You think it is only the married man like me, the poor husband dreaming day and night of Maria and our two *niños*, who longs to return to his loved spot? You think in your heart you have no *querencia*?"

"Most of these ranch boys—Floyd, Hammer, Joe, Lanny and Tom and others—are crazy eager to see new places," Win said. "I myself dream of far blue mountains, of oceans I have not yet seen. Oh, during the war I got homesick, but Mom and Dad died of the Sickness while I was in Georgia with Hood's brigade. My only home now is the ST with Uncle Sheb. You know Uncle Sheb is a bachelor, never married, so it isn't that much of a home. I have plans for the next few years. I'll bet this is just the start of cattle drives from Texas to Kansas and maybe even up into Montana and Wyoming. I'll bet in the next ten years, millions of longhorns will follow our trail and I'll get rich from it!"

Lopez stood with hammer in hand, laughing. "Betty Sue will go with you on these drives if you ask. She can be the *querencia* you need, even if the *querencia* is no more than a mattress at night in a wagon that moves from place to place. Or she can be the *querencia* you return to after each quest for the million dollars in gold you will earn. In your old age, after you are rich—"

Win spurred his horse and rode around the herd. Sancho nuzzled Lopez's shirt pocket, hunting tobacco.

Hammer McKinsey stopped his monotonous singing as Win rode west of the drag. "Boss man, don't you ever sleep?"

"Now and then, Hammer."

"Well, my eyes are all gravel, but that damned Chum Wade hasn't relieved me yet. Reckon you could roust the lazy son out of his roost?"

Back at the camp fire, Jones shook his head and said, "Wade disappeared right after he ate supper."

"Yeah," Lanny affirmed. "And you don't dare holler for him. That'd spook these nervous demons. We keep them moving this fast a couple more days, they'll settle down."

"Maybe he went to converse with those fellows who are slow-trailing us," Tom said. "Win, I should've told you at supper, but you was still riding around. I saw these men today. Six of them, no cattle. I dropped back to ask who they were and what they wanted, and they rode off over the hill. I know I've seen a couple of them in the saloon back in town."

Floyd stood up. "I'll take my brother's place, let him get some shut-eye. When you find that no-good Chum Wade, make him take the next shift."

An hour later, Chum rode in, slow and quiet. Win braced him. "You knew you were supposed to ride drag second shift tonight."

Chum was surly. "Hell, nobody uses that tone of voice to me."

"I'll use any tone I want to use, and I'll take my bare hands and whip your butt until you cry like a baby! Come off your horse and let me show you how it feels to be slapped around!"

Cautious of Chum's gun, Win stepped quickly to the ground, waited. Chum rolled off his horse, his hand darting toward his pistol as he came. Win flipped his own Colt out of holster and jammed the barrel deep in the soft flesh of Chum's belly. Chum went "Oof!" and doubled over. Then he stood with mouth open, groggy. He held both hands out in surrender.

Win stood rock-hard and glaring even though Chum couldn't see him that well in soft darkness with only a half-moon overhead. "Get on your horse and relieve Floyd at drag. Now! You'll pull a double shift tonight!"

Slow day followed slow day as steers munched grass, traveled, munched grass and moved north and farther north. They crossed the Brazos at Waco. Rain fell and the steers bunched together, for the first time acting as a cohesive group.

Sancho had tried several times to break into the chuck wagon after tamales or biscuits or just any human food. Pete's long whip had flicked out and bit him every time. Now and then Sancho dropped back to drag and tried to head south. He still had to be staked and tied every night, always near the chuck wagon and always by Lopez.

The ground became mud-churned as more rain fell. Twice the six men who slow-trailed the drive were seen. Twice, when Win rode to investigate, rifle in hand, the men rode away.

Near Fort Worth, the rain stopped and sun shone. The west fork of the Trinity was swollen and muddy. The drive halted for two days.

On the third day, with sun still shining and water lowered, Win threw a loop around Sancho's great white horns and led him to the ford. Carefully loosing his end of the rope from the saddle horn, making sure his chestnut would not get tangled if Sancho fought water, the tall drover leaned from the saddle, held out a tamale. The steer opened his big maw and his long tongue licked out eagerly. The banana-shaped concoction of peppers and chopped beef wrapped in corn shuck disappeared as Sancho chewed and chewed and then burped.

When Win put his gelding in water and held two more tamales in his hand, Sancho followed, swimming easily as they hit high water. The steer kept his head high, mouth open and tongue curling toward the tamales as they crossed. Behind them the ranchers hoorawed the other steers into following Sancho.

On the other side of the west fork, Win fed the two tamales to the steer and rubbed his head. "By damn, we know what to do when we get to Red River, don't we?"

Later, when they reached Sivell's Bend in Red River, the place was almost deserted. The water was still high from rains upstream. Trees had been uprooted and sawyers and floaters could trap cattle—if you could get them into the treacherous current in the first place.

If it had been three or four years later, there would have been a mass of cattle ahead of them, several herds, waiting their turn to cross. But in 1869, the drives had barely started, and there was no waiting line.

Win Macoy remained on the Texas side of Red River, moved the herd in a westerly direction, more or less, until he was even with the old Civil War Texas Ranger outpost known as Red River Station. That place, too, was almost deserted in 1869. Later, as an important crossing in what would be known as the Chisolm Trail, it would be a crowded rendezvous for Texas herds.

The river here was less hazardous, except for possible quicksand. That wasn't as much danger in high water. Macoy waited another day while steers munched grass. The steers had become even more of a group, recognizing each other and eager to stay together. If they stampeded, as they had threatened to do several times, they would stay together. If they did not stampede, they would bunch together at nights—all except Sancho, who always seemed to be plotting to return to his *querencia*.

At mid-afternoon, with sun shining and water not so bad now, Win held out a tamale to Sancho. The steer loped forward, making glad noises. Win roped him, held the rope loose so he could let go at any moment. Then he tolled the big brown and white longhorn across the Red while the herd followed.

Everybody got wringing wet. A chill wind, late in the season though it was, took away late spring and made wet clothes, chaps, and boots feel winter-cold. Two miles north of Red River, at an open place suitable to bed the herd, Win called a halt. Since most of Pete's firewood had gotten wet, two men with axes took the lead wagon and found wood that would burn. They built as big a fire as they could between the lead wagon and the chuck wagon, and those who could be spared from duty put boots and chaps on sticks in the smoke of the fire, hoping to dry things out. Men changed from water-soaked clothes to spare clothes that had been protected by tarp rolls in the wagon or behind saddle cantles protected by paulin and slicker. Four men, still in wet clothes, rode around and around the herd, singing, trying to get the steers to settle down.

Win Macoy had opened the lid of his box desk and was writing the trail report when Pete Lopez came in.

"Señor," Pete said. "What do you think of Sancho now?"

"He's spoiled."

"Useful, is he not? Ah, it is sad. He realizes he has just left Texas. He stands looking south, not chewing cud, making low moans and looking homesick. Ah, I myself think of Maria and our children, and I know how he feels. Do we have to sell him for beef when we hit Kansas, or do we keep him to lead future drives?"

"He's Tanner Logan's steer. Tanner said sell him."

"You can buy him and give him to Betty Sue for a wedding present."

"Dammit, Pete, I hadn't heard she was getting married. Sancho is a steer, and steers were born to be sold for meat. I don't want to hear a damn bit more about it!"

He got on his horse and rode around the herd. Around the fire now, men stretched out, some talking in low tones, others sleeping. Steers bunched together, looking restless. Preacher Jones and Pitchfork Kelly passed each other as

Win neared. They sang religious hymns in a soothing monotone, and Win wondered if this wasn't a strain on Kelly. Several times he'd heard Kelly sing songs more fit for a brothel than for Preacher Jones's company.

A full moon shone. A night bird cried from near the Red River and wolves howled from somewhere on the prairie.

"Howdy, Win." Preacher Jones and Pitchfork Kelly both stopped. Preacher asked, "Don't you ever sleep?"

"I would if I could hear you preach a sermon."

"Peaceful night," the preacher insisted.

"Oh, no, it isn't," Pitchfork Kelly contradicted. "It was peaceful, but back yonder, one of them steers jumped up and looked around real spooky a few minutes ago. The he calmed and lay back down. Some other steers at another place looked up, sniffed the air like they was something or someone strange circling the herd."

"I'll tell your relief to be on guard," Win promised.

"If my relief is Chum Wade, you better find him first," Kelly said. "Somebody rode west of me a half hour ago, headed toward the river. I figure it was Chum Wade. I feel he has business with those six men who've been following."

"We'll take care of those men later," Win promised. "When we hit the hills, there's a narrow pass and it's the only road through. We'll keep the cattle moving, but four or five of us will drop back with rifles and wait for these fellows. Just be patient. And don't mention this to Chum Wade."

Win kept his horse moving slow, checking every area. He began a slow cattle sing-song, a lullaby, and all seemed to be normal. Coffee is what I need, he decided after a while. Coffee. It'll be stale and bitter by now, but it'll be coffee.

Sancho was tethered on the west side of the chuck wagon, away from sleeping men and the dim reflection of low fire. He made a soft noise, plaintive, sorrowful, as Win rode past him.

The tall drover got a cup from the chuck wagon. An enameled coffeepot still hung near hot coals. Pouring a cup of bitter brew, Win sipped it.

Sancho bawled. Win went back to where the steer stood, shaking his enormous white horns. Win held out his cup, and Sancho licked toward it.

"You want coffee, huh?" Win said. With his left hand, he rubbed the short hairs between the steer's horns. "Damned if you don't grow on a fellow."

Sancho tried to get the coffee cup. Win slapped him, and Sancho tried to lick his face.

Win was laughing aloud when something cold and hard jabbed the back of his neck. He froze, then heard the loud whisper, "Don't make a sound, Trail Boss!"

Chum Wade! Thinking fast, he dropped the coffee cup, eased his right hand toward his belt gun.

A small, ferret-faced man stepped forward, pointed an Arkansas toothpick knife at his gut. "Do what Chum says, mister. No noise. Raise your hands nice and slow. I'll take your hardware and that belt knife you got."

The small man was outlined, black and white, in the moonlight. *He's not professional, or he wouldn't get this close to me,* Win thought. *I can double over on top of him, kick Chum in the groin. No, Chum would shoot, probably kill me, and the sounds would stampede the herd. Careful. Easy.*

Behind him, Chum laughed, a low mocking sound. "You move or you try to yell, and I'll blow your neckbone in two. Start walking nice and slow toward the river—"

Nice and slow toward the river, Win thought. *They'll get me there and throw my body in the swift current.* Aloud, he asked, "But why, Chum?"

The ferret-faced man looked up at him. "Mr. Ruddels is not going to let these ranchers pay their mortgages, Trail Boss. We got people in Kansas waiting. This herd will be stole by Indians and ever' rancher here will be kilt by Indians. We got friends trailing you. First, you'll disappear, then another man or two, and it'll be easy when we get the herd in the right place."

I can yell, get myself killed, and at least the others will be alerted, Win thought. *Chum and his pal will get away as the stampede starts.* He kept his face forward, even when Ferret-face took his gun and knife. Chum's bad breath circled him, Chum's body odor stifled him. Win could even smell the twist tobacco Chum had in his shirt pocket.

Aloud, he said, "Ruddels is smarter than I thought."

Chum laughed. "You'll never know just how smart, Trail Boss. Inside of a year, we'll own Calamity County and some other places. We took care of Banker Lennox, we got control of the bank—"

Sancho moved suddenly, enormous white horns swinging, big nostrils flaring, huge mouth opening and tongue licking for the tobacco in Chum's shirt pocket. Chum stumbled back and

Win doubled over and dived for Ferret-face, grabbing his gun from the man's hand as he did so. Rolling under the chuck wagon, in shadow, he shot Chum, who was backing away from Sancho. Then he shot Ferret-face.

Chum backpedaled, windmilling, arms flailing. He screamed, fell flat. Win leaned over, put his Colt against the man's forehead, gave the coup de grace. Then he shot Ferret-face once more to make sure he was dead.

Steers jumped to their feet, bawling. Men ran, some toward Win, some toward horses. Some never got their wet boots on, but they rode bareback, circling the frightened animals, making soothing noises. Amazingly, the herd stood fast. No stampede.

"Guess after crossing Red River today, they was too tired to be fractious," Hammer conjectured after the fire had built up and calm had been restored and Pete had made more coffee.

"A miracle," Floyd pronounced. "A blue-eyed wonder them steers ain't scattered from here to Hades."

"Way I see it, Sancho saved your life and our bacon," Lopez stated.

"He didn't do it on purpose," Win explained. "He was just after tobacco."

"You owe him," Floyd insisted. "He saved your hide."

"Popcorn!"

"Is that all your life is worth?"

"Look, we got troubles. From what I just heard, Ruddels has fake Indians who will try to kill all of us and steal the herd."

Preacher Jones stood up, gave a prayer for help and a prayer for thanks that the herd had not stampeded, then orated, "We must send word back home, tell the ranchers there what

Ruddels has done and is planning. One of us must carry the message."

Win moved beside him, shook his head. "No. No, we can't spare one man. I'll get this herd through, but everybody stays with us."

Pete Lopez laughed suddenly. "Trail Boss—"

"Shut up, Pete. I know what you're going to say. No!"

"Señor Macoy, Sancho will make it. Tie a note to his horns."

"Dammit, Pete, no!"

"You owe him your life," Floyd kept on. "That big baby will hide by day and travel by night and he'll get back to Betty Sue. Now, if Betty Sue had the hots for me like she does for you—"

"Shut up, Floyd!"

Everybody except Win started laughing. Hammer laughed so hard he rolled on the ground. Win Macoy flung his coffee on the ground, stomped to the wagon, lit the lantern, and opened his box-type desk. Taking pen and ink, he wrote a letter to his uncle Sheb and Tanner Logan, explaining what he'd learned about Gage Ruddels. He put this in an oilskin wrapping, went outside and tied the letter securely to Sancho's right horn at hair base.

Then he stood scratching the short hairs atop the longhorn's head. He stood there a while, thinking of Betty Sue and the way she kissed and how she'd waited for him ever since she'd been ten and eleven years old. Abruptly he wheeled, jumped back inside the wagon, reached for pen and ink. Before he came to his senses, it was too late. He'd written a letter to Betty Sue. He'd promised they would be married next time he saw her. He didn't say he loved her. That would be a sign of weakness. Damnation, if a man asked a girl to marry him, she should *know* he loved her. No use saying something that didn't need to be said.

Next day, after the herd was moving fast on prairie to the north, Win and Pitchfork Kelly herded Sancho south. Win made sure the brown and white beast swam Red River. The last he saw of the bastard, Sancho was headed south in a long lope.

The way Mrs. Logan told it, Sancho came in early one morning. He started bellowing two miles out, and kept it up even as he stood at the gate, getting everybody out of bed. "Lord God, his hooves was wore almost to the hair, but he wasn't lame. He was rib-showing and thin-bellied like he hadn't stopped to graze. Betty Sue went out of her mind, hugging him and crying. Then we saw two letters tied to his horns. Tanner read the one about Gage Ruddels. Next day the ranchers here went in to talk to Gage. You know about that. Wasn't it nice of Mr. Ruddels to write that letter confessing his sins and saying the bank really belonged to Mrs. Lennox? And in his letter he said he was going to hang hisself so he wouldn't do no more bad deeds. How that poor man tied his hands behind his back before he hung hisself I'll never know, but at least he repented his bad deeds before he went to Judgment. It shows there's some good in even the worst people.

"When Betty Sue read that letter from Win—the one addressed to her—well, my Lord A'mighty! I tell you, Tanner spoils his daughter too much, now and then. They're both on their way north, riding fast to catch the herd. My, won't Win be surprised! Preacher Jones can marry them."

Meantime, not knowing how quickly matrimony was closing in on him, Win Macoy felt good every time he thought of Sancho running fast toward his *querencia*. Hell, the big nuisance had saved his life, even if he hadn't meant to. A man ought to be a man and pay his debts and not be beholden to anybody or anything, and he, Win Macoy, lived by that code. You paid your debts even to a pet steer. Any anyway, Win thought, Sancho wasn't his problem anymore.

THE GAMBLER,
by Bill Pronzini

Bill Pronzini has edited, or co-edited with Martin H. Greenberg, more than a score of Western fiction anthologies. Among his forty-five novels are half a dozen Westerns; these include Starvation Camp *(1984)*, The Last Days of Horse-Shy Halloran *(1987)*, The Hangings *(1988)*, and Firewind *(1989)*. A collection of his Western short stories will be published this year by Ohio University Press. "The Gambler," about the life and death of a nineteenth-century "sporting man," is perhaps the best of his shorter work in the field.

• THE GAMBLER •
by Bill Pronzini

For most of his life, he said, nigh on fifty years, he'd been a sporting man.

Faro, that was his game, he said. He'd operated faro banks all over the West, been a mechanic in some of the fanciest gambling houses from one end of the frontier to the other. Poker? Sure, that too. He'd played poker and Brag for big stakes. Three-card monte and twenty-one and pitch and just about any other card game you could name. His hands weren't much to look at now, all crippled up with arthritis like they were, but once, why he could hold one deck in the palm of his hand while he shuffled up another. That wasn't the least of what he could do, neither. He'd always been a square gambler ... well, almost always, fella sometimes hit a losing streak and he had to eat then too, didn't he? Not that he'd ever worked any big-time gyps or cons, mind. Just every now and then held out an ace or stacked a deck whilst shuffling or reversed a cut—and done it in the company of men like Dick Clark and Frank Tarbeaux and Luke Short and the Earp brothers, with them watching with their hawk's eyes and never suspecting a thing. That was how good a mechanic *he* was in his prime.

Those had been wild times, he said, desperate times. But from soda to hock, they'd also been

grand times. Oh Lordy, what grand times they
had been!

Thing was, he hadn't set out to enter the Life.
No, when he'd left Ohio for California that summer of '54, it had been gold-mining that was on
his mind. Just sixteen that summer, all fixed to
help work his brother John's claim in the
Mother Lode. But when he got to Columbia, the
gem of the southern mines, he'd found poor
John a month dead of consumption and his
claim sold off to pay debts—and *him* with just
two dollars left out of his traveling money. Only
job he could get was swamping at the Long
Tom.

Hardly a man left now that remembers the
Long Tom, he said, but in its day it was the
swellest gambling house in Columbia, and Columbia itself the ripsnortin'est town in the
whole of the Mother Lode. Thirty saloons, a sta-
dium for bull and bear fights, close to a hundred and fifty faro banks . . . why there hadn't
been a town like it since, except maybe Tombstone in the eighties. And that Long Tom, well,
that Long Tom was so big it ran from one street
clean through to another, with a doorway at either end. Twenty-four tables, twelve on each
side of a center aisle wide as a stagecoach run-
way. Guards on both doors, two armed floormen, and when there was a ruckus those guards
would draw their pistols and shoot out the big
whale-oil lamps that hung over the aisle and
then the doormen would lock the doors and the
floormen would shine dark lanterns on the gents
that were cheating or otherwise causing trouble and put an end to it, peaceable or unpeace-
able. Then the floormen would rig up new lights
and the games would commence again just as
though nothing had happened.

Well, the Long Tom was owned by the Mitchell brothers, and what they did was, they rented out those twenty-four tables to professional gamblers like Charles Cora, who later on got himself hung for murder by the vigilantes in San Francisco, and Ad Pence and Governor Hobbs and John Milton Strain. Now, John Milton Strain was a gold-hunter as well as a gambler, and he didn't mind taking a young buck along with him to do some of the hard labor. Also didn't mind teaching a young buck the ins and outs of the sporting trade. So that was how he'd learned cards, he said—from John Milton Strain, one of the best of the old-time card sharps. (Wasn't any slouch when it came to prospecting, neither, was John Milton. One day he found a gold nugget big as an adobe brick, ten inches wide and five inches thick—all high-grade ore that he melted down into a bar weighing more than thirty pounds. Sleeper's Gold Exchange paid him $7500 for that bar. Seventy-five hundred dollars for one bar of pure gold!)

He'd worked at the Long Tom three years, he said, learning the gambling trade from John Milton Strain ... well enough finally so that he'd rented his own faro layout right alongside John Milton's. He might have stayed on longer, except that a fire burned the Long Tom down in '57—burned twelve square blocks of Columbia's business district along with it. The Mitchell brothers put up a new building, but John Milton had had his fill of Columbia by then and he decided he'd had his too. So the two of 'em set out together for greener pastures.

He'd spent nearly ten years touring the mining camps in California and Nevada, about half that time with John Milton Strain for a partner. During those years he learned to hold his own with just about anybody in a "hard cards" game for big stakes. Won more than he lost, consistent, and if it hadn't been for a fondness for hard spirits and the company of fast women, why he'd have been a rich man before he was thirty. Yes sir, a rich man. But money was made to be spent, that was his philosophy. The more he made, the hotter it got sitting there in his pockets; and when it commenced to burn holes, well, what was there to do then but take it out and spend it?

By early '66 he'd had enough of the mining camps; he craved a look at other parts of the frontier, a chance to play with the bigger names in the sporting trade. So he'd drifted east and north, he said, up to Montana and then down to Cheyenne, Wyoming, which was a wide-open town in those days. Plenty of sports there, all right, most of them with the "Hell-on-Wheels" crowd that was following the construction of the Union Pacific Railroad west from Omaha to Promontory Point, Utah.

Now along that Union Pacific route, he said, the railroad set up supply points and camp-grounds for track workers and other laborers—impermanent tent towns for thousands of men. Well, those railroaders played as hard as they worked, so it was only natural that the honky-tonkers would gravitate to the camps to oblige them. In Cheyenne, one of the few real towns along the route, he'd found scores of gamblers, square and sure-thing both, and dozens of small-timers working as ropers, cappers, and steerers. Madams and whores and pimps, too. And saloon operators and confidence men and dips and yeggs—the whole shebang. And what they'd do, every time the railroad moved its base of operations a little farther west, was to pack up *their* equipment and move right along with 'em. That was how the whole business came to be called Hell-on-Wheels.

He'd joined up with 'em in Cheyenne and stayed on through Fort Saunders and Laramie and Benton City. Crazy wild, those days were, he said. He'd teamed with Ornery Ed Meeker on a brace faro game, and in Fort Saunders he found out Meeker was holding out on him and they'd had it out and one Sunday afternoon he'd shot Meeker dead. Yes sir, one clean shot right in his whiskers. First man he'd ever killed, but not the last. Then he fell in with one of Eleanore Dumont's working girls, to his sorrow, for she stole three thousand dollars he'd won at faro and decamped with the money and a fellow named Peavey, one of Corn-Hole Johnny Gallagher's steerers.

Well, it was just crazy wild. And the wildest place of all was Benton City, which they came into the summer of '68. Hot? Lordy, it was hot that summer! North Platte River was two miles away and the water-haulers charged a dollar a barrel and ten cents a bucket; they had the best graft in town, by a damn sight. He'd worked the Empire Tent there, on account of it was the biggest operation and got the heaviest play and he figured he could make more than he could with his own box. Fellow who ran the Buffalo Hump Corral wanted him in there, too—offered him a piece of the action—but the Buffalo Hump specialized in a game called rondo coolo, which you played with a stick and ivory balls on a billiard table, and what did he know about a game like that? He was a card man, a faro dealer and poker sharp. That was what he knew and that was how he made his living.

He was working the Empire Tent when *he* got

shot. Railroad worker accused him of marking cards, which he hadn't been, and hauled out a Colt's six-gun and put a slug in his left arm before he could bring his own weapon to bear. Well, he almost died. Almost lost his left arm and almost died, but if he *had* lost that arm he'd have wished he *had* died, he said, because how could a one-armed gambler expect to make out?

Took him three months to recover, and by then the Hell-on-Wheels bunch was getting ready to move on to the next stop. They left a hundred dead behind them, their own and railroaders both—a hundred in three months. And him with that busted wing and most of his cash gone for doctoring and whatnot. So he'd called it quits, right then and there. Hell-on-Wheels wasn't for him. Killed a man and almost been killed himself . . . no sir, that wasn't for him anymore.

So he'd commenced to drifting again, building up stakes and losing 'em and building 'em back up again. Out to Kansas for a spell, Dodge City and the other cowtowns. Shot a man in the Long Branch in Dodge one day but the fellow didn't die; wasn't his fault that time neither, he said. Then, in '73, he'd got wind of a big silver strike in California, down in the Panamint Mountains, and of a new camp that had sprung up there called Panamint City.

Town was wide open when he got there, he said. They called it "a suburb of Hell," which he didn't think it was so far as sin was concerned, not after Hell-on-Wheels—but Lordy, it was *hot* as hell, up there above the floor of Death Valley like it was. Made the Wyoming plain seem like a cool riverside retreat.

First thing, he'd gone to work as a mechanic for Jim Bruce at the Dempsey and Boultinghouse Saloon. Now Bruce was a hard case, having ridden the Missouri-Kansas border with Quantrill, and he didn't take kindly to insults and troublemakers. Another dealer, name of Bob McKenny, ran afoul of Bruce and tried to kill him, and what happened was, Jim Bruce blew his fool head off. And what did he do then, straightaway? Why, he took Bob McKenny right out and buried him, that's what he did, on account of Jim Bruce wasn't just a gambler, he was also Panamint City's undertaker!

Well, he said, after a year or so he started dealing for Dave Neagle at Dave's resort, the Oriental, which had a fancy black walnut bar and some of the spiciest paintings of the female form divine that a man ever set eyes on. He stayed on there for four years, and would have stayed longer, likely, for he and Dave Neagle got on fine and he'd taken up with one of the girls at Martha Camp's bawdy house, Sadie her name was, blond and plump like the women in the paintings over the Oriental's black walnut bar. But then a big rainstorm hit the Panamints and a flash flood came boiling down from the heights and swept up more than a hundred buildings as if they were bunches of sticks, the Oriental among 'em, and washed the wreckage all the way down Surprise Canyon and spread it over a mile of the Panamint Valley. Hadn't been for somebody up at one of the stamp mills spotting the flood and raising an alarm, he said, him and most of the other townspeople would have gone sailing down Surprise Canyon too.

From there he'd gone up to Bodie for a while, and then on back to Kansas and the queen of the cowtowns. But Dodge wasn't what she had been a decade earlier, he said, leastways not so far as a sporting man was concerned, and he hadn't stayed long—just long enough to get wind that Dick Clark and Lou Rickabaugh and Bill Harris, who had once owned the Long Branch, had gone into partnership and opened a resort out in Tombstone. Well, he'd never met Dick Clark and wished he had, for Clark was a legend among sporting men, so he'd set out for Arizona Territory. And when he arrived in Tombstone, why Dick Clark was every bit the gentleman he was reputed to be, and his Oriental Saloon and Gambling Hall at Allen and Fifth streets was by far the grandest gambling house in town. Fancy chandeliers and colored crystals set into the bar, which was finished in white and gilt, and a club room to knock the eye out of a Victorian swell . . . oh, it was grand! He'd never been in a grander place before nor since, he said.

Now Dick Clark, as befitted his station, had some mighty important gents dealing for him. He had Luke Short and Bat Masterson and Wyatt Earp and Doc Holliday, among others, and he paid them twenty-five dollars for a six-hour shift—princely wages for those times. That was where *he* wanted to work, no question about that, so he'd talked to Dick Clark and danged if Dick Clark hadn't hired him. And there he was, he said, dealing at the Oriental Saloon with Luke Short and Wyatt Earp and Doc Holliday and Bat Masterson, all of them swell fellows and don't let anybody tell you different.

Bat Masterson didn't stay long, having fish to fry elsewhere, but Wyatt and Doc, they stayed, and everybody knows what happened with them. Well, sure—they and Wyatt's brothers Virgil and Morgan got into a feud with the Clantons and the McLaury brothers and Curly Bill Brocius and John Ringo, and it all came to a head late in '81 when Morgan Earp got himself ambushed and then Wyatt went out in a vengeful rage and done for Curly Bill and a couple of others in the Clanton crowd. That was when they had the big shootout at the O.K. Corral. He was there that day and he'd seen it all, he said. He'd seen the whole thing from soda to hock.

Nor was that all he'd seen that year, he said. He'd seen Luke Short gun down Charlie Storms, a hard case who'd been one of the Hell-on-Wheels bunch. Happened right there in the Oriental, right smack in front of *his* table. It was Charlie Storms's doing, he said, no question about that, for he was a mean one and had been in several gunfights in Cheyenne and Deadwood and Leadville, and wanted to add an important name to his list of victims. But he met his match in Luke Short. He goaded little Luke, and goaded him some more, and then when push came to shove, why Luke outdrew him cool as you please and Charlie Storms died a surprised man.

Tombstone in the eighties was a fine place to be, he said, and he'd felt settled there, working for Dick Clark. Now and then he'd develop an itch, same as Dick Clark himself would, and get on a stagecoach and see what Lady Luck had in store in places like Tucson and Phoenix and Prescott and Las Vegas, New Mexico. But he never stayed long in any of those places—particularly not in Las Vegas, where he himself had been goaded into killing his second and last man, this time in a misunderstanding over a woman. He always went back to Tombstone and the Oriental Saloon and Gambling Hall. He was still dealing there, he said, when Dick Clark sold out his interest in '94 and retired from the Life.

He was likewise of retirement age by then,

but unlike Dick Clark and some of the other old-timers who'd made their fortunes and bought houses and saloons and other property, or invested their money in stocks and bonds and such, and were comfortably fixed for the rest of their days, *he* was still just a mechanic. Flush some of the time, broke more often. Never saved any of his winnings, never invested any of it or bought any property other than what he could carry in a pair of carpetbags. Sport like him couldn't afford to retire. All he could do, he said, was keep right on dealing cards.

So after Dick Clark sold out his interest in the Oriental, he'd gone on down to Bisbee, which was still a fair hot town in the mid-nineties, and worked for a time in Cobweb Hall. Then he'd moved on to Phoenix and Prescott, and then up to Virginia City, Nevada, and then over to Albuquerque. He was in Albuquerque when the new century came in, he said, sixty-two years old and stony broke in Albuquerque, New Mexico. But then he'd won a stake and moved on to Taos, and then over into Texas—San Antonio and El Paso and Austin and Tascosa—and then back into Arizona Territory, to see if Tombstone was anything like it had been in the old days. But it wasn't. No sir, *none* of the towns were like they'd been in the old days. They were all changed, and still changing so fast you could almost see it happening right before your eyes.

Once, he said, the sporting man had commanded respect. Not just the high rollers like Dick Clark, no, ordinary sports like himself. Why, you could walk down the street in just about any town and gents would doff their hats and smile and wish you good day. Women would smile, too, some of them, and more than you'd think would do more than smile. Oh, you were somebody in those days, he said. You had a skill few had, and you made big money, and you were somebody and you had respect.

But not after the new century came in. Not after all the people moved west and shrank the land and tamed it. Everything changed then. Men quit smiling and doffing their hats and wishing you good day. Women wouldn't have anything to do with you, none except the whores. They all whispered behind your back and gave you dirty looks and shunned you like you were a common thief. And then the territorial leaders that wanted statehood, they went and put those laws in, all those antigambling laws. Blamed gambling and sporting men for society's ills and took away their livelihood and made them outlaws and outcasts.

It wasn't fair, he said, it wasn't right. What could men like him do, men who'd been in the Life for nigh on fifty years? Where could they go? Some took to running illegal games, sure, but those were the young ones. What about the ones past their prime, old men with hands starting to cripple with arthritis? What about them?

Memories, that was all they left him. Fifty years of memories ... all the places he'd been, all the things he'd seen and done, all the men and women he'd known. He'd seen it all in those fifty years, by grab. He'd *lived* it all. Been a part of the wildness, and of the slow taming too. But now ... now the land was too tame, it was like a tiger that had become a pussycat. This wasn't the frontier anymore, a place with growl and howl; this was just a tamed tiger meowing in the sun.

Well, *he* remembered the old days, he said. *He* knew how wild and desperate those times had been. And how grand too. Oh Lordy, what grand times they had been!

They found him one morning in the dust behind Simpson's Barber Shop, lying crumpled in the dust with his nightshirt pulled up to expose the swollen veins in his pipestem legs. He must have come out during the night to use the outhouse, the town marshal said. Left his room at the rear of the shop, where Simpson had let him live in exchange for sweeping up, and set out for the privy and had a seizure before he got there. He hadn't died right away, though. He'd crawled a ways, ten feet or so toward the privy; the marks were plain in the dust.

That afternoon, the undertaker and his assistant put the corpse in a plain pine box, loaded the box into the mortuary wagon, and drove up the hill to the cemetery. The only other citizen to go along with them was the preacher, but he didn't tarry long. The old man hadn't been religious and had never attended church services; it was only out of common decency that the preacher had decided to speak a few words over the grave. Besides, it was hot that day. Hot as the hinges of Hell, the preacher said just before he rode his horse back down the hill.

The undertaker and his assistant made short work of the burying and laid their tools in the wagon. The assistant mopped his sweating face with his handkerchief, spoke then for the first time since their arrival.

"You think he *was* a sporting man?"

"That old coot?" the undertaker said. "Now what makes you ask that?"

"Well, all those stories he would tell . . ."

"Stories, that's all they were. Old man's imaginings. He had nothing when he come here and nothing when he died. No money, no kin, no friends to speak of—nobody, even, to buy him a marker for his final resting place. And him supposed to have been a fancy card sharp rubbing elbows with Wyatt Earp and Bat Masterson? Pshaw!"

The undertaker shook his head, turned to look down the dry brown hill at the dry brown town crouching in the summer heat; at the desert beyond, rolling away like a dead sea toward the horizon.

"Wasn't nobody at all," he said.

BALM FOR A BROKEN HEART,
by Leo P. Kelley

Although Leo P. Kelley hails from Pennsylvania and lives in upstate New York, he writes primarily about the Old West. He has nearly thirty Western novels to his credit, including nine in his popular action-adventure series about an outrider named Luke Sutton. His recent titles include Luke Sutton: Bounty Hunter (1985), A Man Named Dundee (1988), and Luke Sutton: Lawman (1989). "Balm for a Broken Heart" is a considerable departure from the hard-edged Luke Sutton stories—a quietly evocative tale of a Texas "granny woman" and the kind of wisdom that comes only through harsh personal experience.

• BALM FOR A BROKEN HEART •
by Leo P. Kelley

"She needs tending to, Granny Garvey," her mother, Fay, said when she brought Annalee over to me that night right in the middle of all the dancing and the general jubilation at the Harvest Home Barn Dance.

"Child, you've gone and growed up faster than a spring calf in sweet pasture," I told Annalee but she just stood there with her head hanging down and sniffling like a cat with a cold.

"She's ailing, Granny Garvey," Fay said, wrapping an arm around her only offspring and hugging her close up. "She's been feeling real poorly for some time now. I pray you have a poultice or a potion that will cure her."

Folk down through the years, they taken to coming to me for doctoring the way Fay brought Annalee to me that night. What happens is folk take to moping about, feeling off their feed, and first thing you know they come calling on old Granny Garvey to fashion something out of crushed dandelion root or beeswax gathered by the light of a new moon.

If it's an out-of-sorts nursing mother who shows up on my doorstep, more often than not she just needs to drink some of the juice of the bedstraw milkweed to set herself to rights. Indian turnip pounded to a powder has cured more headaches than you could shake a stick at. For unsettled stomachs, I boil up a batch of my special elixir of wild mint that has a pinch of this and a bit of that thrown in it.

Some say I work wonders but what it all is, is mostly good common sense combined with getting to know over a period of years of trial and error what herbs and plants work best for whatever ailment a fellow happens to have. Like, for instance, how the Indians round this part of Texas take to chewing the tiny cones of spruce trees to ease the pain of a sore throat. Works nine times out of the gate and the tenth time—well, nothing and nobody's perfect, I always say.

But sitting there that night I had a funny feeling about Annalee Matlock. I wasn't all that sure I could find a cure for whatever it was that ailed her. She looked to me for sure and certain to be in a bad way. What with her teary red eyes and red nose and the way she was all a-tremble like a willow in a wind, she looked about as sorry as something the cat dragged in.

Funny thing was, even though she was a-sniffling and a-shuddering and looking for all the world like her favorite dog just died on her, she was still the prettiest little thing you ever laid an eye on. Hair the color of ripe corn and eyes as dark blue as huckleberries. Skin as smooth as a blue clay hill after a rainstorm and lips as soft as goosedown. She'd spent just sixteen years on this good green earth but she was already womanly enough to turn the head and stir the heart of any man who wasn't blind.

"What is it ails you, child?" I asked her.

Annalee didn't say a thing. She just got all teary and trembly again and looked over to where the fiddler was playing his heart out and twenty-year-old Luke Warner, who was bean-

pole lean and actor handsome, was standing
with a look on his face that made me think he
might be moonstruck. Only he couldn't have
been, not the way he was staring so wide-eyed
and field-hand hungry at the young and buxom
Widow Ransom, who was smiling up at him like
she was a rose and he was her sun.

"I've got soothing syrups and sweet teas and
all sorts and manner of other things to cure
most any ill known to man," I told Fay, "but
I'm not so sure I know what to do for Annalee."

"You've got to do something!" Fay said. "The
girl's wasting away right before my eyes. Talk
to her, Granny Garvey. She'll tell you what you
need to know to work one of your cures. I'm
sure she will. You've got to help her. I don't
know anybody else who can. This that she's suf-
fering from, whatever it is—it's not the sort of
thing what gets better under regular doctoring.
It needs a granny woman like you to get to the
bottom of it."

"Leave her here with me, Fay," I said. "You
go dance with your mister. I'll talk to the child.
Go on now. *Shooo!*"

When Fay had gone, I patted the seat of the
empty chair next to mine and told Annalee to
sit herself down before she fell down, she
looked that bad. Once she was sitting, I said,
"Now then, tell me what's wrong."

She looked across at the fiddler. Or so I
thought at first. Then I saw it was really Luke
Warner she was looking at. With tears in her
eyes. I got to recalling how I heard Miz Idalou
Hayes say in the General Mercantile in town one
day not far back, "That Annalee Matlock has
taken to walking out with Luke Warner from
over on Owl Creek."

It was right about then that a gent stepped up

alongside the fiddler and he started in a-calling a square dance.

"Gents chase and put on style.
Rehash and a little more style.
Little more style, gents,
a little more style."

Annalee groaned as she watched Luke Warner step out, the Widow Ransom on his arm, and fit the pair of them into one of the sets that was forming on the barn's floor while the fiddler fiddled and the caller called the turns.

"Swing the man who stole the sheep,
Now the one that hauled it home,
Now the one that eat the meat,
And now the one that gnawed the bone."

Annalee's face turned white as a bleached sheet as Luke Warner stole a kiss from the Widow Ransom.

The Widow Ransom's face, on the other hand, was all flushed as Luke swung her this way, then that way, their hands touching, their eyes locked on each other.

I thought I saw now how the land lay. "Luke Warner's the one who's made you feel so poorly, isn't he?" I up and right out asked Annalee.

She looked at me like I'd just gone and discovered the secret at the very center of the universe and nodded.

I waited. Then I waited some more.

Finally, Annalee said, "It's the Widow Ransom. She's turned Luke's head with her teasing and her perfume she *claims* comes from Paris, France, though I happen to know it came from Philadelphia and costs twenty cents the bottle."

"Annalee," I said with a sigh, "there's something you have got to understand and now's as good a time as any for you to do that understanding. Men have been hurting the hearts of women since time began, not to mention vice versa. I don't know of nobody who's as yet found a cure for that other than old Father Time his own self."

"It's all the Widow Ransom's fault," Annalee pouted. "No, it's not. Luke's as much to blame as she is. She come sashaying up to us one night about a week back and started sweet-talking lies to Luke, and before I knew which way was up she had him on a string like he was her pet pup and she hasn't let loose of him since.

"They say she's got eyes for anything in pants, and I, for one, believe it with my whole heart. Since her husband passed on, there's been a regular mob of gentlemen callers at her front door both day and night. Now she's cast her line and caught Luke like he was any old fish in the brook and he's forgotten I even exist!"

I knew well what the gossips had to say about the Widow Ransom, the least unkind remark I'd heard being, "She don't have the least bit of trouble getting a rake to gather her hay crop."

Annalee give me a soulful look. "You don't have any potion that would make me feel better than I do?"

She looked at me so hopeful, I like to have died, knowing I didn't have a thing in my cupboards at home to give her that would help her in her hour of need. If she had bruised her knee or cut herself someplace, I could give her dried yarrow to put on the places that hurt. If she had got the scurvy, I could have told her to eat the raw bulbs of wild garlic which would have her feeling tip-top in no time. But I had no balm to give her to help heal her broken heart.

Both of us just sat there then as Luke Warner and the Widow Ransom snuck off into a corner where there weren't no lantern.

"Then there's nothing you can do to help me?" Annalee asked me.

I shook my head and told her no, there was nothing I could do to help her.

"I don't care!" she declared with a saucy toss of her yellow hair. "It's not as if I were in love with Luke Warner or anything serious like that. If I were, then maybe I would try to patch things up with him. But since I don't love him, I'm certainly not going to go crawling to him and beg him to come calling on me again. I have my pride after all."

Hearing Annalee's last words sent me tumbling back in time to when I was as young and foolish as she was and my man, whose name was Judah Garvey, up and disappeared one day like smoke in the wind.

I had cried my heart out when I first found out he'd gone. I'd carried on and near had me a conniption fit. Then I got a good grip on myself. "He's only one fish," I told myself right out loud. "Remember, the sea's full of fishes. Stop thinking on how you're going to get him back. You don't even know where or when he went. Besides which, you have your pride to think of."

I have my pride after all.

Annalee's words. And my very own—almost—spoken all those long years ago.

Thinking on them and on Judah and Annalee and Luke Warner and the Widow Ransom, I reckoned I might maybe have a way after all to heal the hurt that had come to pester Annalee's young heart.

I started telling Annalee all about me and Judah Garvey and how we lived and loved in bygone days when we were both young and had eyes only for each other.

Judah, he drifted into town one day in the spring of the year the way a tumbleweed drifts before the wind. Folk said a drifter like him'd be gone soon enough, probably sooner than any one of us could get ourselves a real good look at him.

But I got myself a real good look when we went to town after he had come to West Bend, Texas, from nobody knew where or why. I was with my ma and pa and all my younger sisters and brothers. The tads went with their saved-up cents to buy licorice and the like and ma and pa, they went to the general store to buy provisions.

Me, I went strolling down the boardwalk and stopped in front of the milliner's shop window to gawk at the fancy hats with all the ribbons and gewgaws perched on them. I was marveling over a red felt bonnet with a band of pink roses round it when I heard somebody ride up behind me. Then I saw him in the window glass and he about took my breath away.

It was Judah Garvey, sitting his horse free and easy, and looking for all the world, with his black mustache and sideburns, his big brown eyes, and his even white teeth that flashed in the sun as he smiled at me, like every young girl's dream of romance come to life right there in front of the milliner's shop in stodgy old West Bend, Texas.

"You don't need it," he said in a voice that sent shivers through me.

"Beg pardon?" says I, turning right around to look up at him.

"You don't need that hat," said he. "You're pretty enough without it. So why waste your money?"

Well, I didn't know what in the world to say to that. Or to him. Only one other person had ever in my life told me I was pretty and that person was pa, who used to bounce me on his knee and say things like, "You light up my world, darlin'. Who needs the sun when he's got you?"

"Name's Garvey," he said. "Judah Garvey. Aren't you going to tell me your name?"

"Meriah Soames," I told him whilst thinking he was just about the finest-looking man who ever stepped into stirrups.

"Meriah," says he. "Now that is one lovely name. Sounds just like the wind soughing soft across the prairie. You live in town, do you, Meriah?"

I told him I didn't and then, when he asked me, I told him where I did live just north of Armstead's Pass.

He showed up at the homeplace the very next night. Said he was just passing by. Said he just happened to recollect as how I lived nearby and he thought it would be the neighborly thing to do to stop by and say howdy.

And him no neighbor of us Soameses at all!

Before he left, I walked with him down through the pasture to the crick on account of he invited me to. The moon shone on the crick so bright it almost blinded me. You could see your reflection in the water. I saw Judah's.

He come back again the next night and we walked out some more that time. Then we did it again when he come to call the following week.

My brothers and sisters took to teasing me,

saying, "Meriah's got a beau, Meriah's got a beau," like a tree full of screech owls or magpies or something noisome like that. They claimed they all heard me talking out loud to Judah and speaking his name in my sleep, which was probably true enough since I have had the bad habit of sleep-talking since I was ten years old.

By June of that year everybody knew Judah was courting me, me most of all, and did it ever put wings on my feet and a dream in my head.

That dream of mine came true in August when we were married in the clapboard church in West Bend by Parson Carlyle and afterward went to live in the cabin Judah had built for us out in Sweet Valley. We didn't sleep a wink that first night on account of how our friends and neighbors shivareed us something fierce all our wedding night long.

We were so in love it hardly ever entered my head that I didn't know a thing about Judah's life before he showed up in West Bend, while he knew practically everything there was to know about me since the day I was born till the day I met him in front of the milliner's.

So after a while, I started asking him about his folks, where he had come from, things like that. He answered me plain enough at first but when I kept at it—you see, I wanted to know all there was to know about the man I loved and had married—he said, with that imp's grin of his, "Meriah, honey"—he always called me "honey"—"the past's dead and gone and ought to be forgotten. What counts is the present and the future."

I took the hint and stopped asking questions and went on living and loving and admiring the way my man was so well liked by just about everybody everywhere. Nobody had a mean word to say about Judah Garvey. They praised him for organizing barn raisings and for things like lending his plow to a farmer who broke his and couldn't get a new one right away on account of how he was a mite short on cash money and wouldn't take credit if you paid him to.

Judah was the kind of man who just couldn't stop giving to folk and who never did learn how to take from them. If he went fishing and caught a good stringful, he wouldn't dry those that weren't eaten whilst they were fresh. No, he'd send me off to the neighbors to share his bounty with them. If a woman's milk dried up and she couldn't find herself a wet nurse anywhere, Judah would tie our milch cow to the wagon and take the critter over to where the mother and baby were in need.

For us in those times everything, by and large, was fine and dandy.

Until the day seven months later when Judah disappeared.

I didn't know at first that he had disappeared. That bitter knowledge came to me later.

He had gone to town on his saddle horse to buy me a sack of sugar I was in need of and to buy a sack of the green coffee he doted on so. He was late coming home but at first I didn't pay the matter no mind. He'd stopped to talk to somebody he'd met or to visit along the way, was what I told myself at the time. But then sundown came. Then night. Still he didn't come calling out like always, "Honey, I'm home."

That there was one long night, let me tell you. I walked the floor. Practically wore out the planks in it, I did. Didn't sleep one wink. Could his horse have shied at the sight of a grass snake and thrown Judah and him be lying somewhere too hurt to get help? But, if something like that had happened, I reckoned somebody or other would have found him and brought him home or took him to the doctor in town and brought me word of what happened.

Come dawn, I was about wore out. I thought I would go to town and ask after Judah. Ask had folk seen him and did they know where he was or went. But if I did that I'd soon be the laughingstock of West Bend, Texas, and known as the woman Judah Garvey ditched.

I just sat and wept the rest of that morning away.

I thought I knew now what had happened. Judah had grown tired of me and drifted out of my life just as easy and unexpected as he'd drifted into it. I like to have cried my eyes out over losing him. I called out his name. I pounded my fists on the tabletop in a regular fit of fury and I tore at my hair the way a woman sick with love for a man who's scorned her will do.

I thought of how his strong arms felt when they held me tight. Like a safe harbor from any and every storm this life can stir up is how they felt to me. When I thought about what it was like to be loved by him, I cried out in pain like as if somebody had struck a sharp knife right into the middle of my heart. I thought of what my friend Darcy Leland had said to me the day she first found out Judah had took to courting me. "You'd best learn to keep a tight rein on him, Meriah," she'd said. "You don't and you're likely to wake up one day and find that drifter long gone and you left all alone and heartsick."

I confess I even damned Judah to hell for what he'd gone and done to me. In my misery, I damned Darcy Leland too for her second sight about Judah and me. I even, may the good Lord forgive me, damned the baby-to-be that was growing inside me.

When a thought come to me. Was it the fact of him going to be a father that had spooked Judah, made him run off without so much as a fare-thee-well? Not likely. I hadn't told him yet. I'd planned on telling him the very night he didn't come home from town.

I quick took down the cracked glass that hung on a nail next the door and held it this way and then that way. No, I wasn't showing as of yet. So he couldn't have known I was with child. It was clear as well water to me by then that he'd just decided it was time to drift on to greener pastures and to some girl he had in the back of his mind who'd be—for a time, the poor thing—the apple of his roving eye.

Right then and there it was that I made up my mind that no fiddlefooted Judah Garvey was going to ruin my life, mine and the life of his child I was carrying. We two'd get along just fine without him. So let him go on his merry way. Let him make calf eyes at some other woman somewhere and good riddance to bad rubbish. He's only one fish, I thought. Just keep in mind the sea's full of them.

My mind set straight, I felt not one whit better, I must confess. But, truth to tell, I wasn't about to let people like Darcy Leland have the last laugh on me for being foolish enough to marry a drifter. After all, I had my pride to think of. I would hold my head up high, I vowed, and the first time anybody asked me about Judah Garvey, I planned to say, "Who?"

But like the poet somewhere said, the best-laid schemes of mice and men sometimes go haywire. Which is what happened to me.

To put it plain, Clyde Nesbitt showed up at my door that afternoon. I didn't know his name then. I found it out later.

When I opened the door after he knocked on it, I bade him good day but he just said, "I'm here hunting Judah Garvey. I was in West Bend asking after him yesterday and folk told me this here was where he lived."

"He's not here," I said, eyeing the gun he had in his hand and making up my mind not to tell him how Judah had gone and run off on me.

"Mind if I have a look around inside?"

Before I could say a word, he pushed right past me and rampaged through the cabin looking for Judah.

"What's this all about?" I asked him, pretending I wasn't one bit scared. "Who are you and what business have you with my husband?"

At that, he give me an evil grin which made my skin crawl and my heart sink.

"You want to know what business I have with your husband, do you?" he said. "Then I'll tell you. Your man, he killed a fella up in Montana. The law up there was all set to put his neck in a noose when he escaped from jail. They put a bounty on his head and I set out to trail him, which I've been doing for some long time now, so I could collect that bounty."

Don't you dare faint, Meriah, I told myself without opening my lips. Fear had got a good strong grip on me by that time and it had turned my knees wobbly and set my heart to hammering.

That was when Nesbitt grabbed me and shook me hard enough to make my teeth rattle. He asked me again where was Judah and once again I told him Judah had gone to town yesterday to buy sugar and coffee.

"Well," he said, "I'm going to stay here and wait for him to come home."

And that's exactly what Nesbitt did. He stayed the night and the better part of the next day too. But when Judah didn't put in an appearance, he finally left, cursing a blue streak and taking the name of the Lord in vain.

Once he'd gone, I made myself calm down and think real careful about what had just happened and what I now knew. When I was through thinking, I had some hope in my heart. Nesbitt had been in town and so had Judah, both of them on the selfsame day. Which maybe meant that Judah hadn't run off on me after all. Maybe it meant that he'd spotted Nesbitt in town and had given him the slip. I made myself think slow and steady as I figured out what I had to do and how to do it.

I went to the barn and saddled up Bessie, my mare, so quick she must have thought I had four hands and twenty fingers. I went back to the cabin and got Judah's hunting rifle down from over the door and then I went riding hell-bent for leather. Riding like Satan himself was on my backtrail.

I rode toward town and soon enough picked up Judah's trail where he'd left the beaten track and cut to the left, heading for our homeplace. It was real easy following his sign; his horse had one chipped shoe. Of course, I've always been a pretty good tracker. Judah used to say I could track bees in a blizzard.

Halfway to our homeplace, Judah had stopped his horse. The ground was tore up some round where he'd sat his saddle for a spell and his horse had moved about. Then he headed north—away from our homeplace. I rode north after him.

By the time I got to Indian River, I knew Nesbitt was on my backtrail because I'd spotted him. Well, I forded the river where Judah had, and when I came out on the other side he himself come stalking out of some woods that was there and he said to me, "I saw you backtrailing me. What do you think you're doing, woman?"

Not honey. Woman. I could tell he was mad as a wet hen.

"We got to move downriver a ways," I told him, not even letting on I'd heard the question he'd flung at me. "Get your horse and come on!"

I practically had to drag him into the woods to get his horse and then led him downriver for a quarter of a mile to a spot I knew.

"What—why—" he spluttered.

"He's been trailing me," I cut in fast. "I spotted him but didn't let on. Now, you just stand right here alongside me and he'll show up any minute."

"You mean Clyde Nesbitt? Is that who you're talking about?"

I nodded and said, "He's been trailing me for some time now." I told Judah how I found the spot where he'd left the trail from town and headed for our homeplace before turning north. "I reckon Nesbitt must have done the selfsame thing I did and only a little later than I did it. Or else he might have been waiting and spying on me from someplace, figuring I knew where you were and would lead him straight to you."

"And so you did," Judah said, but not in a sad or heartsick way. More like in a way that says there's nothing to be done about a situation which has just got to run its course.

"Not *straight* to you," I said. I reminded Judah how we had moved a quarter mile away from where we'd each forded the Indian River.

"Why did you want to do that?" he asked me. But before I could answer him, Nesbitt rode into view and spotted us a-standing on the riverbank. I handed the rifle to Judah.

As Nesbitt rode down along the other bank until he was straight across from us, he taken his carbine out of his saddle boot and aimed it at Judah.

"Drop that squirrel gun, Garvey!" he yelled.

But Judah didn't drop it. He raised it and pointed it at Nesbitt, who just grinned and said, "I'll wager I'm faster than you, Garvey. Bet I could drill you twice before you could get off a single shot."

Then he rode into the river and started toward the two of us. He was halfway across when his horse faltered so bad Nesbitt dropped his gun and it fell into the river. The animal fought the quicksand I'd always known was in that particular part of the river but to no good purpose. The horse was sinking fast. Nesbitt climbed up onto his saddle but then his horse went under and in just another minute he was down in the water and caught in the quicksand.

Judah and I watched him go under. His hat floated on the top of the water like a monument for a short spell, until the current floated it downriver and out of our sight.

"You took yourself an awful chance coming out here after me," Judah said.

"I thought you'd drifted off on me at first," I told him.

"I couldn't ever do that, honey. I started for the homeplace after I'd spotted Nesbitt in town and he hadn't yet seen me. I was already halfway there when—"

"When you had some second thoughts," I interrupted. "I saw where you sat your saddle for a spell to do some pondering."

"I finally decided I couldn't go home and drag you into the same mess I was in."

"But I got dragged into it," I said. "Nesbitt came to the cabin looking for you. He told me about how you'd killed a man up in Montana and he was after you for the bounty the law up there had put on your head. He said he'd tracked you to West Bend where somebody or other told him where you and me lived. I told him you'd gone to town and hadn't come home. He spent the night waiting for you to show up and when you didn't he left the next day.

"I reckon when he couldn't find you in town he might have guessed you'd spotted him when he was there before and lit a shuck. He must have gone tracking you and found your trail like I did—or maybe he found mine, I don't know which—and trailed us here."

Judah didn't say anything. He just stood there staring at the spot where Nesbitt had gone under.

"Why'd you run, Judah?" I asked him.

"I told you," he said. "I didn't want to drag you into the mess I'd made of things since that shooting. I figured if you knew I'd killed a man, you'd want nothing more to do with me. I would have told you it was self-defense, which it was, but I figured you wouldn't believe me any more than anybody up in Montana did.

"You see, it was just me and a drunken buckaroo name of Jake Meriden. We had words and he threw down on me, shot me in the shoulder and was about to shoot me again. I dropped him with a round in the heart. I told the judge he shot me first but he didn't believe me. I had a reputation at the time as a hot-tempered sort and had been in a scrape or two before. When the judge said I had to hang I broke out of jail and ran.

"I'd been on the run for nearly two years when I drifted into West Bend and saw you and it was love at first sight for me. So I took a chance. I decided my trail was cold enough by now. And I was a long way from Montana. I thought maybe I'd finally given Nesbitt the slip. He'd almost got me up in Indian Territory last year but I got past him."

"I believe you shot that buckaroo in self-defense," I told Judah as I took his hand in mine.

"You do?" He looked at me with eyes awash with hope.

"You're not a killer," I said. "You could have killed Clyde Nesbitt when he lost his carbine in the river. You didn't know there was quicksand there and it had got his horse and was about to get him. A man who had good reason to kill Nesbitt like you did would have shot him down the minute he lost his gun. But you didn't. That's how I know you killed Jake Meriden in self-defense."

"It's been a rough day for you, Meriah," Judah said. "Maybe you ought to rest on account of your delicate condition."

"How'd you know about my delicate condition?" I asked him, surprised as Sodom must have been when the Lord leveled it. "It don't show as yet and I've never told a single soul about it."

"I heard you naming the baby in your sleep," he explained. "You chose the name James if it turns out to be a boy and Ruth if it turns out to be a girl. You were wondering in your sleep-talking would I agree to those two names."

"Do you?" I hoped he would.

"I do," he said and I tell you it reminded me of the first day he said "I do"—the wonderful day him and me married.

"That's about the end of my story about Judah Garvey, my best beloved," I told Annalee. "Except to say that Judah and me, we lived happily together, except for a spat or two from time to time which just added spice to us being together, till the day he died a year ago last August. We had us twins to start out with and we named them James and Ruth and they were followed in later years by quite a brood, seven in all. But what I want to get to is, did you see any sort of moral in the tale I just told you, child?"

"I think so," Annalee said. "You fought to save the man you loved."

I nodded. "You've got that part right as rain. But there's another part. A part about pride. You recollect how I was damning Judah and trying to wipe his very memory out of my mind when I thought he'd up and left me in the lurch? That's the important part. Now just suppose Clyde Nesbitt hadn't come to the homeplace hunting Judah. I would've gone on acting like Judah didn't amount to so much as a hill of beans in my prideful opinion and the days would have passed by and maybe Clyde Nesbitt would have tracked Judah down and shot my best beloved to death for the bounty that was on his head."

"But Clyde Nesbitt *did* come to you," Annalee said.

"But he might not have," I pointed out to her. "And," I added on, "there's no Clyde Nesbitt to come to you tonight to talk about what's going on over there between Luke Warner and the

Widow Ransom. So are you going to let your
pridefulness stand between you and Luke or are
you going to heed the Bible's words that tell us,
'Pride goeth before destruction, and an haughty
spirit before a fall'?''

"Destruction," Annalee breathed, awed.

"A fall," I reminded her and then said,
"Whilst I was tale-telling just now, I saw the
Widower Aberswift—a moneyed man, folk
say—step outside for a breath of fresh air. I also
happened to see the Widow Ransom step outside not two minutes later. So fast, in fact, it's
a wonder to me she didn't trip on the Widower
Aberswift's coattails."

Annalee shot a glance at Luke Warner who
was still standing next to the fiddler. Then she
shot another glance at the open door of the
barn.

"I thank you kindly for the story of you and
your best beloved, Granny Garvey," she said.
"Now, I must ask you to excuse me so I can go
and set things to right with *my* best beloved."

Well, sir, Annalee, she did just that! She
marched out the barn door and then she
marched back in through the selfsame door and
grabbed Luke Warner by the arm and marched
him outside. You could hear her saying Luke
was to look there at the Widow Ransom who
was, she said, all wrapped up in the Widower
Aberswift's arms whilst his hands went a-
roaming and the Widow Ransom did nary a
thing to discourage them in their scandalous
journeying.

Is that what Luke wanted? we all heard Annalee shout. A faithless woman who was no better than she should be which, Annalee claimed
at the top of her voice, wasn't the best by any

stretch of the imagination as anyone with half an eye could plainly see.

Or did he want a woman, she went right on, who loved him with all her heart and soul and then some and who would make him a good wife and bear him children they could raise up to be proud of—did he, to cut things short, want *her*?

None of us heard how Luke answered her question but all of us saw him walk back into the barn a few minutes later hand in hand with Annalee, smiles lighting up both their faces. Right behind them came the brazen Widow Ransom on the arm of the Widower Aberswift. And I, for one, reckoned it wouldn't be long before her hand was in his purse.

That night at the Harvest Home Barn Dance was a year ago. Since then, Luke and Annalee got themselves hitched and I took part in the shivaree that kept them sleepless and fidgety as a cricket on a too-hot hearth their whole wedding night long. At one point during that night, Annalee peeked out an open window and saw me banging an iron spoon on a cake pan. She give me a wink and I give her one and then she beckoned me over. When I went to the window she told me that the balm I give her at the Harvest Home Barn Dance for her broken heart had worked like a charm. I told her hearing that made me as happy as a cat lapping cream.

NATURE OF THE BEAST,
by Bryce Walton

Bryce Walton (1918–1988) began writing Western, mystery, adventure, and science fiction stories for the pulp magazines in 1945. His Westerns appeared in Ranch Romances, Western Story, Fifteen Western Tales, Gunsmoke, and Wagon Train, among others, and later in a number of anthologies. He remained a full-time writer until the last year of his life, selling stories and articles to a wide variety of publications, including The Saturday Evening Post; he also published seven novels and wrote for radio and TV. "Nature of the Beast," a grim and powerful contemporary Western about more than one type of hunter and hunting, is one of several fine, offbeat stories that unaccountably remained unpublished at the time of his death.

• NATURE OF THE BEAST •
by Bryce Walton

Sheriff Braude pointed down through a stand of jack pines. "Let's figure Sammy left his gal along about here."

I coasted the patrol car down into a clearing beside Zuni Creek and cut the motor. Braude opened his door and eased out slow, looking and listening. I did the same. It was near noon, hot and still. All I heard was a wren rustling in the brush and creek water running through rocks.

Braude hauled out our .30/06 Winchester bolt guns and tossed mine across the hood of the Olds. I managed to catch it with the kind of easy, one-handed snatch that Braude inspired, and followed him down onto wet black sand at the creek edge. He was a big man built like a tree stump, but he moved over rocks and fall-down timber with a hefty lightness that made me think of the smooth rolling power of a grizzly bear.

A ways up the creek, we still hadn't found her. Braude stopped again and studied the timber across the creek, then the shadows under the pines on our right and the brown hills sloping up to the sawtoothed ridge of the Chocolate Mountains. He tilted his Stetson back and dragged a blue bandanna out of his whipcords and mopped a face the color of red clay and all wrinkled like the underside of a goose's foot.

"Maybe it's a false alarm," I said.

He gave me a tolerant grin. "You forgetting this is called Fosdyke County, son? Guy Wellman Fosdyke's ranch covers this whole valley and if he says he sees a thing you'd better believe it."

"But you said he saw it from somewhere up there along the ridge. Maybe he didn't see it all that clear."

"He was glassing with ten-x binoculars."

"But from where? That's a long stretch of ridge. How do we know—?"

He gave an impatient snort. "Guy's been after a scruffy old grizzly sow that's got her den just up there under Camelhump Ridge. He was up there setting bear traps and baiting-in with rotten fish. He said he heard screams and glassed right down here to the creek and saw Sammy working his gal over with a rock."

"Even with ten-x glasses, how could he be sure she was dead?"

Braude frowned at me, then turned away. "You wouldn't be trying to talk us out of anything?"

I just looked at him. I didn't know the answer. Yet.

I was twenty-three then, less than a year back from Nam. My folks had hauled on down to Texas. My last girlfriend had a dream and hitchhiked to Hollywood. But I stayed on in Gullyville. Had no reason to go or stay. Things started to come up on me. A car backfiring dropped me to my knees. I had bad dreams, the kind that wake you up choking in the dark. Lonely days with no work or purpose, nothing adding up. Until I started rolling my own smokes again and hanging out in the park with a greasy sleeping bag and a sad crew of other stoned-out cockroach kickers.

Sheriff Braude and my dad had been buddies from the same gun club. He found me in the park counting how many grass blades in a square foot. "Lie down with dogs," he said, "and you get up with fleas." He dusted me off, dried me out, checked my war record and my skills with a rifle. Then he had me fitted out with a County Highway Patrol uniform, gave me a deputy badge, and said it was time to get off my ass and make my run.

It felt like a right turn. What it seemed to mean was a chance for things to start clean again and run clear. I mean on the right side of law and order, in a uniform people respected and depended on. And if I had to hunt anybody down now, I could find him and know he was the bad guy.

But Braude had deputized me less than a month ago. I was touchy. I didn't want to mess up or admit I wasn't exactly gung ho about starting another body count.

She was right there around the next creek bend. Floating facedown in a still pool. And I knew for sure she was dead. That was one thing I'd never have any doubts about.

"Sammy's gal, all right," Braude said. "Same striped shirt she was wearing yesterday over at Steve's Market."

The shirt was all she wore now and it was mostly ripped off her. Tatters of cloth wriggled on the current along with strands of her long black hair. Her body looked like it had been worked over by a wild animal. Some blood was still leaking away into clear water bubbling over rocks. Her right arm was out floating, bobbing in the current like a snag. Her hand still clutched a loop of braided black leather torn in two, and up close to her fist was a lump of Indian jewelry, a glint of green jade and silver.

The sun glared off the water. The surface came and went at me, and I felt dizzy and shut my eyes. The sun still burned through the lids and for a second I heard fire crackling in napalmed thatch, kids screaming. Then I didn't think of her but about the dragonfly hovering over the pool with blue wings, the brown-speckled frog plopping into the water, and that watersnake going along with its head up like a periscope.

Braude's words came back on me from a distance and I opened my eyes. "Little Sammy sure did a job on this one."

He was looking at me like I was next up on a quiz show. The dizziness was gone. This was *now*. "It's hot," I said.

"Yeah, maybe it scrambled Sammy's brain. But then he was always kind of mean. Still, I never figured—"

"Who's Sammy?'"

"Sammy Snapping Turtle. Maybe a dozen left of his people scrounging along the crick. Daddy drunk hisself to death. His ma whored over in Sun City till some clown gave her canned heat to drink and she died with her stomach burned out. That bastard won't joke anymore where I put him."

"She's just a kid," I said.

"Old enough to get Sammy crazy jealous over at Steve's Market yesterday. Steve called me on it, said Sammy and his gal was in there buying tortilla flour and whiskey. Said he was cussing her out and knocking her around. Accused her of messing with a migrant down from the north with a surplus of beet-topping money. I drove over there but the gal had no complaints and Sammy was all smiles and offering me his jug. If I'd had any idea he would—" He shrugged and slipped his rifle bolt and snapped it back. "Well, now with hindsight we got a sure motive."

He started up away from the creek. "What about her?" I said. "I mean we just going to leave her?"

"We've given Sammy enough time. We got to move on him."

"But I can get her up out of the water." Minnows were there now, a damned school of nibbling minnows.

He raised his voice. "The timing will be off. We have to move up. Come on!"

I started to wade out to where her fist still bobbed on the water, clenching that torn leather thong and the Indian jewelry. "Guess we ought to take this in as evidence—"

"Leave it be, dammit! And come the hell on. She ain't going anywhere, and the grip she's got on that thing won't come loose. We won't need to mess around with evidence. We got Sammy."

I followed him up across the dirt road, on up a steeper slope until we were digging up the sharp slip-slide gravel of an old fire trail. Braude drew up every now and then to look around. He'd look, then just stand with his head angled like he was hearing things I couldn't.

It came to me that if Fosdyke had drove into town and told us direct instead of going clear up valley to his ranchhouse and phoning us, we'd have been here a good three hours earlier.

"Sammy could be long gone," I said. "In the next state."

"He ain't far. Take my word for it."

"Sure, but you talk like you *know*, like we already got him nailed down."

"We do." Braude eased up again and mopped his face. He was breathing a little hard. "I know his kind. They tend to hunker near home, specially when they're in heavy trouble. Thing is to give him time. Time enough to get good and scared. A scared animal runs on pure instinct. He doesn't think, doesn't plan, just does what nature's programmed him to do. So any big trophy hunter is just a dude who knows his animal, knows just what he'll do and how he'll do it."

I watched a chicken hawk coasting down an updraft of air like a kite. I didn't say anything. But Braude didn't need to be prodded when it came to hunting talk.

"That's what put the sand in your motor over in Nam. Didn't know your animal. Sure, a man's just a more complex kind of animal. He's smarter. He can think ahead, make plans. He can be unpredictable. But get him running scared enough and he reverts to primitive instinct, does what he was programmed to do a few hundred million years back. Just know the nature of the beast, like they say, and you'll anchor yourself a prize trophy every time."

I had to point out something I'd learned. That some beasts didn't scare so easy.

"Just didn't know him well enough. There's species and subspecies, with variations in flight patterns and the like. You know baboons, chimps, and gorillas don't run the same. Hear what I'm saying? A coyote don't move like a mountain lion or a grizzly. You don't hunt a wild pig like you plink jackrabbits. Let's move up."

We went on up a long steep rise of shale. The

sun burned hotter. The sky had a bleached look, almost white, and I was sucking air and slipping around, but Braude pushed on up until we got into shade under an overhang. He caught up on some breath, then brought his bolt gun up slowly and took aim.

I looked higher up along the general angle of his sight and thought I saw a movement, a quick blur, among the scattered chunks of rock and brush. He adjusted his scope a little, then sighed and lowered the gun and leaned it against a shelf of shale.

"Run, Sammy, run," he whispered.

"You figure it's him?"

"Could be. He's close. Sammy and his ma live no more than a hundred yards up the crick from where he left his gal. So we know Sammy didn't plan the killing. He knew he'd be liable to get spotted by somebody along that stretch fishing for cutthroat trout. He'd have done it off in the boonies and tried to hide her. No, he went ape and started killing in a burst of temper. And he's acting according."

"And how's that?"

"He took off right up the hill here like I figured he would."

"Why couldn't he just as easily have cut on down south of the creek into the valley and headed west?"

"They don't ever run that way." He squinted up against the sun. Then, all at once, he snapped his rifle up and let one off. The sharp crack cut into me and I almost fell backward down the slope; I caught myself and if Braude saw it he didn't let on. I felt queasy. Something in my belly turned cold as a frog.

Rock dust hung in the air up there. Maybe I heard a little crying sound. Maybe I didn't.

What I know I heard was my heart thumping too hard. And the way bullets come down after you through the sunny air.

Braude lowered his bolt gun and leaned back. "Now he knows we're on his tail and he's running on course."

I ventured the humble suggestion that maybe one of us ought to work in around behind so he couldn't cut down the other side of the mountain.

But Braude assured me he wouldn't do that. "You know how a human runs when he's scared and going on instinct?"

I didn't.

"Pretty much like a rabbit. That's right. A rabbit. That's how I knew he'd be up here. Flush them out, they always run up. Maybe it's from way back when they had to run up a tree. Anyway, they go up every time. Up a tree, a building, a hill. By the same token we know he won't kite off north. That'd be away from his hutch. No, he'll go on up, then circle, cut back."

He yawned and mopped his face again, then spread his wet bandanna out on a flat rock. "Course if Sammy hadn't been scared, if he could have used his head a little, he wouldn't have run up here. He'd been better off down low in short brush and tall grass. Better for us, too, more the sporting way. Flatland's best for hunting. Where there's plenty of weedy ditches, fence rows, and little hills. Snow's fun too. You can track 'em right to the hutch."

"You ought to write a book about it," I said.

"Been thinking about that. I'd call it *The Sporting Way*."

We dug on up another few hundred yards, and Braude suddenly went into a crouch and this time hardly even took the time to aim. The shot cracked and echoed but it sounded unreal and went through me like a tiny sliver of glass. Rock chips and dust flew up and a shadow jumped between two high splinters of cliff.

Braude didn't go up there to check.

"Maybe you bagged him," I said.

"No, not yet. Cut a little hair maybe, but what we want is to work him back down."

"You must have been at this kind of thing a long time," I said.

We rested in the shade of some brush and Braude told how he'd been a hunter before he could walk. How his daddy used to take him along when he went hunting, carried little Braude on his back in a rucksack. "I was poppin' jacks when I was so little Daddy had to lift the rifle for me. He was the best I ever knew, but he liked open country. On that account I never have catered to mountain goat or cougar."

"Popping jacks is good sport, right?"

"And grouse. Fact is, I'm a bird man, like my daddy was. You know where one's going, specially with grouse. You lay it all out. Pick your opening in the foliage ahead where it's going to jump and you're ready to open fire. But like I said, you got to know your animal. Or bird. If there's any distance, you'll never bring a man down with a few stray O-O pellets from a twelve-gauge. Shot spreads too thin."

Braude looked and listened for a while, then went on about birds. "Geese are the hardest damned things to kill. A wounded goose'll hold on to living worse than any old mud turtle around. Daddy passed onto me the obligation to be merciful to all God's creatures. And the quick merciful way to end a goose is whirl it around by the head. Dislocates the neck—

snap—like that. No pain. And the bird's appearance don't get spoiled. Quick and merciful way with a rabbit—you just clap it behind the head with the edge of your hand."

All of a sudden, without a word, he jumped up and headed back down the trail. It was all I could do to keep up with the old sportsman.

Sammy's shack was in a little clearing with a white sand floor walled off with a windbreak of brush and dwarf pine. The shack was maybe fifteen feet square, made of scrap wood, flattened tin cans, and beer bottles. There was an oil drum with charred tortillas smoking on top. There was a smell of burnt corn. A dried-out old woman lay on her stomach nearby. Her gray hair was full of dust. She was wailing and beating the ground with her fists, then throwing sand and dust all over herself.

"Check the hutch." Braude was in a wall of brush on my left, covering the clearing. He was on one knee, rifle up and ready, angled through a break in the foliage. "He's had just about time to make his circle, like I told you. Might even have beaten us in. Check the hutch but watch yourself."

I started walking. The air had a deadly pull and the stillness grew in all around me like everything was slowing down. I seemed to walk forever through the hot dust and there was a sound, a smell like Son Thang under a monsoon sky. It was the inside of their shack . . . the dirt floor that had been used for forty years, some old handmade willow furniture oiled by bodies, the smell of cooked beans, tortillas, fried meat, old washings, killed rabbits, old blood, and the sour-sweet smell of old age and pain and time passed.

I remember two orange crates, tins of food,

piles of ragged bedding and a scrawny dog cringing back and getting out one scared little snarl. But for a long time what happened after that was muzzy. Like one of my dreams, wavery and slow and focused weird like I was seeing it underwater. I can still see it, see and hear it all . . .

Braude's eager whisper: "Get down, boy. He's coming in." And the old woman sitting up with her hands on the ground in front of her, palms up, not making a sound now, hardly breathing. No sound anywhere. No bird sounds or creek sounds. Until a branch cracked loud as a firecracker and a familiar dude drifted out from the wall of brush and stumbled across the clearing—a born loser at the end of his string. A thin little guy in a half-falling run, face a bloody mask, black beard and hair matted with blood and dust, patched Levi's, a torn warsurplus khaki air force shirt, a loose sole flapping on a burned-out sneaker.

I don't remember any warning like, "Freeze, this is the sheriff." Just that flat jarring roar of Braude's bolt gun and Sammy Snapping Turtle turning once and floating down to the ground and lying there like he was too beat to try it anymore.

It all melted away for a while, then came back. But I was all right then. I found that I had an ache locked in my chest. A big ache of hurt and rage.

When we took the pickup out and brought the girl and Sammy back in to the funeral home, I got a look at the jewelry on the ripped leather thong that she was still holding on to for us. It was a fast look because the first thing Braude did was pry it out of her deadlocked fingers and push it into his pocket. But the look was long enough to make out the green jade initials on what turned out to be a cowboy tie—GWF. Then I noticed there weren't any sneaker tracks in the wet black sand. Just the tracks of well-heeled cowboy boots mixed with those of small bare feet.

No need to mention these facts to Braude. They were no longer relevant. I could imagine Fosdyke leaving those clues behind because he was panicked by the approach of fishermen looking for cutthroat trout.

Maybe Sammy knew Fosdyke had done it. Also knew that his word wouldn't count. He was set up. He'd be the rabbit. So he ran.

But I let it ride. Live and learn and wait your turn. I learned fast and didn't have long to wait.

Folks still talk about those two freak hunting accidents that happened during the first week of the deer season. How Guy Wellman Fosdyke shot himself in the lungs while crawling through a barbed-wire fence. Seems he got a bit reckless with his .375 Magnum. It was primed with a 300-grain Nosler soft-point bullet that opened a fist-sized hole in his chest. And how less than three days later that experienced old sportsman, Sheriff Braude, got stuck in an old bear trap Fosdyke had set and forgotten about up near Camelhump Hill.

We were up there stalking whitetail. He walked the south side of the ridge, I the north. But we didn't meet at the agreed point. It was hours before I found him. Seems the good sheriff panicked with pain and shock when those big steel teeth chewed into his leg. What can a man do to get out of a trap made to hold a nine-hundred-pound grizzly?

Seems that in his crazed struggle he dislodged the boulder the trap was chained to and

the boulder took him with it down about four hundred feet of rocky slope. There wasn't much left of the old sportsman when I brought him in.

That's how I saw and reported the unfortunate accidents of our two good citizens. Of course my reports were accepted without question. No reason why they shouldn't be. A lot of sportsmen die by accident every year during the hunting season. And to my knowledge none of those deaths are ever suspected of being anything else.

Sometimes, like now, I bring it back to make sure I've done things right. Otherwise I've learned to forget the past. Best forget the dead and let them lie—all of them. It's the present that counts. We keep our faith with the living.

Susan got cured of her dream and came back to Gulleyville. We've got two great kids now and a nice condo the developers put up on a big chunk of old Fosdyke real estate.

And the voters just reelected me sheriff again for the fourth time.

THE PRODIGAL,
by Dan Parkinson

A former journalist, and for twenty-six years an executive with a Texas city's chamber of commerce, Dan Parkinson turned to the production of fiction several years ago and is now a full-time writer. He has published historical and science fiction novels, but most of his work is in the Western field. His novels of the Old West include The Slanted Colt, Gunpowder Glory, Blood Arrow, Jubilation Gap, Shadow of the Hawk, and The Way to Wyoming. "The Prodigal" is one of his rare short stories—a dark, almost mystical account of what happens when two strangers chance upon a lynching in a bleak place called Jenks' Hole.

• THE PRODIGAL •
by Dan Parkinson

He was tall and quiet, a man of the lean high hills with the solitude of them in his manner. Our paths had joined among those hills and had not yet parted. So we rode together, as is the way of the land. In raw and lonely country two are better than one.

He rode a blood sorrel and led a pack mare, and on the trail his worn old shotgun was never far from hand. We shared our game, kept our peace, and put miles behind us with each sun. And at each day's end I noticed he would draw off to himself for a time, his manner thoughtful as he thumbed through an old Bible, reading a page here and there.

Where trails forked sometimes he would pause and gaze about him as though drawing from deep memory, then move on, and each time our path had been the same.

At a place where tumbled stone lined a shallow creek the mare broke a shoe. He looked around, then ahead along the trail. "Moulton should be near," he said, and we set off, slower now to avoid the stones and stump roots that could injure an unshod hoof.

A mile along we topped a high ridge. Down in the hollow was a settlement—a defeated place of worn structures and gaunt fields, but there would be people. He looked down upon it, squinted his eyes and shook his head. "I don't know," he said.

We met a man coming up and stopped him. "How is that place called?" my companion asked.

The man edged away. "Jenks' Hole. But was I you I'd not go there. This is a hard day."

"Was it ever called Moulton?"

The man nodded. "In better times it was, but no more." He looked at us with suspicion. "Are you strangers here?"

"We are."

"Then, so you'll know, this has been feud land these fifteen years gone. Brothers-in-law fought over a whiskey still to start it. The feud has burned out but Old Jenks carries the scars of it, and he and his sons say what passes here."

"What scars does he carry?"

"The scars on his body from a barn that burned . . . and some say soul scars from lost sons. His firstborn, that his wife took away when she left him long ago. Another to the feuding and now a third. If you must go in today, strangers, it's a time for a body to mind his own affairs."

My companion studied him in silence for a moment. Then he asked, "Is there a smith?"

"There, where the wagon wheels are."

It was a low, leaning shed at the top of a bare rise. Below it a gaunt oak tree grew beside the creek and there were people gathering.

"You said this is a hard day."

The man nodded. "Old Jenks has lost another son. The two left have come to hang the one that done it."

Jenks' Hole was a sad, worn-out place. The smith met us at his door, a tired and discouraged man. He raised the mare's hoof. "I'll fix it.

I'd rather be working than see what's happening down there."

We had come in from above the place and not passed the crowd below. There was commotion down there now and voices raised.

"Can you grain our horses and water them?" I asked.

"I have no grain," he said. "If you want water you'll take them down to the creek."

A one-armed old man with a crippled leg worked the bellows under the shed. His tattered campaign jacket had once borne sergeant's stripes. He hobbled to the door and looked at us.

There was more commotion below and a woman screamed. "No! Don't hang my son! He's just a child!"

The crippled man came out of shadow, clutching a hammer. "Had I two arms and good legs, that would not be going on." His face was hard with outrage. He turned away.

The scream came again from the bottom of the hill and the crowd parted as a heavy-shouldered man swung backhand at the woman, knocking her to the ground.

"A man don't like to see a thing like that," the smith said, glancing up at each of us in turn. We were both armed and he had noted it. "Not much anybody here can do, though."

The woman got to her feet as one dazed. Two small children clutched wide-eyed at her skirt. She turned and came stumbling and sobbing up the hill. Behind her a girl broke loose from the man who held her and came after the woman, calling, "Ma! They're gonna hang him, Ma!"

I had my rifle out and was leaned to spur, but my companion's arm blocked me. "It isn't your concern nor mine," he said softly.

At this the one-armed man swung to face him, looking up. "Mister, they're fixin' to hang a child down there! Can't you see?"

The woman had gained the hilltop. She stared around, bewildered, then hurried to us. "Strangers," she panted, "please! Those men, they're hanging my boy. He ain't fifteen yet."

"What did he do, mam?"

"He tried to help his father. Those men killed his father, and he killed one of them." She sagged, near to fainting, and caught his boot for support. "In the name of God, sir . . ." Her hand slid off and she slumped to the ground.

He looked around at me and distant fires were in his eyes. He drew his worn shotgun from its boot. "Will you watch my back?" I nodded.

He went down the hill, somber on his tall sorrel, and pushed among them. People turned, startled, and moved back. I followed partway, rifle on my arm. Where they parted I could see under the oak. A towheaded boy on the back of a black mule, two men holding him, putting a rope around his neck. At sight of the man on the sorrel they stopped.

"What's going on here?" he asked.

There was arrogance in their appraisal. "It's none of your damn business," the larger one said. "You best turn around and ride out. You ain't welcome here."

My companion didn't move. "It looks to me like you're hanging that boy."

"That's right," the smaller one barked. "He killed our brother and we are sure as hell gonna hang him."

My companion looked at the frightened boy, then again at them. "Are there witnesses?"

"You damn right. We was both witnesses. And him," pointing to a man in the crowd. "You,

Toby. Tell him if you saw this boy kill our brother."

The man didn't look up. "Yeah, I seen that. I did." He eased back into the crowd.

"That satisfy you, stranger?"

"I reckon. But there's a thing needs doing first."

"Ain't none of your business," the larger one said, wary now, "but what is it needs doin'?"

"In the first place, that loop on his neck. Can't anybody here tie a proper knot? And no slack. You won't break his neck. He'll just strangle. And another thing. Has that boy prayed and been prayed for? Does he know his Savior?"

"It don't matter."

"It does matter," my companion said, and I've never heard a voice so cold. "I see no preachers hereabouts, so I will talk to him myself."

The two men reddened. They closed together and stepped toward him. "You ain't gonna do nothin' but leave this place!" the larger one said, and their hands went to guns at their belts, then stopped. They were looking into twin bores of a big shotgun and the hammers were back.

"Both of you back away," my companion said. "I'll talk with this boy about his soul."

"You're tryin' to stop this hangin'!"

"Whether the lad hangs rests with the Lord's will. But I'll know he's prepared before it happens."

They stepped back and he eased down from his horse. Keeping them in sight, he stepped back to where the boy sat on the nervous black mule. Reaching up he slipped the loop off his neck.

The larger of the hangmen spat, "You will be sorry for this, mister. You should've minded your own business!" But he ignored them.

On the mule the boy was pleading, his teeth chattering, his voice failing him. "They killed my pa. Now they're gonna kill me. Dear God. Help me, please, somebody. Help me, God."

My companion reached an arm around him and lowered him to the ground, supporting him so his knees would not buckle. For the first time, the boy seemed to realize he was there. Wide, wet eyes looked up at him.

"Listen to me, boy," he said. "I have questions for you, that you must answer. First, do you know your Savior?"

"I . . . I don't understand."

"They're fixing to hang you, boy. Are you ready to die?"

The boy almost collapsed. "I'm scared, sir. I'm scared to death. Please . . ."

"Straighten up, boy. Tell me now, do you know God? What He did for you? That He let His son die on the cross for you?"

The two men near him were furious. But the big gun and the stranger's eyes held them where they were.

"If your soul is saved, boy," he said, "then should you die this day you will awaken in Heaven."

The boy caught his sobbing breath. With an effort he tightened his knees to stop their shaking and drew an arm across his wet face. "I don't know how to get my soul saved, sir."

"Do you believe in the Son of God?"

"I guess so. Pa told me to."

"Well, the Son of God is your Savior. Do you know the Bible?"

The boy nodded. "Ma has one."

"It says in there, in the book of John, that God so loved the world that He sent his Son, and if you believe in Him you can have ever-lasting life. Do you believe, boy?"

"Yes. Yes, I think I do. I know I do."

The two hangmen stepped forward, murder on their faces. "You've wasted enough time, mister. Now get the hell out of here and let us get on with this."

"You move fast enough an' far enough," the smaller one said, "maybe we won't find you when we get done here."

But the shotgun didn't waver. My companion fixed cold, level eyes on them and they backed off. "You all heard this boy." He raised his voice to the crowd. "He has made confession to his belief. He should be baptized in that belief."

Leading the boy, keeping the gun on the two glaring at him, he backed into the creek and had the boy kneel there in the water. He placed his hand on the boy's head. Still staring at the two angry men, the silent crowd beyond them, he said, "Here now, in the name of the Father, the name of the Son . . ."

It was too much for the livid hangmen. As one they drew their pistols and rushed him. The shotgun bucked in his hand as he triggered it. The smaller man pitched backward, lifted from his feet by the load that caught him in chest, neck, and face. The big one was taken dead center, and he stopped as though he had hit a wall. He backed one step and fell.

". . . and the name of the Holy Ghost, I baptize you." The boy's eyes and mouth were open wide as he was pushed beneath the water. He came up coughing and spitting. "You . . . you killed them!"

"Seems to me, boy, the Lord took a hand here."

Stunned silence held the crowd. Then a voice

was raised. "You done it now, mister. Them was Jenks' sons you killed." The crowd milled, dread robbing them of their senses as Old Jenks' name was invoked. They might have rushed him then, but I raised my rifle and my voice. Faces came around. "He's not alone."

From behind me came a voice. "Damn right he's not!"

On the hill stood the smith with an ancient gun in his hands, and the one-armed man with his hammer.

They came out of the water, and my companion picked out the man who had been the witness. "You said you saw this boy kill those two men's brother. Now say it all." As he spoke he was reloading the shotgun.

The man tried to run, but the crowd blocked him. There were hard, accusing eyes around him. He turned back. "They was beating the boy's pa, the three of 'em. They found him milkin' a cow an' said he stole it. That one, the big one, he hit him with a gun butt and killed him. That boy there, he grabbed his pa's gun and killed one of 'em. I swear, that's how it come about."

My companion finished loading his shotgun. "I know why they call this place Jenks' Hole. Anyplace a man can't defend his own, that place is a hole and nothing more."

"Those was Old Jenks' sons, mister. He owns this place. He'll be waitin' at his house down the creek. What's he gonna do now? What're we gonna do?"

He looked around at them, then to the boy. "You go to your mother, son. Go now." To some of the men there he said, "Put those two in a wagon and bring them to me. I'll take them home." Mounting, he rode back to the top of the hill and I followed along.

The smith said, "I'll have your mare ready when you want to leave."

They brought the dead men in a wagon, pulled by the black mule. My companion tied his horse's reins to the tailgate and climbed aboard.

"I'll follow along," I told him.

From somewhere the boy came running, his father's old long rifle in his hand. "You're going to Old Jenks' house," he said. "I want to go, too."

From the wagon seat my companion looked down at the boy and shook his head. "You do what I said, boy. Go to your mother, pack what you have, and get her and your family out of this place. It's no fit place to be."

The boy held his eyes stubbornly for a moment, then turned and walked away. His mother and the children waited for him.

The smith said, "Jenks' house is a mile out, down the creek. There's a road, an' you'll see a big block house of logs and stone."

The road wound down along the creek, then up the backside of a bluff. The house sat high above the land around it, back from an open-gated fence.

"Will you watch my back again?" my companion asked, and I nodded.

We came up to the house. The old man sat on the porch, motionless in a rocking chair, a quilt covering his lap, his hands buried beneath it. The scar of an old burn covered half his face, and his head was bald on that side. His mouth was drawn into a tight line, and only his eyes moved to stare at what was in the wagon.

My companion climbed down and faced him

from the ground. "These men tried to kill me," he said. "I brought them home."

An old Negro woman appeared in the open door, looked out at the wagon and the two bodies in it, at me briefly, and then at the man standing on the ground. For a long moment she studied him, then turned and went back inside.

For a time the old man said nothing. He sat under his quilt in the noontime sun, staring through his scarred face, eyes as hard as burnished steel. Finally he said, "A man does what he has to do."

The man on the ground touched his hat and turned away. He walked around the wagon to unhitch his sorrel, and I watched him, a feeling of strangeness in me. Motion at the house caught my eye and I jerked around. The old man was standing, swaying slightly, his face gone cold and gray. He held a pistol in a trembling hand, but even as I raised my rifle the old black woman was there beside him, pushing his gun down, her voice toneless and hardly more than a whisper.

"It all done now. Just let it end."

He didn't even seem to hear her, but as she spoke his arm went limp and the gun slipped from his fingers and fell. Eyes gone too old stared at my companion, seeing no one but him . . . or maybe seeing nothing at all.

He swayed again, then a spasm shook him and his hand clawed at his breast. Still his eyes didn't waver from the one who held his gaze. A moment longer he stood, then his head dropped, hiding sightless eyes, and he crumpled to the porch planking. He didn't move again.

The old black woman looked down at him, expressionless. Then she stepped around him to the edge of the porch and gazed long at the man standing by the wagon.

"I know you," she said. She turned away and went into the house.

We walked over and looked at the old man.

"He would have killed you," I said.

My companion shook his head. "Maybe there are some things a man just can't do."

As we rode out the gate I looked back. The old black woman came from the house, carrying her meager belongings. She looked at the man on the porch and the dead ones in the wagon, then turned from them and walked away.

As we neared the settlement we passed people going the other way, toward Jenks' house. The mare was ready at the smithy, and we took the grade at a good pace. From the top we looked back, across Jenks' Hole, to where a column of smoke stood in the distance.

"They're burning the house," I said.

He nodded. "Fire purifies."

"The old woman said she knew you."

"She knew me. She helped raise me, my early years. The old man knew me, too. I'm Abel Jenks. He was my father."

STALKING-WOMAN,
by Ardath Mayhar

Like many writers, Ardath Mayhar has worked at an odd assortment of jobs: dairy farmer, postal clerk, proofreader, raiser of broiler chickens, bookstore owner/operator, writing teacher and lecturer. She made her first professional sale, of a poem to Arizona Quarterly, at the age of nineteen; since then she has published numerous other poems, many short stories (one of her Western tales, "Night of the Cougar," was a finalist for a 1986 Western Writers of America Spur Award), and more than a score of young adult, fantasy, science fiction, and Western novels. A grim chronicle of revenge, "Stalking-Woman" is set in those long-ago days when East Texas was the domain of Indian tribes and the first intruders were the "Turtle-Men," Spaniards under the leadership of such adventurers as Cortez.

· STALKING-WOMAN ·
by Ardath Mayhar

Nahadichka broke her first knife on the shell of
the Turtle-Man she caught relieving himself behind a clump of huckleberry bushes. Squatting
as he was, the blade should have slipped neatly
between his shoulder blades and into his heart
from behind . . . but the hard thing that encased
his torso snapped the flint, leaving her with a
stub.

If the man had not been entangled with his
own clothing, that would not have been enough.
As it was, she managed a rough slice through
his jugular before he could do anything to prevent it. The knife, however, was lost. Only the
fact that her victim carried one of bright metal,
worth any number of hers, comforted her for
its loss. She used the new weapon to sever one
of the ears, which she strung on the thong she
had brought for such a purpose.

The first of her son's killers was now dead,
his ear anchoring the string of ears that she
hoped to lay on the mound covering Bear-boy's
burial place. There were now five more to catch
and to kill, in order to complete her tally of vengeance.

She did not remain in the thicket. The others
would come to find their lost companion. She
slipped backward through the brush, replacing

disturbed branches as she went. One of her own kind would be able to see where she had gone, but these blind newcomers would not, she felt certain.

Moving in a wide arc, she went through the trees, down a shallow creek to pass the point nearest the campfire where the other Turtle-Men talked in their strange tongue, and around to a thick cluster of sumac on the side opposite that in which the body lay. Only one of these remaining men had taken part in the death of her son, and she waited to catch him apart from his fellows. Then she would leave these survivors to their own devices and follow the group in which the other three traveled.

It was some time before one of the men called out for the other. *"Capitán! Capitán Escobedo! Como está usted?"*

The tallest of the armored figures stood when there was no reply, and said something to his fellows. When he strode away through the bushes and disappeared behind the trees, Nahadichka flattened herself among the dead leaves and waited.

In just a moment, there came an exclamation, followed by a cry of *"Venga! Venga! El está muerto! Aquí!"*

As the other three men rose to their feet, dropping the gear they had been mending while they rested, Nahadichka stared hard at the back of the one they called Ho-an. It had been he who caught her son as he played with the bright metal things he had found in the shelter of the white men. He had beaten the child, for Bear-boy had lived long enough to speak to his mother.

"The one whose hair burns, he caught me and beat me. And then the others came, and they beat me, too. Why? I had not taken those things away. I only wanted to look at them." His dark eyes had been filled with astonishment, even as he died.

She had not been able to tell him. She only hoped, as she stalked those who had killed him, that they were as puzzled about the death that tracked after them as her son had been.

She furrowed her brow, staring at the back of the man whose hair flamed in the firelight. As his companions crashed away toward the call for help, this man turned, as if unwillingly, to gaze into the circle of brush about the small clearing.

"Juan! Juan! *Aquí!*" came the call again, and he shrugged and turned to go.

She was upon him before he knew what had happened. Her arm locked about his neck from behind, and that sharp steel knife that had belonged to his fellow parted the flesh of his neck smoothly. He fell at her feet, and she stared down for an instant before leaning over to sever a circle of scalp, with its bright hair hanging long from it. That joined his ear on her string, once she regained the shelter of the forest that covered the land from the Big Water to the Flat Ground.

She did not wait to see what the three survivors might do. They were no concern of hers. That other group had been going west, and they now had two days on their journey while she had stalked this group. That much larger number of armored men would be harder to deal with, she was sure, and so she had made certain of this manageable one.

The Deer-things that the Turtle-Men rode moved fast, and Nahadichka traveled most of the night, pausing only to chew some dried meat and to rest for a short time. She ran through the trees, taking shortcuts when the ancient trail followed by her prey made one of its curves so as to avoid difficult ground or deep streams. One afoot could go where those awkward beasts could not.

She felt that the men ahead of her could not know that they were pursued. She had seen how they regarded her people, how they had scorned the women as of no account, much to the amusement of the entire tribe. Her people knew well that without the work of the women, life would have been almost impossible. Men liked to hunt and to fish and to battle among themselves, but they were not at all dependable when it came to farming and preparing hides and making the stores of food that kept the people alive in winter.

So the Turtle-Men would not expect to be stalked by the mother of the child they had beaten to death. That thought helped her to keep her wearying feet moving at top speed. It woke her from her brief bouts of exhausted sleep, and it bore her up as she crossed the rivers in which alligators sometimes lay sluggishly, watching as she swam or waded or walked over fallen trees.

Her people had traveled all the forest country for countless generations. Their trails were many, though that oldest of roads that the Turtle-Men used was the best marked and easiest. Nahadichka knew others, however, that crisscrossed the forests, linking up bits of other tracks, sometimes faster to travel than that easier road. She used them, making a wide angle southwestward that brought her out of the woodlands in less than two more days.

When she examined the trail of the Old Ones,

there were no tracks of the hooves of the beasts, no droppings in neat piles. She had beaten her prey to this point, and she knew they were still in the forest country. Something inside her relaxed when she found a spot from which she could see the track without being seen; she slept, her ear flat to the ground, for a long while.

There was no vibration of hoof on earth to wake her, and when she rose it was with her strength renewed. She took up an easy trot, again along a minor set of trails, that sent her again into the forests. She watched the crows, the circling hawks, as she ran, and at last, before the sun was overhead, she heard a raucous chorus of caws from the direction of the road.

It wasn't difficult to keep her prey in sight without being seen. Those Turtle-Men were as blind as new puppies. She kept pace with the group, staying well downwind of them. She could track them by the stink of their rank bodies, as well as the strong scent of the beasts they rode.

She felt sure they would camp before darkness fell, for a convenient stream offered a comfortable site. They were a people who liked their ease, as her people had learned by watching them. She scurried ahead and found herself a spot in which to rest and wait, with the stream and the clearing edging it within easy distance.

They were noisy and careless. Their beasts made the whinnying noises as they neared the water, and the men shouted in their coarse voices as they made their camp. She felt nothing but contempt for them. Children were valuable, and these creatures thought nothing of killing one simply because he was curious. The thought made her dry eyes burn with rage as she slid through the tangle of brush along the edge of the water and found a spot from which to watch them.

There was no moon that night, which was helpful. Their watchfire flared red against the darkness, and the four sentries thumped about the perimeter of the camp, as easy to hear as the crackle of the flames. She had marked, while they cooked and ate and sat about the fire, the three she wanted. One had gone into the shelter set up at the farther edge of the clearing. Two were together in one nearer the fire. The four shelters held three hands of men, though they took turns watching through the night.

Nahadichka crept easily around the circle, avoiding the sentries without effort. Their heavy feet, their audible breathing, and their occasional comments as they met and passed made them irrelevant. She reached the dark tangle of grapevine and sweetgum and oak and hickory for which she had aimed herself, and then she lay waiting for a chance to slip across the narrow span of grass to the shelter.

The fire burned down, and the shadows grew darker. She found her chance and reached the side of the shelter without trouble. Her keen blade made a long slit, soundlessly, in the material, allowing her to peer through.

Three men lay cramped together in the narrow space. The flap was thrown back, and by the flicker of the coals outside, she could see them. The long one—that was the one she wanted! The others she would leave as they were, for they would fear greatly, and such was worse than death.

The knife moved, slick and silent, and the long legs flexed, straightened, twitched. She took the

ear and slipped backward again, into the con-
cealing forest. There was another camping spot,
a day's travel westward. She would be waiting
there.

The next camp the group made was much
more secure than the first. She watched them
from a clump of brush as they cut away en-
croaching growth that might conceal an enemy.
The Deer-things were hobbled, and six sentries
patrolled the perimeter, instead of four. The
men kept their metal shells on their backs, instead of setting them aside for comfort, and a
few even kept their heads covered with the high
metal pots they wore.

She found herself able to laugh quietly at the
nervousness of the group. When an owl
mourned shrilly downstream, they all jerked
and turned to stare. She found that very grati-
fying. She was making them suffer.

There was no way to reach either of the others as she had done their fellow, and so she did
not wait for full darkness. Again, a man went
behind a clump of brush to relieve himself. He
was not one she wanted, so she waited patiently
until he was done. After a time another came,
his sword in his hand, his gaze flicking from
right to left, before and behind him. She lay
curled around her bush, secure in the knowledge that he was as blind as his fellows.

When he had his clothing all undone and dis-
arranged, she uncurled silently, slithered over
the ground as quietly as a rattlesnake, and took
him from behind. Having learned with her first
attempt, she went for the throat, always, knowing that the armor would foil a stab at the back.
He died as easily as the others had done, and
she dropped him into his own mess and retired

downstream, crossed the water, and sped southward and westward, paralleling the old road.

Only one of the killers was left alive. She told herself that she should be satisfied, should return through the forest to her own Caddoan people while yet she could. Her stealth and cunning had been great, but she knew that fortune had favored her, as well. One could not depend upon that to continue.

Yet every time she thought to turn back, her son's bewildered eyes stared at her from the leafy crowns of the trees or the muddy purls of the river water. No, she must go on to complete the task she had taken upon herself.

She did not wait for the Turtle-Men to camp, this last time. She knew they would be so cautious that there would be little chance for success. She must attack from some hidden place, at a time when they least expected it. That meant that she could not use a stream or a river as her hiding place. They would now expect that.

She must rise from the earth itself, ready to kill that last slayer no matter what happened to her. Nahadichka was a woman of the forest now, but she had been born in the plains of a warrior people. She knew how to mislead an enemy into thinking himself safe, and she set about doing that.

The forest had been damp, for there had been rain in the east. But the flatlands were much dryer, and the grass, the soil, and the bushes and scrub oaks were dusty. She became a heap of dusty weeds beside the faint track that generations of travelers had worn into the prairie.

The sun burned up the east, traveled overhead slowly, and at last she heard the thud of hooves through the earth against which she lay. The group came closer, and she opened her eyes to stare through the mesh of grass she had arranged so as to hide her face. First came the heavy man who led the Turtle-Men. Then the one in black robes who raised his hands so often.

Behind came the others, riding in pairs, their hands on their weapons and their eyes busy studying the terrain about them. The last of the killers rode on the side nearest her. Fortune still was kind. Two pairs rode before him and three behind. There would be time.

As he drew nearer, she gathered herself into a tense knot of muscle and resolve. The horse stepped steadily forward, and she sprang upright almost beneath its hooves. The knife flew unerringly from her hand and buried itself to the hilt in the eyesocket of her victim.

There was a circle of riders about her, weapons in hand, their eyes burning with anger. Anger and astonishment.

"Una mujer? No lo creo! Donde están los hombres?" Their words meant nothing to her.

She stood proudly, waiting, as several of the riders pulled away and circled, wider and wider, searching, she suspected, for a band of warriors that had harried them across the countryside. She smiled as the blade lifted, holding her neck still for its impact.

Her son was avenged, and she had no other child. Her man had two wives to comfort him. It was her time to die.

She waited for the impact of the blade . . . the descent of darkness to free her of effort. The string of ears would not go onto her son's mound ... but perhaps she would find Bear-boy there in the Other Place, where the deer were fat, and the fruit was sweet and plentiful.

That would be enough.

THE PISTOLEER,
by H. Edward Hunsburger

H. Edward Hunsburger is another writer who is equally at home in the mystery and Western fields. He has published several novels and short stories in both genres, most notably an action Western novel, Crossfire *(1985)*, and the first of a series of mysteries about a teacher of deaf children in Minneapolis, Death Signs *(1988)*. In its evocative portrait of an aging gunfighter, "The Pistoleer" is reminiscent of such celebrated novels as Glendon Swarthout's The Shootist *and* Lewis B. Patten's Death of a Gunfighter, *yet it stands on its own merits and offers its own thoughtful conclusions.*

• THE PISTOLEER •
by H. Edward Hunsburger

At the sound of the shots Flood stiffened, crouching motionless beside the grave. He counted six of them in all. They were slow and evenly spaced at four, maybe five seconds apart. They had come from the other side of the cemetery, or just below it where a rocky slope gave way to the town's Mexican quarter and, farther down, the warehouses that lined the banks of the Colorado. Flood stayed hunkered down by the tombstone.

When everything was quiet again, he stood up and let his hand fall away from the butt of his holstered Smith and Wesson. Yuma was getting too damn big, overcrowded, with everyone shoved in on top of one another. There was no peace and quiet left, not even in a graveyard. Not even for the dead and those who came to mourn them.

Sighing, Flood took out a handkerchief and wiped the sweat from his forehead. It seemed as though the heat bothered him a little bit more with every passing year. He was only forty-seven but he looked as least a decade older. Time and circumstance had stripped away all the softness from his face leaving weathered skin stretched taut over angular cheekbones, a jutting chin, and a sharp, narrow blade of a nose. His neatly barbered hair was silvery gray. A matching mustache framed the hard, straight line of his mouth. Dressed in a brown sack suit, Stetson, and polished Judsons, he looked like a prosperous cattleman. But only until you looked into his eyes. They were deepset and a flat, smoky blue in color. They seemed to hold the kind of memories that set men apart. Someone had once described them as having a haunted, empty look.

Putting the handkerchief away, Flood knelt down again and placed a small bouquet of flowers on the grave. He spent a moment adjusting them so that they were centered and resting against the base of the marker. In this heat the flowers would be wilted by sundown. Not that that made any difference. Bringing them, that's what counted. Flood closed his eyes for a few seconds, shutting out the sun's intensive glare. His hand rested on the curved top of the tombstone. He could feel the stored heat of the day seeping up from the granite, warming his hand like a fire. He enjoyed the sensation. It was almost like touching something human, something alive. After a few seconds more he forced his eyes open and slowly rose to his feet.

Just as suddenly as it had stopped, the gunfire started up again. There were six shots, the same as before, with a few seconds separating each one from the next. Flood's irritation turned to anger. This was a cemetery, not a goddamned shooting range. Freeing his own Smith and Wesson from its holster, Flood threaded his way through the maze of wood and stone markers. Five sparse cottonwoods shaded the cemetery. The sun poured through their leaves and twisted branches, laying down a shadow pattern that covered the graves and scrub grass like the black lace on a widow's veil. Flood stayed in the shadows, moving quickly and quietly until he reached the other side of the graveyard where a waist-high fence of ornamental wrought iron separated the burial ground from the land below.

He stopped and drew a slow, deep, breath. There wasn't any sign of the shooter yet. He was probably somewhere downslope among the rocky outcroppings, cutbacks, and arroyos. All Flood had to do was look over the fence to find him. Still he hesitated, standing there rigid with his sweaty hand wrapped around the butt of his .45. He wasn't afraid. He was wary. There was something about gunfire and graveyards that was like a lick of cold wind that raised the hairs on the back of your neck. It was almost like an omen or an Indian sign. One that prophesied trouble but never bothered to tell you when or where.

Shaking his head as if to clear it, Flood stepped forward and peered cautiously over the fence. He caught sight of the shooter immediately. He was positioned about midway down the slope, standing at one end of a narrow dry wash. He appeared to be a young man, thick-shouldered and stocky. He was wearing sun-faded range clothes, Levi's, and a colorless shirt that was patchworked with sweat stains across the back and shoulders. Flood couldn't see the man's face from this angle, only the battered brim and crown of a gray Stetson. The man was looking down, his head bent as he concentrated on feeding shells into the chambers of a seventeen-dollar mail-order Colt.

Flood put his own gun away. He had nothing to fear from some young cowhand getting in a little shooting practice. Flood watched as the puncher reholstered the Peacemaker. Taking a stance, he shifted his weight from one leg to the other and then yanked the Colt out, his fingers clumsy and clawing. Jerking the single-action to chest height, he aimed and fired. Flood assumed that the target was a tin beer pail propped up on some rocks at the other end of the wash. He wasn't entirely sure what was going on. But if this was some kind of contest, the beer pail was winning.

Unaware of Flood's observation, the puncher continued to draw, aim, and fire until he'd emptied all six chambers of the Colt. He'd only managed to hit the target once. And as far as Flood could tell, that single hit had been more a matter of divine intervention than marksmanship. The sound of the shots faded, and Flood could hear the cowhand swearing softly to himself. A moment later he pushed the brim of his Stetson back and dragged a shirt sleeve across his glistening forehead. That was when Flood finally got a look at his face. It was young and even-featured, a face untouched as yet by trouble or time. The smooth skin was reddened either by the sun or embarrassment. In contrast, the puncher's eyes were the clearest, lightest blue that Flood had ever seen. He was even younger than Flood had first imagined. Late teens at best. Little more than a kid.

Flood leaned over the fence and called out, "Don't you have any respect for the dead?"

The kid looked up, startled, squinting his eyes as he focused on Flood, who was backlit by the sun. "I've got a certain amount of respect," he said in a slow, soft voice. "Tempered by a strong desire not to join them." With this last he looked at the beer-pail target and shook his head.

"You're going about it all wrong." Flood

hadn't meant to interfere. He didn't want to become involved, but he just couldn't help himself. The words came out as though they were driven by a separate, somehow stronger, will of their own.

The young puncher didn't say anything. He seemed to be waiting for Flood, who stood very still for a moment, as though debating something, forcing himself to come to a decision. A slight smile flickered, then died, as he remembered something, a memory fragment from another part and place in his life. Finally he turned and followed the line of the ornamental fence until he reached the gate. Passing through it, he began to make his way down the rock-littered slope. The kid continued to watch him, his face expressionless, the Colt held loosely at his side. Around his feet, cartridge cases were scattered in the dust, the bright metal winking in the sunlight like fool's gold.

Reaching the dry wash, Flood took up a stance alongside the boy. "You're too tense," he said without preamble. "You're too damn anxious. Try to relax your shoulders and arms. When your hand grips the gun, don't try to jerk it out of the holster, *ease* it out and then up in a single motion. Forget about speed for a while and concentrate on drawing the weapon properly and hitting the target. All the *fast* in the world isn't going to do you a bit of good unless you hit what you're aiming at."

"That's easy enough to say, but—"

The rest of his words were lost as Flood turned, drew, and fired his .45 in a single unbroken blur of motion. The bullet slammed the tin beer pail with a metallic thud that set it spinning wildly until it backflipped over the rocks and out of the wash altogether. Flood calmly reholstered the gun, and then, taking out his handkerchief, dabbed at the line of sweat across his forehead.

"Son of a bitch." The boy's tone was a mixture of respectful amazement and more than just a little fear. He regarded Flood cautiously, then looked down at the ground and swallowed hard. "I've got some money saved up. It's not much—"

Flood cut him short. "I don't do gun work for money. Not anymore. And when I did, it was never for kids. You understand that?" His voice was whispery soft and edged with anger.

The young puncher nodded. "I didn't mean it the way you think," he insisted. "I just wanted to hire you to *teach* me, nothing more. The other part of what has to be done, I can take care of that myself."

"I take it that this is important to you. Not just something you're fooling around with?"

"It's important."

"Tell me about it," Flood prodded him.

Hesitating for a few seconds, the boy looked down at his cracked boots. "It happened last month," he said finally, "over on the other side of the territory, in Benson. My brother, Evan, got into this claims dispute, and the other side, a combine, brought in a professional gunman to settle the matter. Evan never had a chance. Not against Phil Sutherland. Sutherland cut him down in the street. Right there in broad daylight." The kid's voice was tight and dry, all the words coming out in a rush, crowding in on each other. "I'm getting ready for the bastard now. He's coming to town at the end of the month. I'm going to call him out and meet him face-to-face. That's a damn sight more than he ever did for Evan."

"How do you know Sutherland's coming to Yuma?"

The kid said, "He left a Sharps for cleaning and repair with the gunsmith over on Range Street. The smith swore that Sutherland said that he'd be picking the rifle up when he passed through town on the thirtieth. But I got a boy watching the shop just in case he shows up early."

Flood stared at him in stony silence. "Do you know who Phil Sutherland is?" he demanded.

"Yeah, I know who he is . . . the gunman who murdered my brother."

"He's not a gunman," Flood said softly. "He's a *gunfighter.*"

"What the hell's the difference?"

The older man took a deep breath. "The difference is what you're going to have to learn if you want to live to see next month." He paused to let that sink in. Turning away for a second, he watched two overloaded mackinaws go drifting down the Colorado. "Now, a gunman," Flood continued, "works in close where he can't possibly miss. He relies more on the element of surprise than a fast draw, and he's likely as not to back-shoot you. But a gunfighter is a marksman, a true pistoleer. If you're fighting at a distance of twenty feet or more, he'll take you down with his first shot while you're busy showering lead all over the street."

Flood glanced down at the kid's shiny-new mail-order Colt. "Anything past seven yards and you've got to aim in order to hit it. Accurate distance shooting takes a lot of practice. You've also got to learn to clear leather a hell of a lot faster than that. It won't be much of a fight if you never get your gun out of the holster."

"I've got three and a half weeks," the youngster said defiantly. He squared his heavy shoulders and met Flood's eyes with a hard, level stare. "I know I'm new at this and not very good. I don't need anyone to remind me." He left it at that, looking quickly away, his body suddenly tense and motionless.

Flood wanted to turn and walk away, but he couldn't bring himself to do it. Without somebody's help the kid didn't stand a chance. Sighing, he hauled out his stem-winder and studied it for a second. The watch was a Waltham in a gold hunting case that caught and reflected the harsh sunlight. Flood snapped the protective lid shut and put it away. Then he looked up and smiled. "It's just past two," he said. "We've got the better part of the afternoon left." He nodded toward the end of the dry wash. "Why don't you go and set that pail up again. And put some rocks in it this time so we won't have to go chasing it all over the slope."

Understanding softened the youngster's face until he was grinning openly at Flood. "That means you're going to teach me. Right?"

"Right," Flood said. "Now go get the damn pail before I change my mind."

Instead the young puncher thrust out a callused hand. "My name is Hagen, Charlie Hagen." After a moment's hesitation Flood gave his own name, and the two of them shook hands in that awkward, hesitant way that strangers have when they're still a little bit suspicious of each other's honesty and intent.

With a tight smile Hagen turned and started up the wash. Halfway along, he stopped suddenly and wheeled around to where he was facing Flood again. "How come you're helping me?" he demanded.

The older man studied him for a moment

through narrowed eyes. "Maybe it's because somebody helped me once," Flood said finally. "Maybe not. Don't look for a reason behind everything, son. Because half the time there just isn't one there."

Having said his piece, Flood turned his back to the kid. Hagen stared at him for a few more seconds. Then, with a thoughtful expression, he turned and headed up the wash again.

Hagen finished the last of the chicken, tossed the bone away, and listened to it go clattering down the rocks. He wiped his greasy hands on his faded denim trousers and then dragged a shirt sleeve across his mouth. The midday meal, eaten picnic-style among the rocks, should have left him feeling full and contented. But these past weeks his stomach, full or empty, had been twisted tight in a cold knot of fear. He never knew that a feeling could hold you like that. Hold you and never let go. This fear had become something that he slept with. This fear was a bitter, coppery taste in his mouth, a taste he couldn't swallow or wash away. But what really troubled Hagen the most was a hard, inner certainty that he would carry, and be carried by, this fear into an early grave.

"Let's get back to it. The day's not getting any younger."

At the sound of Flood's voice Hagen nodded wearily and staggered to his feet. He was beginning to hate the harsh, measured resonance of Flood's commands: *Higher . . . lower . . . keep the gun steady . . . don't jerk the trigger . . . do it again . . . do it again . . . do it . . .* The old man's curt orders had even begun to invade his dreams, along with the stench of gunpowder and its swirling gray smoke that billowed fog-like across a black, barren landscape that was not of this world. In the dream Flood's voice mixed in with gunfire and cries of pain and desolation.

Reaching the end of the dry wash, Hagen turned and studied the target, a man-sized plank and scrap-wood affair that had long ago replaced the bullet-ridden pail. Hagen took a steadying breath, drew his Colt slowly, steadied it, then thumbed the hammer back and fired. The sound of the shots echoed off the rocks. The bullet splintered wood in the crude circle painted at chest height on the target. Hagen leveled the gun, thumbed the hammer back, and fired again. He kept it up until he emptied the Colt's chambers, all the rounds cutting a tight, clustered pattern in the splintered wood. Hagen allowed himself a tight smile as he emptied the Colt and began to feed fresh cartridges into the chambers. He was pretty good at distance shooting now. He could hit the target damn near every time. After three weeks of intensive practice and drilling, it was his fast draw that was still giving him trouble. No matter how hard he tried, he just couldn't clear leather fast enough. He only had a couple more days to go. Then it would be the thirtieth. The last day of the month. The day he had to face Phil Sutherland.

Just the thought of it made Hagen sweat. He could almost smell the fear on himself, clinging to his clothes and hair like the stink of gunpowder, a stink that he couldn't get to go away.

"What are you doing?" Flood demanded. "Wool-gathering? Posing for a monument?"

Hagen jerked his head around to where the old man was leaning against a boulder, studying Hagen through narrowed eyes. "We better make the most of the time we've got," Flood said, looking up at a sky turned dark and heavy with thunderheads. It didn't rain very much or very often in the territory, but today you could feel it on the wind and in the air.

"It's time for some more draw and fire," the old man said. "Just one round on each time out of the holster. Right."

Hagen nodded. What the hell difference did it make? He might as well admit that he was as good as dead. After everything that Flood had done for him, he couldn't back out now. But facing a man as fast as Sutherland, he'd be dead before he even had a chance to get off a shot. He suddenly realized that it didn't matter. That none of it mattered anymore. That in death he'd be beyond caring or foolish pride, beyond even the cold, constant touch of fear itself.

Squaring off about twenty feet from the target, Hagen shifted his weight from one foot to the other and rolled his shoulders, trying to shake loose of the tension that held them tight. Staring dully at the target, he drew, leveled, and fired the Colt in a single blur of motion that was so like Flood's, it was almost eerie. Hagen could hardly believe it himself. Not only had his draw been deadly fast, but he'd hit the painted center of the target, too. It was as if all the hours of constant repetition and practice had finally come together. He'd accepted death as inevitable, and somehow not caring anymore had suddenly made everything fall into place.

"Stay with it. You don't want to lose it now." The old man could be a stern teacher, but there was no disguising the pleasure in his voice.

Grinning, Hagen turned to the target again and slid the Colt back into its holster. Distant thunder rumbled across the nightlike sky. As if it were a signal, Hagen drew, leveled, and fired the .45 with the same blinding speed and accuracy as before. He emptied the gun with the same smooth, easy rhythm, reloaded, and began to fire again, the bullets chewing up the splintered planking as though it were paperthin.

Flood watched Hagen with a feeling that was part relief and part pure wonder. He'd seen it happen once or twice before. A man working so hard at something that he was all thumbs until suddenly he steps back from it and he's got the knack as sure and certain as though he'd been born with it. Shivering, Flood looked up at the ever-darkening sky. It was going to rain any minute now.

Jamming his hands in his pockets, he walked over to stand beside Hagen. "Let's get out of here," he said, "or the sky's going to burst open before we make cover."

Hagen looked up from reloading and grinned at Flood. His face was flushed with excitement, and his eyes had a bright, almost feverish glaze to them. "Am I as fast as Phil Sutherland?" he demanded. A vein pulsed along his neck, as though something were trying to push its way through the sun-darkened skin.

Flood went suddenly still. "What makes you think I know Phil Sutherland?" he asked softly.

Hagen's grin lost something around the edges. "I just figured you would," he muttered, "seeing the way you handle a gun yourself. I didn't mean anything by it. No disrespect."

Sighing, Flood turned his collar up against the wind that was whispering through the cottonwoods and ruffling their leaves in its wake. "I knew Phil Sutherland," he said, meeting Hagen's eyes. "But that was a long time ago. Hell, probably back before you were even born. We were both up in the Dakota Territory, working out of Bismarck as deputy U.S. Marshals. It was a lot of risks and too damn little pay, but we were young then and everything seemed like it would go on forever." Flood paused, and there was a look in his eyes as though he'd caught some fragment of memory that he wanted to hold on to. "Phil was damn fast when I knew him," he continued, "but like I said, it was a long time ago. Back before he started to play both sides of the law against the middle ... before he turned into a gun for hire. But after seeing you today, I don't think you have anything to worry about. I think you're going to do just fine."

Hagen started to say something in reply, but his words were swallowed by the roar of thunder. Lightning splintered the sky, and the clouds cut open, splattering the rocks with dollar-sized raindrops. Swearing, the two men ran for the cover of the trees.

The lobby of the Fairfield Hotel was small, narrow, and dark, overcrowded now by men who'd taken refuge from the rain-swept streets. A knot of them stood by the entrance, smoking and staring out at the steady downpour. Their tobacco smoke hung in the stale air, mixing in with the odor of furniture polish, wet wool, and damp leather. Dressed in dry clothes again, Flood leaned against the front desk and read the telegram a second time, slowly and carefully. The lobby was lit from overhead by the dim glow of Rochester lamps. In the murky half-light he had to squint in order to clearly see the words. When he read the message twice through, he carefully folded the flimsy square of paper and tucked it away in his jacket pocket.

His face was hard-set, almost expressionless, but there was something in his eyes that was part memory and part pain. He shifted his gaze to the open double doors. The rain was beginning to slack off; it would be over in a couple of minutes. Already men, singly and in pairs, were beginning to drift out onto the covered pineboard landing.

Flood took a long-nine from his pocket, scraped a sulfur match against the wall, and lit up. Smoking silently, he continued to stare at the street. He'd already decided to tell the kid. He just hadn't figured out yet the right way to break it to him. It was almost a joke, one of life's small, dark ironies, the kind that makes you figure that if there is a god, he's got one hell of a sense of humor. At first Flood had thought that he might be able to ignore the wire. There was no debt involved, nothing owing on either side. But that didn't make any difference. He'd go, just as he'd known he would from the start. It shouldn't take him more than a day or two, maybe even less if the situation were as bad as the wire made it out to be. Adjusting the brim of his hat to the proper angle, Flood strode across the lobby and out the double doors.

The rain had stopped, but runoff still dripped from the sloping overhang that sheltered the landing. On impulse, Flood stuck out his hand and caught a drop of rainwater in his leathery palm. He stared at it for a moment. Then he rubbed his hands together and it disappeared, as fleeting and insubstantial as life itself. Swearing, he wiped his palms dry on his trouser legs. He was getting too damn morbid in his old age. It wasn't a very good sign. If he kept it up, he wouldn't be fit for anything except sitting around, like the old men who lined the

Comstock's veranda, just sitting there and waiting until it was time to die.

Flood moved purposefully down the landing, forcing his mind to concentrate on other things. He'd go to the saloon and tell Hagen first. The kid deserved to know. Then he'd go back to his room, pack his war bag, and head over to the livery stable to hire a mount. If the roads weren't too muddy, it shouldn't take him more than two or three hours to reach Clairmont.

Hagen leaned against the bar, feeling a comfortable whiskey glow that smoothed all the rough edges off reality. The long, narrow barroom was hot and crowded. A blue haze of tobacco smoke eddied and swirled around the hanging lamps. Below, the rough pine floorboards were thick with mud, the earthy smell mixing in with the odor of spilled beer, coal oil, and whiskey. None of it bothered Hagen. None of it touched him at all. Tossing back a shot, he capped it with a long pull from his schooner of beer. He knew he was spending too much money. Spending it recklessly. But trapped in the warm, half-drunk glow, he just didn't care.

Grinning, Hagen poured himself another shot of whiskey, overfilling the glass until the liquor spilled over the sides to soak into the scarred mahogany bartop. This was a day for celebration. He could draw a gun as fast as Flood now. And the old man knew it. It stood to reason that he had to be faster than Sutherland, too. But that wasn't the best part. The fear that he'd lived with night and day had suddenly vanished, breaking up and drifting away like ground fog in the morning sunlight. And it wasn't just the drink. It was something else, stronger, deep down inside him. Something that told him that he was never going to be afraid again.

"Bill . . . Bill Ford?"

Hagen felt a stiff finger prodding his back. Scowling, he swung around and looked down at a short, shabbily dressed stranger. "Go away," Hagen said thickly. "Find someplace else to stand."

But the man just peered up at him through bloodshot eyes, his lips spread wide to expose tobacco-yellowed teeth. His face was thin with that furtive, closed-in quality that some men get when they spend too much time alone. Through a grizzled salt-and-pepper beard, Hagen could see the puckered channel of a knife scar. More hair, dull black and threaded with silver, spilled out from beneath the brim of a weathered Stetson.

"Bill, don't you remember me? It's Morgan, Morgan Farrel." His voice was low-pitched, and the words had that soft, slushy sound to them that comes from too much drinking. Bony fingers clutched at Hagen's sleeve, the ragged nails digging into the soft flesh of his forearm. Up close, the little man smelled like something that had been left out in the rain to die.

"You've got the wrong man," Hagen told him. He pushed the offending hand away and then wiped his own on his jeans. "My name is Charlie, Charlie Hagen. If I happen to look like someone you know, there isn't a hell of a lot I can do about that."

Frowning, Farrel shook his head. "Bill . . . Bill." He repeated the name softly, almost wistfully. "If you're still concerned about that business over in Bisbee, put it out of your mind. It's all done with. Forgotten." He grinned at Hagen.

"So there's no need to be calling yourself by any other name than your own."

His irritation turning to steadily mounting anger, Hagen put his hand out flat against Farrel's bony chest and pushed the man back a couple of stumbling paces. "Now leave off," Hagen said in a low, hard voice. "I'm not your damned friend. So just leave me to drink in peace."

Farrel's face was mottled with dark color. "Think you're too good for me now," he said. "Don't want to remember who your real friends are." He lurched forward, his thin fingers closing around Hagen's arm again.

"Damn it. I told you to keep away." He shoved Farrel, who went staggering back, while Hagen, in a single, smooth motion, swept the Colt from its holster, raised it, aimed, and—

"Don't do it," Flood said. His voice was level and hard. In the silence that followed his words, the only thing that could be heard was the metallic click as he thumbed back the single-action's hammer to full cock.

"What are you doing here?" Hagen demanded. In his warm, alcoholic haze he'd missed something, some damned connection.

"Put the gun down, Hagen."

The young cowhand nodded dumbly and returned the weapon to its holster. "What's all the excitement? I was just . . . well, you know what I mean."

Beneath the curving brim of his hat, Flood's eyes burned bright with anger. "He's only a drunk, Hagen. A nuisance. You could have knocked him out easy enough. No reason to draw down on him. He's not even armed." Flood looked at Hagen and then spat as though he wanted to rid his mouth of some lingering bad taste.

Grabbing Hagen by the upper arm, Flood marched him through the parting crowd and out the bat-wing doors. The cool, rain-fresh air hit Hagen like a slap across the face. He blinked and shook his head to clear it. Muttering to himself, he sagged against Flood. The older, more slightly built man pushed Hagen against the outer wall of the saloon.

"Don't ever do that again," Flood said in a dead-cold, expressionless voice. "Do you understand me?"

Hagen nodded, but his eyes were unfocused and his mouth hung open in a lazy, lopsided grin. "I understand," he mumbled.

Flood sighed. "I'm going out of town for a few days. But I'll be back before the thirtieth. All right? Now go back to your room and sleep it off. You've already gotten yourself into enough trouble for one night."

Nodding again, Hagen pushed off from the saloon wall and began to weave and stumble his way down the plankboard landing, a thick-shouldered, swaying figure. Keeping half a block back, Flood trailed him. In his current condition he was easy pickings for any jack-roller or hard case that happened to catch sight of him.

When Hagen reached his hotel door without incident, Flood abruptly wheeled around, heading back the way he came. He still had to pack his bag and hire a horse if he was going to make it to Clairmont tonight. It occurred to him suddenly that he'd never told Hagen what he'd come to tell him. It was too late now. Considering what had happened in the saloon tonight, maybe that was for the best.

* * *

Hagen lay back on the narrow bed smoking and watching the girl. Now that she was done with it, she was all business, silent and hurrying as she rebuttoned her dress and brushed a stray wisp of auburn hair back from her face. Adjusting the lace around her collar, she turned and smiled at Hagen. "It was nice," she said softly. "Come see me anytime you want."

Hagen nodded but didn't stir. When it became obvious that she could see her own way out, the girl shot him a venomous glance, yanked the door open, and slammed it behind her. On the pine washstand a chipped pitcher and basin rattled in the aftershock. Hagen listened to the sharp clatter of her heels until the sound faded into the silence of the empty hallway. The sickly-sweet aroma of her violet scent still lay heavy in the air, intermingling with the smells of tobacco smoke and gun oil. A whisper of wind rustled the dirty curtain on the half-open window. Hagen pinched out the cigarette and shifted around in the damp, twisted sheets.

He'd thought the girl would help. Ease things up a bit. But all he felt was a curious emptiness, a greater sense of being alone. Already he could feel the fear taking hold of him again.

Flood had been gone for two days now. Tomorrow was the thirtieth; Phil Sutherland would be passing through Yuma and stopping at the gunsmith's to pick up the Sharps he'd left for repair. It was the last day of the month. It just might turn out to be Hagen's last day ever. All his wild, whiskey-born confidence had deserted him. He knew he was good with a gun. But his fear told him he wasn't good enough. One way or the other, he'd find out tomorrow, his fate decided by cold fear or his newfound skill with a gun.

Hagen slept fitfully, tossing and turning in the hot, airless room while he drifted in and out of dreams until the edges began to blur and nightmare spilled into reality. In the dead quiet hours of the morning he awoke to the sound of footsteps outside his door. He was halfway upright and reaching for his gun when the door slammed open, silhouetting a tall figure in the dim, predawn light. Hagen lunged for the Colt. He almost had it out of the holster when a hand closed over his arm, pinning it to the bed.

"You don't need that quite yet," Flood said in a harsh whisper.

Hagen smiled up at him, still too bleary-eyed to figure out what was going on. Flood let go of his arm, then turned and, gathering up Hagen's clothes, tossed them to him. "Get dressed," Flood ordered him. "Then strap on your gun belt and splash some water on your face. I want you awake for this."

"What's it all about?"

Flood shook his head. "I'll tell you about it downstairs."

A few minutes later Hagen followed the old man through the peaceful quiet of the hotel and out into the narrow alley behind it. Light from the rising sun was just beginning to touch the rooftops and trees, but the alley was still thick with shadows and the stench of piled-up garbage.

"All right," Hagen said. "So what's the big secret?"

"You stole my watch," Flood told him in a cold, expressionless voice. "I figure you lifted it when you were leaning on me outside the saloon. But maybe you were too drunk to remember that."

"What the hell," Hagen sputtered. "I'd never do anything like that. If I'd happened to grab it when I was drunk, I would have given it back to you."

"It's too late for that," Flood said. "After everything I've done for you, it's too late by half." He began to back away from Hagen, his arms held loosely at his sides. "Draw," Flood prodded him. "Make your move."

"I can't. I don't . . ."

"Draw."

This was crazy, Hagen thought. Crazy and horribly wrong. He was supposed to be facing Sutherland, not Flood. And it should have been on a bright, sunlit street lined with hushed, almost reverent spectators, not out here alone in the predawn chill in an alley filled with shadows and stinking refuse.

Hagen took a deep, calming breath and drew the Colt. Before he had it halfway clear of the holster, he felt the bullet slam him. The noise and the pain seemed to blend together as he fell back into the warm, waiting darkness.

Crouching beside the grave, Flood put fresh flowers in front of the tombstone. He heard footsteps behind him, soft and muted by the grass. Quickly he stood up and turned around to see Charlie Hagen standing there, smiling hesitantly. His right arm was in a sling, and his ruddy face had lost some of its color. He looked embarrassed, as though he didn't know what to say.

"How are you feeling?" Flood asked him finally.

"I'm on the mend. There'll be a little stiffness

in the arm, but nothing I can't live with. The doctor said you brought me in yourself and that you'd already paid the bill."

"Least I could do."

Looking down at his cracked boots, Hagen pulled something out of his pocket and handed it to Flood. It was the old man's gold watch and chain. "I found it under the washstand in my room," Hagen muttered. "I still don't remember taking it, but I guess I must have. Anyway, I'm sorry as hell."

"As far as I'm concerned, the whole matter is over and done with," Flood said as he looped the heavy chain through a buttonhole in his vest. "On reflection I figure that you really never meant to take it in the first place."

Hagen smiled gratefully, then sighed. "I guess you know I missed Phil Sutherland. The doc kept me at his place all of yesterday. Said I'd lost a lot of blood and needed the rest." He looked down at his hips where his gun belt used to rest. "I'm not going to go after him. I don't think I'm cut out to be a gunfighter. Horses, that's what I know best. I'm going back to wrangling as soon as the arm heals."

Flood nodded. "I think that's a good idea." He took out a couple of long-nines, offering one to the kid, who refused. Flood lit up and leaned back against the trunk of a cottonwood.

"Can you tell me something?" Hagen asked abruptly.

"Maybe."

"I know I must of lifted your watch when I was drunk," he began. "But did you call me out and wound me just to keep me from getting killed by Sutherland? I figure you knew I wasn't fast enough and that was the only way you could work out to keep me alive."

Flood studied him for a long, thoughtful moment. "Maybe yes, maybe no," he said finally. "The truth of it isn't all that important. Just that everything came out for the best."

"I guess it did at that," Hagen agreed. As the conversation died and the silence deepened, he turned and looked back toward town. He cleared his throat. "I better get back to my room. The doctor said I should stay off of my feet for the next few days. I probably won't see you again. So good-bye, Flood—and thanks, I think. Hell, you know what I mean."

Flood nodded. "Good-bye, kid."

They didn't shake hands as they'd done when they'd met. It was as if they both knew they'd gone beyond that. Leaning against the tree, Flood smoked and watched Hagen until his distance-diminished figure disappeared among the adobes on the fringe of town. Maybe their trails would cross again, but he didn't think it was likely.

Flood had come damn close to telling him the truth, that he'd planted the watch in the room just after he'd burst through the door. It had been easy enough in the darkness. He'd done it, and the shooting that followed, to save Hagen, not from Sutherland but from himself. The incident in the saloon had shown Flood that the kid could handle a gun, but he couldn't handle himself. Liquor and an inflated sense of his own importance makes for a deadly combination in what might otherwise be a decent man. If he'd stuck with the gun, Hagen would have become a killer for hire, a killer with or without good reason. It wasn't that Hagen was bad by nature. It was just the effect that a gun had on certain men.

Ironically Hagen had gone through all that

training for nothing. Phil Sutherland had passed through Yuma on the last day of the month, but in a pineboard coffin bound for California, across the river where the outlaw still had family. It was Sutherland who'd wired Flood, asking, on the strength of older and better days, if Flood would come to his bedside and help him through the last days and hours of his life. Flood had ridden to Clairmont and a dingy hotel room where time and cancer had reduced a man who was once bigger than life to something that barely contained it. If it hadn't been for the dark, troubled eyes and the long brown Hickok-style hair, Flood wouldn't have recognized him.

They talked all through the night and into the next morning. Not about anything important. Just small, everyday things and scraps of memory out of a common past. A little past dawn, Sutherland fell asleep, and Flood tipped the room's only chair back against the wall and angled his hat brim down over his face. The room was thick with trapped heat that held the stink of slow death and the sweet smell of opium that Sutherland smoked to ease the pain. In spite of that, Flood managed to doze off. He awoke a few hours later to find Sutherland dead. Flood spent the rest of the day making the funeral arrangements. Sutherland had died broke, leaving just enough for his coffin and the transport of it back to California. Before he died, Flood had asked him about Evan Hagen. Sutherland admitted to the killing but insisted that the puncher's brother had provoked the fight and had drawn first. Seeing as he was a dying man, Flood had no reason not to believe him.

Flood tossed away the stub of his cigar and turned to look at the grave where he'd placed the flowers. The inscription on the stone read DANIEL RANSOM THE REDOUTABLE PISTOLEER 1840–1877. Ten years ago everyone knew who he was; now only a handful of people remembered. Flood had been a young deputy when he killed Ransom in a shoot-out right here in Yuma. For a year or more after that, Flood had been a local hero. There'd been the reward money and offers of jobs all over the country. But Flood stayed on in Yuma where people knew and respected him. After a while the job offers stopped, a girl he was courting got tired of waiting and married somebody else, another lawman or hero became the new hero of the day. Flood quit being a lawman and invested what was left of the reward money in a hotel. As the years passed, fewer and fewer people remembered Flood or Ransom. Flood kept the grave clean and put fresh flowers there once a week. He was closer to Ransom than anyone else. He'd become caretaker of their shared history. Without him their moment would be lost, slipping away forever through the cracks in time. That was the part he most wanted to save Hagen from. The loneliness.

Flood stayed at the cemetery for another half hour. Then he walked slowly back into town.

THE BLUE ROAN,
Molly Gloss

Oregon native Molly Gloss has published several excellent short stories, most in publications in the science fiction and fantasy field (Universe, The Magazine of Fantasy & Science Fiction, Isaac Asimov's Science Fiction Magazine); *and a young-adult fantasy novel,* Outside the Gates. *Her recently published "woman's western,"* The Jump-Off Creek, *has been highly praised by such readers as A. B. Guthrie, Jr. and William Kittredge. "The Blue Roan," which deals quite poignantly with the effects of a rodeo performer's sudden accidental death on his wife and his best friend, reflects a deep and abiding understanding of the modern West and those who inhabit its landscape.*

• THE BLUE ROAN •
by Molly Gloss

As soon as they had the cast on my leg I loaded the mare in the trailer and drove down to Jim's place in the Indian Valley. I was overnight getting there, on account of my leg would swell up every little while, working that stiff clutch, and I'd have to pull the truck over to the shoulder of the road and prop the cast up on the windowsill or the dashboard and let the ache ease out of it for an hour or two. In the morning, in the town, I asked an old man standing in front of a store if he knew where the Longanecker farm was and I went where he said.

The house I took to be Jim's stood most of the way up a hillside, above a flat, milky creek. There was a long slope of plowed ground between the creek and the house, and a woman working an old tractor across the field, towing a harrow. I don't think she could have heard the truck over the tractor noise, but maybe she saw the dust we raised going up her road because she looked around sudden from under the brim of her hat and then shut the tractor off and stood down from it and walked up across the plowed ground toward the house. It wasn't much of a house. The porch was rotted so it leaned downhill, and the roof had club moss along the eave edges. There was no barn, just a cow shed with manure piled up under it, and a lean-to at the end where she stood her tools. There was a post and wire fence that went around a couple of acres of grass and weed. An old pickup with a fender gone stood in the yard under the only tree.

There wasn't any bridge going over the creek. I had to ford the truck across. I took it slow on account of the trailer and the blue roan, but it was a shallow crossing and the rocks were cleared out of it so the trailer didn't buck too much getting over. The woman had beat me to the house and she was waiting for me when I got up the hill. She had her sleeves rolled up and was hugging herself so I could see she had rough red hands and rough red elbows, but her face under the hat-shadow looked smooth and fine-skinned, only a couple of pinch marks where the corners of her mouth tucked in. She had her hair drawn back in a knot but there was a thick bang of fuzz just under the edge of the hat and more of it leaking out at the neck. She maybe cussed that hair every day, too much of it and all frizzed like that, but it was a good color, gold-brown as wheat, and I can't say I minded the way it made a sort of halo around her face. She had on filthy jeans that fit poor, but I could see why Jim would have married her.

I stayed in the truck. "I'm after Jim Longanecker's place," I said across the windowsill. "I wonder if this is it." I was pretty sure it was, and as soon as I spoke his name those little tucks by her mouth squeezed in.

"Jim's gone rodeoing," she said, in a short way.

I had to ask her, I didn't want to tell it to the wrong woman. "Are you Mrs. Longanecker?"

She watched me, holding her head straight

and keeping her arms folded up on her chest. "I'm Irene Longanecker," she said. "Who are you?"

"I'm a friend of Jim's. I've brought down some news."

Her mouth flattened out a little. It wasn't a frown, but as if she had got tired suddenly, and she spoke like that, too, with a flatness. "Where's he at now? Lakeview?"

There was a big ark of cloud sculling across the sky above the ridge beam of the house and I looked at that while I took off my hat and sleeved the sweat-edge on my forehead. "The news I've got isn't good," I said. I had quit watching her, but I could see from the tail of my eye she had raised her head back a little out of the shadow of the hat and now she had one hand flat above her eyes to shade against the glare. "Jim's dead," I said. I had meant to say, *Your husband Jim has been taken from you*—I had planned it, wooly and formal and old-fashioned like that. But I didn't remember until right afterward, so it came out straight and maybe sounding a little hard-boiled, though I wasn't feeling that way at all.

In the three years I'd known Jim he'd only come down to this place maybe a dozen different times, two or three weeks at a stretch during the off seasons. But he would get a letter now and then with his name spelled out in a spiky woman's hand, spelled all the way out, James Thomas Longanecker, like there might be more than one Jim Longanecker anywhere. And Jim used to speak of his wife like he spoke of his good bird gun or his handmade saddle, like she was something he had that he was proud of. So when I told her he was dead, I didn't know what I ought to expect.

She watched me a minute without moving, with the edge of her hand against her bangs to shade out the sun, and then her mouth moved again, slipping down in that tired way, but there wasn't any sound out of her and the face she made wasn't grief. She began to shake her head like she couldn't believe it. She didn't say anything to me, she just shook her head half a dozen times and then turned around and went up onto the leaning porch and cracked the screen door back and went inside.

I sat quite a while after that, creasing the edge of my hat with my thumbs, and then I eased my cast out of the truck and set it down on the dirt and stood up. I held on to the door of the truck and stood there looking across the plowed hill to where the tractor waited in front of the harrow.

The boy came from behind the hill, driving the cow and calf ahead of him. I could see him watching me while he switched the cow into her little shed, and for a while after that he stood by the buildings just looking down the hill at me. I thought the woman might come out to talk to him but she didn't. Finally he drifted down and stood at the edge of the field, watching me fight the tractor across those furrows, but he tired of that pretty quick and began to sidle up to the mare where I had let her out into the fenced pasture. She was soft-gaited, that horse, and light in the mouth, sweet-tempered and willing as any horse I'd seen. And she had that pretty roan color, that dark charcoal hide veined with white so it showed up blue, like the bluing on a new gun, and where the boy stroked her long stretched-down neck there was a shine I could see sometimes, bright as metal. Jim was killed on account of I loved that horse too much, I guess. So after a while I couldn't watch the boy with her anymore and I called to him, "She's testy. She's been known to bite," and heard it come out hard-boiled again. The sun was high up and hot and the sweat was itching over my ribs and my leg was aching all the way up to the hip. I don't know if he heard me over the tractor, but he gave me a look and went back up to the cow shed. He was maybe seven or eight years old. There was a ditch in his chin, just like Jim had.

Before too long, the woman came out and she said something to the boy and then came downhill to where I was. She had her sleeves rolled down now and her hat was gone so the sun lit up her hair like it was burning along the scalp.

"Dinner," she said. "You'd better come in." She didn't come any closer than the edge of the furrows. She just shouted it out so I'd hear her.

The boy and I took turns at the outside faucet. I didn't know what his mother had said to him and I was afraid he might ask me something about Jim, but he just washed his hands real slow, looking at me sidelong, and then went ahead into the house. I stayed out a while, wetting my hair and combing it back smooth, and I left my hat in the truck when I went inside. The woman was already sitting, spooning food onto the boy's plate, and it felt like quite a while before she looked up and saw me standing in the door.

"Sit down," she said, and that was the last thing anybody said until the meal was done, though that boy kept sneaking looks in my direction. When the woman began to clear the plates, the boy pitched right in. That left me sitting there, so I made as if to help too. She said, "You can go on out and sit in the shade. I'll be out in a minute," and stuck her chin toward the door. So I went outside. I stood a while. Then I walked back down to the tractor and started in at the harrowing again.

After a while the woman came out. She walked down to the edge of the field and said something. I couldn't hear what it was so I shut off the tractor, and she walked across the plowed ground, then, until she was standing right next to me.

"Thank you for the harrowing. Most cowboys don't like to do that work at all." Maybe she meant it as a complaint against Jim but if she did I couldn't hear the sourness in it.

I said, "My folks were farmers. I used to know my way around a tractor pretty well."

She nodded, as if there was a meaning in it. "Well, I can finish it now. I appreciate you helping out."

There was a little speech I had readied while I was driving down here overnight. I said it now. "I'd help you out a while, if you want. I can finish up this field, get it put to seed. Or whatever else you need done. I can't rodeo much with this broken leg but I can do a little farming, I guess. I don't mind working for bed and board. I expect there's room for me to sleep in your tool shed, and I eat about anything."

She gave me a look, like she was hunting for something in my face. Maybe she was just making sure it was a true offer. Then she ducked her head and said, "I guess you're Glenn." That caught me short and I must have looked it. In a minute, watching me, she said, "Jim wrote that you were his friend." I'd seen Jim sweating out a few letters all right, but I'd never figured he would put me in one. I wondered what he had written. I don't know why it made me feel itchy.

"What killed him?" she said, so it came straight out without a warning, and I was caught short again.

I bent my broken leg up and rubbed the knee above the cast. I looked at my hand, my fingers working at the knee. "A horse kicked him," I said. "I guess he didn't feel it. At least that's what they said." She didn't say anything to that, so after a while I let out a little more: "I couldn't make it here right away but I came as soon as I was able. It happened Wednesday night. You don't have a telephone and I didn't think the news ought to be put in a letter if it could be otherwise." I thought it over and then I said, "I can drive you up there tomorrow if you want. Or tonight."

Finally she looked off, away from me, off toward her old house. "I appreciate you coming so far." I couldn't hear grief in it, just that same flat tone, like she was worn out, worn down.

I thought about it. "Jim would've done the same for me," I said.

She raised her head without looking around. "Yes. I guess that's so," she said. "Jim always set his friends high." She said it like she faulted him for it, and there was a look in her face, somewhat of bitterness. After a silence she said, "Were you with him?"

I had to think a minute what she was getting at, and then when it came clear I began to knead my leg again, working my knuckles at the knee. "Yes. I was there."

She nodded in that way she had, as if it meant something serious. Then finally she looked at me again, a straight look. "I want to hear about it."

I had thought I might get away with just telling her he had been kicked by a horse. But she stood there waiting for the rest, so I told her more or less what had happened, though I hadn't got myself ready to tell it.

I told her we had got drunk after the rodeo in Sprague and Jim had started in teasing me about that blue roan I loved so much. Actually, I never did tell her it was the roan. I just said it was a mare Jim had, which I had taken a liking to. She had lately come into heat and every stallion who stood within half a mile of her was probably rubbing himself against a post that night. Jim was kidding me about it, asking if I was man enough to service her myself, and so on. But after a while things took a turn and he started talking in a serious way, as if we weren't both drunk, sitting on our butts under the dark bleachers in the rain.

"Female needs offspring," he said solemnly. "She won't be happy until she throws a colt. I ought to put her in with that good-looking red stud belongs to Chip Lister. She'll get herself a little red roan baby to keep her happy."

"The hell," I believe I said, and kept drinking my beer.

In a while he made a thoughtful sound and stood up. He walked off, dragging his boot heels in the mud in a lazy, strutting way. It was a while before I got up to follow him. I was pretty drunk. By the time I caught up to him, he had the mare in with Chip's stallion and was leaning on the rail watching them.

"Hey," I said. "Hey. What the hell are you doing?"

"If you weren't so blind-drunk you'd see what I'm doing."

I took off my hat and waved it. I don't know

what good I thought that would do. "Jim, damn you, this ain't funny."

Jim clapped me on the shoulder. He was grinning. "The hell it ain't," he said.

The stud was driving the mare just ahead of him around the edge of the corral. In the rain and the darkness the mare looked black, the stallion dark red, the color of old blood. I flapped my hat again. "Get away from her you big bastard."

Jim laughed. "That old boy's going to make her a baby."

I stood holding my hat. Then I said, "The hell he is," and I went over the fence. Chip's horse had her pushed up against the rails by then and he was trying to work around behind her. I went up and just hit him in the muzzle with my fist. I was drunk. I should have got a stick of wood or something but I didn't. I just pushed in between them and started hitting.

I don't know what happened. I guess I got bumped. I was sitting in the mud, all at once, and they were stepping on me. I heard Jim yelling, I still don't know if it was at me or at those horses, but a big drunk yell, and then he came wading in, beating at the stallion like I'd done, with his knuckles. The horse got up on his hind legs, squealing, I saw his big chest and his mane swinging loose, and then I heard the sound the iron shoe made against the solid bone of Jim's head. That was all there was, just that sound, because Jim never made any, just fell back straight as a tree and heavy.

I got up from under him and got hold of a two-by-four and beat hell out of that stallion. I felt bad about it afterward, it wasn't the damn horse's fault. But I beat him off the mare and ran the mare outside, and then I went back and sat down next to Jim, with the rain falling on us in the dark. One of the horses had broken my shinbone and my boot was filled up with blood, but there was no pain there, just the sticky wetness, and I didn't know I was hurt until somebody told me afterward.

Jim's wife never said a word while I told her how Jim had got killed. When I was done she just stood there looking out at the sky edge. Finally she said, "Well, I'll think about the work you offered," and she looked down at her feet and then walked back up the hill to the house. She had a deliberate way of walking, even across the soft field. I'd noticed it before. She walked like somebody who has a long way ahead and has set herself a pace to get there.

By the time I had got the harrowing done, the sun was low. I gave the mare what feed I had from the back of the truck and I was doling out the woman's hay to her cow when the boy walked out to me.

"I'm supposed to do that," he said, mumbling, pointing the words somewhere to the left of where I was.

"Okay," I said, and stood off and watched him do it.

"You're supposed to come in for supper," he said, when he had finished with the cow. "We're both supposed to."

I followed him up to the faucet and we took turns again.

"Did you get bucked off?" he asked me, sideways eyeing the dirty cast.

"Got stepped on," was all I said.

He nodded like his mother, in a solemn way. "Oh."

The woman had brought out a bit of a cold

supper and we ate as before, silently, in the high-ceilinged kitchen. She didn't turn on a lamp, but the daylight began to fail fast while we were sitting there, and when she stood to do up the dishes she pointed with her chin and the boy pulled the chain on the ceiling light without being told. I didn't wait for her to point her chin at the door. I went on outside.

I'd been hoarding the few cigarettes I had left, but I was needing one pretty bad tonight and, hell, that's what they were for, so I got one out. I went partway down the hill and sat down on the grass in the darkness with my cast stuck straight out in front of me while I smoked. I watched the mare grazing on the poor grass in that fenced field. I could hear her ripping the tough stalks with her teeth.

After a while I heard the screen door crack. I kept on sitting there, sucking up the last of my smoke, staring off at the mare like I didn't know, but I could feel the woman's eyes on me—I knew she was standing back there, watching me. I was about to get onto my feet again when she came down from the house and sat a couple of yards away, with her knees pulled up in front of her and her arms clasped around them.

In a bit she said, "Jim never could stay put. I guess you know that, you'd be like that yourself. So the boy and me, we've been alone half his life, and sometimes we get pretty hungry for a man's voice. Both of us do, I won't deny it; we get pretty lonesome." There was a silence. Then she said, "If I was looking for somebody to wear the edge off my lonesomeness, I guess you'd do; you have a kind face, as far as that goes."

I felt a heat start up from my neck. I took a long stem of grass and began to split it down the middle with my thumbnail. I guess I had known all along she might take my offer that way. Afterward, when I thought about it, I wondered if I might even have meant her to take it that way. I don't know. I sat there on the grass in the dark, looking at my hands.

"The truth is, I could use the help," she said. "There's more work than I can do, and no money to pay anybody." She waited again. "But the boy sees you with that good-looking horse, looking like you do, dressing like you do, just smelling of places a long way from here. And I can see his eyes going away from me." I didn't know what she meant, not then, but I figured it out later. She said, "Jim's eyes used to do that," and there was tenderness in it, or pain, the first I'd heard since telling her Jim was dead.

She didn't say anything else for a while. I wondered if she had started to cry. Then she said, "I guess I'm stupid, turning you away when you offer your help. I could use it, that's for sure. But it wasn't your fault, what happened; you don't owe Jim anything. And my saying no doesn't have anything much to do with you." She lifted her chin a little and gave a straight look and then I saw her eyes were tearless. "It's just a lonesome woman isn't any mare in heat," she said in a level voice. I looked away. I looked down at my hands. "I'm just trying to hold on to my son," she said after a wait. Her voice had dropped lower. "I appreciate you harrowing the field. And coming down here with the news. If you don't mind sleeping in the shed, I'll see you get a good breakfast in the morning before you leave."

She stood up without waiting for me to say anything else and walked back up the short hill to the house. I kept sitting where I was for a while. I watched the blue roan, the shadow of her, in that field.

She and the boy made a space for me under the eaves of the lean-to, amid the stacked-up tools, and it was snug there; I'd slept in worse places. But after a while I just gave it up. There was a pretty good wind shaking the tree and my leg was aching and I blamed it on those things. In the dark I had to watch out not to kick over a rake or something, feeling careful with my boot and my cast until I was out in the open, where the moon gave some light to see what I was doing. I sat down and wrote on a scrap of paper the name of the mortuary where Jim's body was, in Sprague, and below that I wrote, *His horse and gear was sold, this is the sum of what it came to. The truck was his too.* Jim had had a little money and I put it with my own money, all I had, in a stack on the piece of paper, and I folded it so it was a flat packet. Then I went up and set it under a rock on the porch, where she would find it. I lugged the saddle out of the truck and put it on the mare. I had a hell of a time getting her saddled and a worse time getting myself up on her with that damn cast. I had to lead her up next to the house so I could stand on the porch and clamber up. I was afraid maybe the woman would hear me bumping around, but if she heard, she didn't come out to see what it was.

I left her the truck sitting there with the keys in it. It was a better one than she had, and the trailer was damn near new. Half of the rig was Jim's anyway, and I didn't have the money to buy him out, after giving her the money for the horse. Driving up here, I had thought I would give her the blue roan too, but I could see, now, she wouldn't have wanted it there, around the boy. So that was the only thing of Jim's I held on to.

DANCE GIRL,
by Edward Gorman

Edward Gorman is highly proficient in a variety of fictional fields: Westerns, mysteries, and horror. He is also an accomplished anthologist (Westeryear) and co-publisher of an excellent magazine devoted to the enjoyment of contemporary genre fiction, Mystery Scene. His Western novels include two about a middle-aged and sharply individuated bounty hunter named Leo Guild, Guild (1987) and Death Ground (1988); and two set in his native Iowa, Graves' Retreat (1989) and Night of Shadows (1989). Gorman is at his most mordant in this haunting story of murder, revenge, and other human tragedy in old Cedar Rapids.

• DANCE GIRL •
by Edward Gorman

At the time of her murder, Madge Tucker had been living in Cedar Rapids, two blocks west of the train depot, for seven years.

After several quick interviews with other boarders in the large frame rooming house, investigating officers learned that Madge Evelyn Tucker had first come to the city from a farm near Holbrook in 1883. At the time she'd been seventeen years old. After working as a clerk in a millinery store, where her soft good looks made her a mark for young suitors in straw boaters and eager smiles, she met a man named Marley who owned four taverns in and around the area of the Star Wagon Company and the Chicago and Northwestern Railyards. She spent the final five years of her life being a dance girl in these places. All this came to an end when someone entered her room on the night of August 14, 1890.

A Dr. Baines, who was substituting for the vacationing doctor the police ordinarily used, brought a most peculiar piece of information to the officer in charge. After examining Madge Evelyn Tucker, he had come to two conclusions—one being that she'd been stabbed twice in the chest and the second being that she had died a virgin.

One did not expect to hear about a dance girl dying a virgin.

Three months later, just as autumn was turning treetops red and gold and brown, a tall, slender young man in a dark Edwardian suit and a homburg stepped from the early morning Rock Island train and surveyed the platform about him. He was surrounded by people embracing each other—sons and mothers, mothers and fathers, daughters and friends. A shadow of sorrow passed over his dark eyes as he watched this happy tableau. Then, with a large-knuckled hand, he lifted his carpetbag and began walking toward the prosperous downtown area, the skyline dominated by a six-story structure that housed the Cedar Rapids Savings Bank.

He found a horse-drawn trolley, asked the driver where he might find a certain cemetery, and sat back and tried to relax as two plump women discussed the forthcoming election for mayor.

For the rest of the ride, he read the letters he kept in his suit coat. The return address was always the same, as was the name. Madge Evelyn Tucker. Just now, staring at her beautiful penmanship, tears formed in his eyes. He realized that the two women who had been arguing about the present mayor had stopped talking and were staring at him.

Rather than face their scrutiny, he got off the trolley at the next block and walked the remaining distance to the cemetery.

He wondered, an hour and a half later, if he had not come to Cedar Rapids on the worst sort of whim. Perhaps his grief over his dead sister

Madge was undoing him. Hadn't Mr. Staley at the bank where Richard Tucker worked suggested a "leave of absence"? What he'd meant, of course, was that Richard was behaving most strangely and that good customers were becoming upset.

Now Richard crouched behind a wide oak tree. In the early October morning, the sky pure blue, a chicken hawk looping and diving against this blue, Richard smelled grass burning in the last of the summer sun and heard the song of jays and bluebirds and the sharp resonating bass of distant prowling dogs.

It would be so pleasant just to sit here uphill from the place where she'd been buried. Just sit here and think of her as she'd been. . . .

But he had things to do. That was why a Navy Colt trembled in his big hand. That was why his other hand kept touching the letters inside his jacket.

By three P.M. the man had not come. By four P.M. the man had not come. By five P.M. the man had not come.

Richard began to grow even more nervous, hidden behind the oak and looking directly down at his sister's headstone. Perhaps the man had come very early in the morning, before Richard's arrival. Or perhaps the man wasn't coming at all.

A rumbling wagon of day workers from a construction site came past the iron cemetery fence, bringing dust and the smell of beer and the cheer of their worn-out laughter with them. Later, a stage coach, one of the few remaining in service anywhere in the Plains states, jerked and jostled past, a solitary passenger looking bored with it all. Finally, a young man and woman on sparkling new bicycles came past the iron fence. He saw in the gentle lines of the woman's face Madge's own gentle lines.

I tried to warn you, Madge.

His remembered words shook him. All his warnings. All his pleadings. For nothing. Madge, good sweet Madge, saw nothing wrong in being a dance girl, not if you kept, as she always said, "your virtue."

Well, the doctor had said at her death that her virtue had indeed remained with her.

But virtue hadn't protected her from the night of August 14. It hadn't protected her at all.

Dusk was chill. Early stars shone in the gray-blue firmament. The distant dogs now sounded lonely.

Crouched behind the oak, Richard pulled his collar up and began blowing on his hands so the knuckles would not feel so raw. Below, the graveyard had become a shadowy place, the tips of granite headstones white in the gloom.

Several times he held his Ingram watch up to the light of the half-moon. He did this at five-minute intervals. The last time, he decided he would leave if nothing happened in the next five minutes.

The man appeared just after Richard had finished consulting his watch.

He was a short man, muscular, dressed in a suit and wearing a Western-style hat. At the cemetery entrance, he looked quickly about, as if he sensed he were being spied upon, and then moved without hesitation to Madge's headstone.

The roses he held in his hand were put into an empty vase next to the headstone. The man then dropped to his knees and made a large and rather dramatic sign of the cross.

He was so involved in his prayers that he did not even turn around until Richard was two steps away. By then it was too late.

Richard shot the man three times in the back of the head—the man who had never been charged with the murder of Richard's sister.

On the train that night, Richard took out the letter in which Madge had made reference to the man in the cemetery. Cletus Boyer, the man's name had been. He'd been a clerk in a haberdasher's and was considered quite a ladies' man.

He met Madge shortly after she became a dance girl. He made one terrible mistake. He fell in love with her. He begged her to give up the taverns but she would not. This only seemed to make his love the more unbearable for him.

He began following her, harassing her, and then he began slapping her.

Finally, Madge gave up the dance hall. By now, she realized how much Cletus loved her. She had grown, in her way, to love him. She took a job briefly with Greene's Opera House. Cletus was to take her home to meet his parents, prominent people on the east side. But over the course of the next month, Madge saw that for all he loved her, he could never accept her past as a dance girl. He pleaded with her to help him in some way—he did not want to feel the rage and shame that boiled up in him whenever he thought of her in the arms of other men. But not even her assurances that she was still a virgin helped. Thinking of her as a dance girl threatened his sanity.

All these things were told Richard in the letter. One more thing was added.

Whenever he called her names and struck her, he became paralyzed with guilt. He brought her gifts of every sort by way of apology. "I don't know what to do, Brother. He is so complicated and tortured a man." Finally, she broke off with him and went back to the taverns.

As the train rattled through the night, the Midwestern plains silver in the dew and moonlight, Richard Tucker sat now feeling sorry for the man he'd just killed.

Richard supposed that in his way Cletus Boyer really had loved Madge.

He sighed, glancing at the letter again.

The passage about Cletus bringing gifts of apology had proved to Richard that Boyer was a sentimental man. And a sentimental killer, Richard had reasoned, was likely to become especially sentimental on the day of a loved one's birthday. That was how Richard had known that Cletus would come to the cemetery today. A sentimental killer.

Richard put the letter away and looked out again at the silver prairie, hoarfrost and pumpkins on the horizon line. A dread came over him as he thought of his job in the bank and the little furnished room where he lived. He felt suffocated now. In the end, his life would come to nothing, just as his sister's life had come to nothing; just as Cletus Boyer's life had come to nothing. There had been a girl once but now there was a girl no longer. There had been the prospect of a better job once, but these days he was too tired to pursue one. Dragging himself daily to the bank was easier—

The prairie rushed past. And the circle of

moon, ancient and secret and indifferent, stood still.

The world was a senseless place, Richard knew as the train plunged onward into the darkness. A senseless place.

McIntosh's Chute,
by Jack Foxx

Jack Foxx is a pseudonym of a well-known writer and anthologist, another of whose stories appears elsewhere in these pages. He has published one historical novel under the Foxx name, a humorous Western mystery called Freebooty (1976). In "McIntosh's Chute," he tells a tale of cowhands in Montana, loggers on Oregon's Black Mountain, a scoundrel named McIntosh and his fabulous 2600-foot-long chute, and "the damnedest sight a man ever laid eyes on."

• McIntosh's Chute •
by Jack Foxx

It was right after supper and we were all settled around the cookfire, smoking, none of us saying much because it was well along in the roundup and we were all dog-tired from the long days of riding and chousing cows out of brush-clogged coulees. I wasn't doing anything except taking in the night—warm Montana fall night, sky all hazed with stars, no moon to speak of. Then, of a sudden, something come streaking across all that velvet-black and silver from east to west: a ball of smoky red-orange with a long fiery tail. Everybody stirred around and commenced to gawping and pointing. But not for long. Quick as it had come, the thing was gone beyond the broken sawteeth of the Rockies.

There was a hush. Then young Poley said, "What in hell was *that*?" He was just eighteen and big for his britches in more ways than one. But that heavenly fireball had taken him down to an awed whisper.

"Comet," Cass Buckram said.

"That fire-tail ... whooee!" Poley said. "I never seen nothing like it. Comet, eh? Well, it's the damnedest sight a man ever set eyes on."

"Damnedest sight a *button* ever set eyes on, maybe."

"I ain't a button!"

"You are from where I sit," Cass said. "Big

shiny man-sized button with your threads still dangling."

Everybody laughed except Poley. Being as he was the youngest on the roundup crew, he'd taken his share of ragging since we'd left the Box 8 and he was about fed up with it. He said, "Well, what do *you* know about it, old-timer?"

That didn't faze Cass. He was close to sixty, though you'd never know it to look at him or watch him when he worked cattle or at anything else, but age didn't mean much to him. He was of a philosophical turn of mind. You were what you were and no sense in pretending otherwise—that was how he looked at it.

In his younger days he'd been an adventuresome gent. Worked at jobs most of us wouldn't have tried in places we'd never even hoped to visit. Oil rigger in Texas and Oklahoma, logger in Oregon, fur trapper in the Canadian Barrens, prospector in the Yukon during the '98 Rush, cowhand in half a dozen states and territories. He'd packed more living into the past forty-odd years than a whole regiment of men, and he didn't mind talking about his experiences. No, he sure didn't mind. First time I met him, I'd taken him for a blowhard. Plenty took him that way in the beginning, on account of his windy nature. But the stories he told were true, or at least every one had a core of truth in it. He had too many facts and a whole warbag full of mementoes and photographs and such to back 'em up.

All you had to do was prime him a little—and without knowing it, young Poley had primed him just now. But that was all right with the rest of us. Cass had honed his storytelling skills over the years; one of his yarns was always worthwhile entertainment.

He said to the kid, "I saw more strange things before I was twenty than you'll ever see."

"Cowflop."

"Correct word is 'bullshit,' " Cass said, solemn, and everybody laughed again. "But neither one is accurate."

"I suppose you seen something stranger and more spectacular than that there comet."

"Twice as strange and three times as spectacular."

"Cowflop."

"Fact. Ninth wonder of the world, in its way."

"Well? What was it?"

"McIntosh and his chute."

"Chute? What chute? Who was McIntosh?"

"Keep our lip buttoned, button, and I'll tell you. I'll tell you about *the* damnedest sight I or any other man ever laid eyes on."

Happened more than twenty years ago [Cass went on], in southern Oregon in the early nineties. I'd had my fill of fur trapping in the Barrens and developed a hankering to see what timber work was like, so I'd come on down into Oregon and hooked on with a logging outfit near Coos Bay. But for the first six months I was just a bullcook, not a timberjack. Low-down work, bullcooking—cleaning up after the jacks, making up their bunks, cutting firewood, helping out in the kitchen. Without experience, that's the only kind of job you can get in a decent logging camp. Boss finally put me on one of the yarding crews, but even then there was no thrill in the work and the wages were low. So I was ready for a change of venue when word filtered in that a man named Saginaw Tom McIntosh was hiring for his camp on Black Mountain.

McIntosh was from Michigan and had made

a pile logging in the North Woods. What had brought him west to Oregon was the opportunity to buy better than 25,000 acres of virgin timberland on Black Mountain. He'd rebuilt an old dam on the Klamath River nearby that had been washed out by high water, built a sawmill and a millpond below the dam, and then started a settlement there that he named after himself. And once he had a camp operating on the mountain, first thing he did was construct a chute, or skidway, down to the river

Word of McIntosh's chute spread just as fast and far as word that he was hiring timber beasts at princely wages. It was supposed to be an engineering marvel, unlike any other logging chute ever built. Some scoffed when they were told about it; claimed it was just one of those tall stories that get flung around among Northwest loggers, like the one about Paul Bunyan and Babe the blue ox. Me, I was willing to give Saginaw Tom McIntosh the benefit of the doubt. I figured that if he was half the man he was talked of being, he could accomplish just about anything he set his mind to.

He had two kinds of reputation. First, as a demon logger—a man who could get timber cut faster and turned into board lumber quicker than any other boss jack. And second, as a ruthless cold-hearted son of a bitch who bullied his men, worked them like animals, and wasn't above using fists, peaveys, calks, and any other handy weapon if the need arose. Rumor had it that he—

What's that, boy? No, I ain't going to say any more about that chute just yet. I'll get to it in good time. You just keep your pants on and let me tell this my own way.

Well, rumor had it that McIntosh was offering top dollar because it was the only way he could get jacks to work steady for him. That and his reputation didn't bother me one way or another. I'd dealt with hard cases before, and have since. So I determined to see what Saginaw Tom and his chute and Black Mountain were all about.

I quit the Coos Bay outfit and traveled down to McIntosh's settlement on the Klamath. Turned out to be bigger than I'd expected. The sawmill was twice the size of the one up at Coos Bay, and there was a blacksmith shop, a box factory, a hotel and half a dozen boarding-houses, two big stores, a school, two churches, and a lodge hall. McIntosh may have been a son of a bitch, but he sure did know how to get maximum production and how to provide for his men and their families.

I hired on at the mill, and the next day a crew chief named Lars Nilson drove me and another new man, a youngster called Johnny Cline, up-river to the Black Mountain camp. Long, hot trip in the back of a buckboard, up steep grades and past gold-mining claims strung along the rough-water river. Nilson told us there was bad blood between McIntosh and those miners. They got gold out of the sand by trapping silt in wing dams, and they didn't like it when McIntosh's river drivers built holding cribs along the banks or herded long chains of logs downstream to the cribs and then on to the mill. There hadn't been any trouble yet, but it could erupt at any time; feelings were running high on both sides.

Heat and flies and hornets deviled us all the way up into scrub timber: lodgepole, jack, and yellow pine. The bigger trees—white sugar pine—grew higher up, and what fine old trees they were. Clean-growing, hardly any under-brush. Huge trunks that rose up straight from brace roots close to four feet broad, and no branches on 'em until thirty to forty feet above the ground. Every lumberman's dream, the cut-log timber on that mountain.

McIntosh was taking full advantage of it too. His camp was twice the size of most—two enor-mous bunkhouses, a cookshack, a barn and blacksmith shop, clusters of sheds and shanties and heavy wagons, corrals full of work horses and oxen. Close to a hundred men, altogether. And better than two dozen big wheels, stinger-tongue and slip-tongue both—

What's a big wheel? Just that, boy—wheels ten and twelve feet high, some made of wood and some of iron, each pair connected by an axle that had a chain and a long tongue poking back from the middle. Four-horse team drew each one. Man on the wheel crew dug a shallow trench under one or two logs, depending on their size; loader pushed the chain through it under the logs and secured it to the axle; driver lunged his team ahead and the tongue slid for-ward and yanked on the chain to lift the front end of the logs off the ground. Harder the horses pulled, the higher the logs hung. When the team came to a stop, the logs dropped and dragged. Only trouble was, sometimes they didn't drop and drag just right—didn't act as a brake like they were supposed to—and the wheel horses got their hind legs smashed. Much safer and faster to use a steam lokey to get cut logs out of the woods, but laying narrow-gauge track takes time and so does ordering a lokey and having it packed in sections up the side of a wilderness mountain. McIntosh figured to have his track laid and a lokey operating by the following spring. Meanwhile, it was the big wheels and the teams of horses and oxen and men that had to do the heavy work.

Now then. The chute—McIntosh's chute.

First I seen of it was across the breadth of the camp, at the edge of a steep drop-off: the chute head, a big two-level platform built of logs. Cut logs were stacked on the top level as they came off the big wheels, by jacks crowhopping over the deck with cant hooks. On the lower level other jacks looped a cable around the foremost log, and a donkey engine wound up the cable and hauled the log forward into a trough built at the outer edge of the platform. You follow me so far?

Well, that was all I could see until Nilson took Johnny Cline and me over close to the chute head. From the edge of the drop-off you had a miles-wide view—long snaky stretches of the Klamath, timberland all the way south to the California border. But it wasn't the vista that had my attention; it was the chute itself. An engineering marvel, all right, that near took my breath away.

McIntosh and his crew had cut a channel in the rocky hillside straight on down to the riverbank, and lined the sides and bottom with flat-hewn logs—big ones at the sides and smaller ones on the bottom, all worn glass-smooth. Midway along was a short trestle that spanned an outcrop and acted as a kind of speed-brake. Nothing legendary about that chute: it was the longest built up to that time, maybe the longest ever. More than twenty-six hundred feet of timber had gone into the construction, top to bottom.

While I was gawking down at it, somebody shouted, "Clear back!" and right away Nilson herded Johnny Cline and me onto a hummock to one side. At the chute head a chain of logs was lined and ready, held back by an iron bar wedged into the rock. Far down below one of the river crew showed a white flag, and as soon as he did the chute tender yanked the iron bar aside and the first log shuddered through and down.

After a hundred feet or so, it began to pick up speed. You could hear it squealing against the sides and bottom of the trough. By the time it went over the trestle and into the lower part of the chute, it was a blur. Took just eighteen seconds for it to drop more than eight hundred feet to the river, and when it hit the splash was bigger than a barn and the fan of water drenched trees on both banks—

"Hell!" young Poley interrupted. "I don't believe none of that. You're funning us, Cass."

"Be damned if I am. What don't you believe?"

"None of it. Chute twenty-six hundred feet long, logs shooting down over eight hundred feet in less than twenty seconds, splashes bigger than a barn . . ."

"Well, it's the gospel truth. So's the rest of it. Sides and bottom a third of the way down were burned black from the friction—black as coal. On cold mornings you could see smoke from the logs going down: that's how fast they traveled. Went even faster when there was frost, so the river crew had to drive spikes in the chute's bottom end to slow 'em up. Even so, sometimes a log would hit the river with enough force to split it in half, clean, like it'd gone through a buzz saw. But I expect you don't believe none of that, either."

Poley grunted. "Not hardly."

I said, "Well, *I* believe it, Cass. Man can do just about anything he sets his mind to, like you said, if he wants it bad enough. That chute must of been something. I can sure see why it was the damnedest thing you ever saw."

"No, it wasn't," Cass said.

"What? But you said—"

"No, I didn't. McIntosh's chute was a wonder but not the damnedest thing I ever saw."

"Then what *is*?" Poley demanded.

"If I wasn't interrupted every few minutes, you'd of found out by now." Cass glared at him. "You going to be quiet and let me get to it or you intend to keep flapping your gums so this here story takes all night?"

Poley wasn't cowed, but he did button his lip. And surprised us all—maybe even himself—by keeping it buttoned for the time being.

I thought I might get put on one of the wheel crews [Cass resumed], but I'd made the mistake of telling Nilson I'd worked a yarding crew up at Coos Bay, so a yarding crew was where I got put on Black Mountain. Working as a choke-setter in the slash out back of the camp—man that sets heavy cable chokers around the end of a log that's fallen down a hillside or into a ravine so the log can be hauled out by means of a donkey engine. Hard, sweaty, dangerous work in the best of camps, and McIntosh's was anything but the best. The rumors had been right about that too. We worked long hours for our pay, seven days a week. And if a man dropped from sheer exhaustion, he was expected to get up under his own power—and docked for the time he spent lying down.

Johnny Cline got put on the same crew, as a whistle-punk on the donkey, and him and me took up friendly. He was a Californian, from down near San Francisco; young and feisty and too smart-ass for his own good ... some like you, Poley. But decent enough, underneath. His brother was a logger somewhere in Canada, and he'd determined to try his hand too. He was about as green as me, but you could see that logging was in his blood in a way that it wasn't in mine. I knew I'd be moving on to other things one day; he knew he'd be a logger till the day he died.

I got along with Nilson and most of the other timber beasts, but Saginaw Tom McIntosh was another matter. If anything, he was worse than his reputation—mean clear through, with about as much decency as a vulture on a fence post waiting for something to die. Giant of a man, face weathered the color of heartwood, droopy yellow mustache stained with juice from the quids of Spearhead tobacco he always kept stowed in one cheek, eyes like pale fire that gave you the feeling you'd been burned whenever they touched you. Stalked around camp in worn cruisers, stagged corduroy pants, and steel-calked boots, yelling out orders, knocking men down with his fists if they didn't ask how high when he hollered jump. Ran that camp the way a hardass warden runs a prison. Everybody hated him, including me and Johnny Cline before long. But most of the jacks feared him, too, which was how he kept them in line.

He drove all his crews hard, demanding that a dozen turns of logs go down his chute every day to feed the saws working twenty-four hours at the mill. Cut lumber was fetching more than a hundred dollars per thousand feet at the time and he wanted to keep production at a fever pitch before the heavy winter rains set in. There was plenty of grumbling among the men, and tempers were short, but nobody quit the camp. Pay was too good, even with all the abuse that went along with it.

I'd been at the Black Mountain camp three weeks when the real trouble started. One of the gold miners down on the Klamath, man named Coogan, got drunk and decided to tear up a holding crib because he blamed McIntosh for ruining his claim. McIntosh flew into a rage when he heard about it. He ranted and raved for half a day about how he'd had enough of those goddamn miners. Then, when he'd worked himself up enough, he ordered a dozen jacks down on a night raid to bust up Coogan's wing dam and raise some hell with the other miners' claims. The jacks didn't want to do it but he bullied them into it with threats and promises of bonus money.

But the miners were expecting retaliation; had joined forces and were waiting when the jacks showed up. There was a riverbank brawl, mostly with fists and ax handles, but with a few shots fired too. Three timber stiffs were hurt bad enough so that they had to be carried back to camp and would be laid up for a while.

The county law came next day and threatened to close McIntosh down if there was any more trouble. That threw him into another fit. Kind of man he was, he took it out on the men in the raiding party.

"What kind of jack lets a gold-grubber beat him down?" he yelled at them. "You buggers ain't worth the name timberjack. If I didn't need your hands and backs, I'd send the lot of you packing. As is, I'm cutting your pay. And you three that can't work—you get no pay at all until you can hoist your peaveys and swing your axes."

One of the jacks challenged him. McIntosh kicked the man in the crotch, knocked him down, and then gave him a case of logger's smallpox: pinned his right arm to the ground with those steel calks of his. There were no other challenges. But in all those bearded faces you could see the hate that was building for McIntosh. You could feel it too; it was in the air, crackles of it like electricity in a storm.

Another week went by. There was no more trouble with the miners, but McIntosh drove his crews with a vengeance. Up to fifteen turns of logs down the chute each day. The big-wheel crews hauling until their horses were ready to drop; and two did drop dead in harness, while another two had to be destroyed when logs crushed their hind legs on the drag. Buckers and fallers working the slash from dawn to dark, so that the skirl of crosscuts and bucksaws and the thud of axes rolled like constant thunder across the face of Black Mountain.

Some men can stand that kind of killing pace without busting down one way or another, and some men can't. Johnny Cline was one of those who couldn't. He was hotheaded, like I said before, and ten times every day and twenty times every night he cursed McIntosh and damned his black soul. Then, one day when he'd had all he could swallow, he made the mistake of cursing and damning McIntosh to the boss logger's face.

The yarding crew we were on was deep in the slash, struggling to get logs out of a small valley. It was coming on dusk and we'd been at it for hours; we were all bone-tired. I set the choker around the end of yet another log, and the hook-tender signaled Johnny Cline, who stood behind him with one hand on the wire running to the whistle on the donkey engine. When Johnny pulled the wire and the short blast sounded, the cable snapped tight and the big log started to move, its nose plowing up dirt and crushing saplings in its path. But as it came up the slope it struck a sunken log, as sometimes happens, and shied off. The hook-tender signaled for slack, but Johnny didn't give it fast enough to keep the log from burying its nose in the roots of a fir stump.

McIntosh saw it. He'd come catfooting up and was ten feet from the donkey engine. He ran up to Johnny yelling, "You stupid goddamn greenhorn!" and gave him a shove that knocked the kid halfway down to where the log was stumped.

Johnny caught himself and scrambled back up the incline. I could see the hate afire in his eyes and I tried to get between him and McIntosh, but he brushed me aside. He put his face up close to the boss logger's, spat out a string of cuss words, and finished up with, "I've had all I'm gonna take from you, you son of a bitch." And then he swung with his right hand.

But all he hit was air. McIntosh had seen it coming; he stepped inside the punch and spat tobacco juice into Johnny's face. The squirt and spatter threw the kid off balance and blinded him at the same time—left him wide open for McIntosh to wade in with fists and knees.

McIntosh seemed to go berserk, as if all the rage and meanness had built to an explosion point inside him and Johnny's words had triggered it. Johnny Cline never had a chance. McIntosh beat him to the ground, kept on beating him even though me and some of the others fought to pull him off. And when he saw his chance he raised up one leg and he stomped the kid's face with his calks—drove those sharp steel spikes down into Johnny's face as if he was grinding a bug under his heel.

Johnny screamed once, went stiff, then lay still. Nilson and some others had come running up by then and it took six of us to drag McIntosh away before he could stomp Johnny Cline a second time. He battled us for a few seconds, like a crazy man; then, all at once, the wildness went out of him. But he was no more human when it did. He tore himself loose, and without a word, without any concern for the boy he'd stomped, he stalked off through the slash.

Johnny Cline's face was a red ruin, pitted and torn by half a hundred steel points. I thought he was dead at first, but when I got down beside him I found a weak pulse. Four of us picked him up and carried him to our bunkhouse.

The bullcook and me cleaned the blood off him and doctored his wounds as best we could. But he was in a bad way. His right eye was gone, pierced by one of McIntosh's calks, and he was hurt inside, too, for he kept coughing up red foam. There just wasn't much we could do for him. The nearest doctor was thirty miles away; by the time somebody went and fetched him back, it would be too late. I reckon we all knew from the first that Johnny Cline would be dead by morning.

There was no more work for any of us that day. None of the jacks in our bunkhouse took any grub, either, nor slept much as the night wore on. We all just sat around in little groups with our lamps lit, talking low, smoking and drinking coffee or tea. Checking on Johnny now and then. Waiting.

He never regained consciousness. An hour before dawn the bullcook went to look at him and announced, "He's gone." The waiting was done. Yes, and so were Saginaw Tom McIntosh and the Black Mountain camp.

Nilson and the other crew chiefs had a meeting outside, between the two bunkhouses. The rest of us kept our places. When Nilson and the two others who bunked in our building came back in, it was plain enough from their expressions what had been decided. And plainer still when the three of them shouldered their peaveys. Loggers will take so much from a boss like Saginaw Tom McIntosh—only so much and no more. What he'd done to Johnne Cline was the next to last straw; Johnny dying was the final one.

At the door Nilson said, "We're on our way to cut down a rotted tree. Rest of you can stay or join us, as you see fit. But you'll all keep your mouths shut either way. Clear?"

Nobody had any objections. Nilson turned and went out with the other two chiefs.

Well, none of the men in our bunkhouse stayed, nor did anybody in the other one. We were all of the same mind. I thought I knew what would happen to McIntosh, but I was wrong. The crew heads weren't fixing to give him the same as he gave Johnny Cline. No, they had other plans. When a logging crew turns, it turns hard—and it gives no quarter.

The near-dawn dark was chill and damp, and I don't mind saying it put a shiver on my back. We all walked quiet through it to McIntosh's shanty—close to a hundred of us, so he heard us coming anyway. But not in time to get up a weapon. He fought with the same wildness he had earlier but he didn't have any more chance than he gave Johnny Cline. Nilson stunned him with his peavey. Then half a dozen men stuffed him into his clothes and his blood-stained boots and took him out.

Straight across the camp we went, with four of the crew heads carrying McIntosh by the arms and legs. He came around just before they got him to the edge of the drop-off. Realized what was going to happen to him, looked like, at about the same time I did.

He was struggling fierce, bellowing curses, when Nilson and the others pitched him into the chute.

He went down slow at first, the way one of the big logs always did. Clawing at the flat-hewn sides, trying to dig his calks into the glass-smooth bottom logs. Then he commenced to pick up speed, and his yells turned to banshee screams. Two hundred feet down the screaming stopped; he was just a blur by then. His clothes started to smoke from the friction, then burst into flame. When he went sailing over the trestle he was a lump of fire that lit up the dark . . . then a streak of fire as he shot down into the lower section . . . then a fireball with a tail longer and brighter than the one on that comet a while ago, so bright the river and the woods on both banks showed plain as day for two or three seconds before he smacked the river— smacked it and went out in a splash and steamy sizzle you could see and hear all the way up at the chute head.

"And that," Cass Buckram finished, "*that*, by God, was the damnedest sight I or any other man ever set eyes on—McIntosh going down McIntosh's chute, eight hundred feet straight into hell.''

None of us argued with him. Not even Poley the button.

COWBOY BLUES,
by Lenore Carroll

A part-time teacher of psychology, composition, and creative writing, Lenore Carroll has written advertising, publicity, trade news, book reviews, and both fiction and nonfiction about the Old West. Her first novel, Abduction from Fort Union, was published in 1988. "Cowboy Blues," about a young Eastern woman who attempts to realize her dream of finding a cowboy to be her boyfriend, is a provocative study of the marked contrasts between the West of romantic myth, as engendered by fiction writers and Hollywood filmmakers, and the modern West as it really is.

· COWBOY BLUES ·
by Lenore Carroll

When I came out to the guest ranch I had this idea about finding a cowboy to be my boyfriend—every Eastern girl's dream. Broad-brimmed hat, boots, tattoo, Coors belt buckle, and a room-temperature IQ. I saved my money and sent references and drove three days; I was going to find me one and see what he was like. Did he wear a down vest indoors? Did he drive a pickup? With a gun rack? He had to have a dog named Bubba. I was looking for something like Joel McCrea in those old movies my dad watched, only modern. I called him Jim Bob.

After my girlfriend, Debbie, and I checked in at the place near Sheridan, I put on my jeans and my new boots and went out to the corral. There they were, lean and battered, with sun-squint eyes and neckerchiefs and Skoal tins in their back pockets. This was what I had dreamed about all winter, watching Busch commercials and reading travel brochures.

My girlfriend, Debbie—she's a word processor at Datatech like me—found one right away and I didn't see much of her. During the first few days I zeroed in on a tall, lean wrangler with battered chaps who kept looking at me when I waited at the fence for my mount. "How about you and me getting together after dinner?" I asked.

"You deserve something better than a cheap fling with an old saddle tramp like me."

I told him I liked *him*, but he just shook his head and said, "No, no, little lady."

I was so mad I wanted to scream, but I tried to maintain some dignity. I left him standing there by the fence, with the Big Horns behind him and a dirt smudge on his battered hat and a rope in his hands. He had the high plains pink over his year-round tan and hands as rough as a backcountry road. Instead of fun and games in the cabin, I was left with bridge in the lodge with old folks. Well, I wasn't going to sit around and feel sorry for myself. I fixed myself up after dinner and borrowed Deb's car and drove into town and walked into the first likely place.

When I stepped inside the Golden Spur, glittering eyes from twenty stuffed heads stared back; I felt like I was a prize mare, up before the judges. I wished Deb was with me. Why was I doing this? Then I remembered the wrangler. I'd find me a *real* cowboy and Not Think about that bastard.

The back bar was an elaborate mirrored affair that I'd seen in dozens of cowboy movies. It looked a hundred years old, with a carved deer head in the center of the mahogany.

The bartender nodded and I ordered a beer. I stood crowded in with a bunch of people my age and listened to the conversation. I swallowed a little Bud, gradually calmed down, and listened. Most of the people seemed to know each other and gossiped about who was doing what.

Besides the staring heads on the walls there was the heroic version of the Battle of the Little Big Horn—Custer was still winning. Bird and horse paintings. Crowded between the heads were beer mirrors, antlers, skulls, announcements for rodeos and a county fair and an art exhibit. And framed photographs of people on horseback doing weird things to cows.

I studied the clientele—local men and girls, dude men and girls, some other guys I couldn't quite figure out who looked more like Ralph Lauren cowboys than the real thing. But they were all friendly and started talking to me, asked me where I was from and hoped I liked it out here and could they buy me a beer?

I gradually relaxed and caught a whiff of something familiar. A guy stood by the jukebox with one hand in his Levi's pocket, fingers angled toward the zipper, thumb hooked over the edge of the pocket. Another young man carefully recentered his hat, revealing biceps as he raised his arms. Tourists and dudes like me were just watching, but the local kids exchanged telling looks, or casually brushed by each other in the crowded room. All of the guys watched one girl with a perfect tush as she maneuvered around the pool table. This wasn't a singles bar, with loud rock music like the places back home, but I recognized the longing and the horniness. That's the same anywhere.

Members of the three-piece combo played on a small platform at the back of the room. Couples crowded the dance floor, swinging each other to the drummer's steady beat. I took my beer and watched, then a guy in a pointy-yoke shirt asked me to dance. Sure. I would drink and have a good time and Not Think about that wrangler.

After a few dances, the guy led me back to the bar and said, "Hey, Curry, you had any accidents lately?" to a big, good-looking guy.

"Yeah, but that sumbitch ain't caught me yet."

"You burned yourself on the propane forge?"

"Naw, we've been putting up hay. I don't get many calls for shoeing this time of year."

Curry was crisply turned out in a laundry-creased shirt, spotless jeans, and a summer straw Stetson that looked riveted in place. Maybe it was the hat, pulled down to half an inch above his eyebrows, that gave him a dim look. Then it registered and I almost dropped my beer. This was my Jim Bob. I found out Curry worked on a ranch east of Ucross, came into town on weekends like a soldier on leave. He had that ground-in tan and muscles straining the plaid shirt and pale, innocent blue eyes.

"This cop stopped me," Curry said. "I was driving in this park in Denver. And when he looked in the pickup, there was this woman giving me a blow job."

People around Curry laughed. I usually ignore stories like that, but I kept listening. And Not Thinking.

"She never even stopped till we were done. And the cop said, 'I don't know what to write on the ticket.' Hell, *I* didn't know what to say. I must have been driving funny. It was a miracle I kept the pickup on the road. Then the cop said, 'I'm going to put down obstructing the view of the driver,' So I said, 'Sounds okay to me.'"

Everybody laughed. Curry was feeling his Coors and he had an audience.

"It cost me thirty-eight hundred dollars to get my shoulder fixed," he said, "so I never did get my wrist taken care of. But except for that I was good at rodeoing." His listeners laughed and one reminded him of all the falls he had taken bull riding.

"Yeah," continued Curry. "But that wasn't how I got hurt. I'm acrobatic. I knew how to fall."

"Then why did you quit?" asked a blond girl.

"Got tired of bull snot in my back pocket," said Curry.

"What?" I asked.

"Bull snot. Dropping down on my backside when I was on the ground."

"What else did you do, rodeoing?" I asked.

"Roping, bronc riding, all that stuff."

"Why'd you quit?"

"Well, I got into trouble with that old sumbitch I was working for, at Arvada. It wasn't nothing. I didn't go to do it on purpose, but he got mean and called the cops on me."

"What'd you do?"

"I set his foreman's house on fire."

"Just like that?"

"Well, I was using this propane branding iron and I got too close to the siding and the next thing I knew, the house was on fire."

"Sounds like you're—"

"Accident-prone, that's what they say. Anyway, I had a choice and I went in the army and that was the end of rodeoing for me."

"What do you do now?"

"Whatever the boss tells me—fix fences, move cattle, put up hay, take care of the horses, shoe them."

"Sounds interesting," I said.

"Not as interesting as being here. Would you like to dance?"

"Sure, if you don't mind getting your feet stepped on."

Curry placed a hand lightly at my back and

we walked onto the dance floor. The combo was doing a slow, non-Willie Nelson version of "Whiskey River" and Curry swung me in front of him and wrapped an arm around my waist and took my hand and gently started the steps. It wasn't very complicated, but when I tried to think of what I should be doing, I stumbled and lost the beat. I would Not Think. I would dance and drink enough to feel the edges soften and listen to Curry bullshit about his accidents. This was the warm cowboy I'd dreamed about all winter.

I laughed, mostly from nervousness, and he just kept steering me back and forth. He sang along with the band and it sounded kind of nice to have his voice soft in my ear, his cheek on mine. Occasionally, I'd knock his hat loose when I lifted my head, but he'd calmly screw it back in place.

The band went into a fast version of "Honky-tonk Man" and I tried to keep up with Curry. For a beefy guy, he was light on his feet and tireless. My awkwardness didn't seem to bother him and he patiently got me back on the beat until I was more or less following him. His hand slipped down my back to my waist, then to my ass, and at first I didn't even notice. It seemed *normal* to have a hand there. Then I remembered I had just met him and pulled it back up.

After half a dozen dances, the band took a break and he led me back to the bar and bought me a beer. I asked him about his work and shoeing and he told me and joked about it.

We danced again and I felt a little drunk. It was easy to lean against Curry and let him lead me around the floor. He did a lot of "sugar, honey, baby, sweetie" stuff, told me I had a great body. He sang some more, his mouth close to my ear. After a while he stopped singing and started kissing and nuzzling my neck. I pulled away, but in a few minutes he was back again and it seemed like too much trouble to stop him. His hand slipped down to my ass again and I let it stay. I just wanted to sway and shuffle and Not Think.

After another round of beer and dancing, he asked, "Would you like to go home with me?"

"Where's home?" I asked. I had trouble concentrating.

"I got this little house outside Sheridan," he said. "Well, it's not mine, but my uncle is off on a pack trip over by Jackson and I stay there on weekends."

"What would we do at your uncle's?" I knew damned well what we'd do, but I wanted to hear what he'd say.

"Well, we could put a pizza in the microwave and turn on the late movie and then we'll *see* what we could do."

For some reason, that sounded appealing. I wouldn't be able to Think about the wrangler if I went. I wouldn't have to think at all. Curry was my Jim Bob. No Coors belt buckle, but all the other qualifications. I tried to think of reasons why I shouldn't, but I was foggy from beer. And I didn't want to talk myself out of it. I wondered if there was a gun rack in his pickup.

I left Deb's car in the parking lot and got in Curry's truck. The floor was littered with rust-red gravel, fast-food containers, and empty beer cans. A brown plaid bath towel covered the shredded upholstery. Curry said his dog tore it up. I looked for the seat belt, but it had disappeared and I wasn't in the mood to dig for it. I felt dizzy and I was riding without a safety belt anyway.

He drove south on the main drag out of Sheridan and turned off the highway at the edge of the city. We bounced down a long gravel drive and around some trees to a small frame house with a dog tied to the front porch. The dog, a sheepdog mix, went berserk, barking and leaping against the rope. I don't know if he was any good scaring away burglars, but he convinced me. Curry hollered, "Shut up, Igor," on his way past and the dog quieted.

Well, a dog named Bubba was too much to expect.

I stood in front of Curry's house and looked west. The moon hit the last of the snow on the peaks of the Big Horns and I expected theme music by Dmitri Tiomkin to swell in my head. It didn't seem possible that this crackerbox house and the mountains were in sight of each other. I wanted a developer to rezone the West and get rid of the trailers and trashy houses and nonphotogenic farms and it would all look like an old B movie. Curry looked okay, but this wasn't turning out the way I'd planned.

I stood beside the pickup with the passenger door handle in a death grip. I couldn't go through with it. I felt sick and wondered if it was the beer, Curry, or myself. I scuffed gravel. I eyed the dog. I looked through the open door to the living room. Curry opened the screen, which didn't hang plumb, and walked out on the porch. He held two cans of Coors in one hand.

"Igor won't bite you. Come on up."

I wasn't afraid of the dog. He looked like a floppy dust mop, once he collapsed by the porch steps. I just wanted out. I didn't want a tussle with Curry, a little old roll in the hay. And I didn't know how I could get out of it. This was what I wanted, wasn't it?

Curry had talked steadily through half a dozen Coors and started repeating himself after two hours. In the pickup I'd heard about the ticket in Denver again. I'd been waiting for the rodeo stories to recycle.

I must have sobered up enough on the drive out to realize I was fooling myself. This warm cowboy wasn't really what I wanted. He'd called me "ma'am," and held the doors for me, and now I was being awful and I didn't care.

He'd been out on the ranch, working hard all week. He'd gotten cleaned up, come to town, petted me and danced, chatted and done all the right things and now I was walking out on the unspoken contract. Bitch. Tease. But I wasn't in love with him and there would be the whole routine with the lies and getting out of our clothes and figuring out what to do after. That wasn't part of my dream.

And there was something unmovable about him. People who work alone get strange. When they finally get out and start socializing, they want other people to behave as they expect, as they've imagined in their aloneness.

He sucked on a beer and I clutched the door handle.

"You gonna stay out there all night?" He sounded stone-hard peeved.

"Take me back to town."

"What the hell? You wanted to come here. Now you change your mind?"

"Yes."

"No you ain't."

"Take me back."

"Not when I had a hard-on for two hours."

"Tough," I said. He'd probably had a hard-on

for a week. I turned on my heel and started walking down the long driveway. He caught up with me, grabbed my arm and spun me around.

"You ain't leaving now."

"It's my period." I shook his hand off.

"No it ain't."

I took a couple of deep breaths. I was weaving a little and things tried to spin, but I was soberer than Curry. "I'm leaving."

I turned to walk away and Curry hit me hard below the shoulder blades. I went off balance and hit the dusty red gravel, grazed my chin, and the air whooshed out of my lungs. I wrenched the hand I flung out to catch my fall. I was jarred more than hurt. I got to my hands and knees, then to my feet, wondering what he would do next.

I started to say something and he backhanded me across the mouth. I could taste salty blood and my face hurt.

"What do you do for an encore?" I said. "Kick the dog?"

He stood with fists clenched, watching me. I stood facing him, weaving and half-drunk. He took a step toward me. I tensed up. The blood and saliva choked me. I took another breath and vomited. The spasms bent me double. Curry backed away. I heard him spit in disgust, but all I could do was stand there and heave till my stomach emptied itself.

When I could breathe without triggering a spasm, I straightened up and started down the driveway again. Curry stood with the dog beside the porch steps.

I was at least two miles out of town, then another mile to the Golden Spur. I hoped my new boots didn't rub a blister. I couldn't think straight. Several cars went by, but I was walking against traffic and nobody stopped.

I felt like I was choking, like I still wanted to throw up, but it wasn't beer. I was sick-disgusted with myself. I wanted a warm cowboy, but what was I going to do with him when I got him? I couldn't take him home. Was I going to wear his scalp on my belt for two weeks in Sheridan?

Walking that gravel shoulder back to town helped sort out what I'd done. It was John Wayne, apple pie, and the American flag—that's what my dream of making love to a warm cowboy was. I'd never once thought about the real person behind the pearly-snap shirt and the Stetson.

The Golden Spur was still open when I got there and I used the ladies' room. My face was starting to swell and ache. I felt awful. I rinsed my mouth over and over, but I couldn't wash the bad taste away.

By the time I got in Deb's car I was more or less sober, and maybe a little smarter. I fell into the driver's seat, headed for the highway, and drove back to the guest ranch.

Can't judge a book by its cover, so why did I try to fall in love with a dust jacket?

KID BOZAL,
by Russ McDonald

In addition to short stories, Californian Russ McDonald writes articles on Western topics, Indian lore, and CB radio; a satirical newspaper column called "The View from the Bottom Rung"; a weekly book review column, "Books Are Us," which appears in several papers; and short humor pieces for a variety of publications. He is also an accomplished cartoonist who has published two books of CB cartoons, Footloose and Fancyfree and Truckin' CBers and Other Liars. His sense of humor is evident in "Kid Bozal," the waggish tale of a loudmouthed young cowhand who had "enough brag in him for three men twice as old," and the outcome of a bet based on the kid's claim that "I ain't never been thrown out of any place I didn't want to leave."

• KID BOZAL •
by Russ McDonald

Jessie Eldon Thrasher issued a nickname to the younger cowhand. He had not asked for one, especially not a handle like Kid Bozal, but the name stuck like a hot brand on a steer's rump. None of the other drovers knew what his rightful name was, and it was not the custom to pry, even into the curiosity of the inglorious name of a halter muzzle used by poor Mexicans.

Kid Bozal, a wiry five feet two with smooth face, looked younger than his twenty years. His hair, uncombed and brown with a tendency to curl, reached almost to his shoulders. The gray-green eyes, under thick eyebrows, sparkled with youth's optimism. He wore the usual cotton shirt and duck pants, and his head was crowned by a wide-brimmed hat, floppy from trail dust and sweat. Shotgun chaps with fringes of old buffalo fur down the sides protected his legs. A reasonably good pair of boots with Spanish spurs jingled loudly when he strutted.

It was obvious from the start that he sat a horse well. When he galloped across open country, Kid Bozal merged as part of the animal, seeming to flow from hill to knob with ease.

It was fortunate for the kid that he had been given a chance to prove himself as a cowhand before the others learned of his one great flaw.

Kid Bozal earned his thirty and found. There

was no question about that. He, like any trail hand pushing and swearing a herd of four-footed steaks from Texas to the railhead in Kansas, did not shirk from duty. Until they reached Dodge City, the cow was the most important thing in their lives. At the start, the trail boss, Seth Morrison, informed them in certain terms.

"Boys," he said, "you watch the cow's feet, the horse's back, and then you worry about your own welfare. A trail hand can be replaced but a pound off a cow means lost money."

With a firm dedication they pulled cows from mud pockets, guided strays back into the main herd, grouped the herd each night, and did hundreds of chores for the safety of the cattle.

There were times in the middle of the night when Seth bellowed out the warning of a stampede: "All hands and the cook!" Kid Bozal was always among the first to grab his boots and swing aboard the nearby night mount, then race for the lead of the thundering mass of long-horned hellions. Pulling his own weight was not the problem with Kid Bozal.

His one great and obvious flaw lay in his mouth. There was enough brag in him for three men twice as old, and it required very little effort to set him off.

Jessie Eldon Thrasher, the top hand, swung into camp for breakfast one day. He dusted his britches with his hat.

"I tell you true," he commented to no one in particular, "I feel like I been on the losing end of a three-day fight."

Kid Bozal swallowed a mouthful of beans, pointed with his spoon, shaking his head.

"This little sortie ain't much. I remember one time in San Antonio I got into a bar fight with the Kirker brothers. Milo Kirker was an even six feet with shoulders the size of a hay wagon and fists that looked like molasses barrels and felt twice as hard. He was the smallest of the lot. I had tipped my hat to the questionable lady named Lulu they were entertaining. I always tip my hat to a lady whether she is or not. The Kirker boys, that fairly set them off and they decided right there they were going to bust something that belonged to me and throw the rest out onto the street."

Kid Bozal helped himself to some more beans. "Now, I tell you for a fact. I never been thrown out of any place I didn't want to leave. So me and the Kirkers exchanged blows. It was like hitting a locked barn door. They sagged and groaned but didn't fall down.

"I knew right off there was no use in just trading blows, although I got some good ones up my sleeves. So I resorted to scientific fisticuffs. I outdanced them and snuck in fast jabs in places that set tears in their eyes and their noses to running. Well, sir, we fought, first one then the other for six straight hours before I had all three down on their knees at the same time.

"You talk about tired. I finished off my drink, tipped my hat to the questionable lady named Lulu, crawled upstairs and slept for two days and nights. No sir, I ain't never been thrown out of any place I didn't want to leave. It's a fact."

Everybody groaned over this recitation and some scowled at Jessie Eldon for giving the kid an opportunity to brag another wild escapade.

The trail cook, Pancake White, suffered with the rest. At one evening chow he brought out a pound of Arbuckle's Coffee, his favorite since each pound contained a peppermint stick. As was his habit, Pancake called out, "Who wants the candy tonight?"

There was a wild scramble but Kid Bozal managed to leap first in line. While the kid turned the coffee grinder as payment for the treat, Pancake happened to mention bedbugs that were unusually large.

Kid Bozal slowed the grinder down. "Why now, it's a fact," he said, "you never seen a bedbug until you've bunked at the Running W on the Concho. I saw 'em as big as dry land turtles. We used to set traps for 'em but they learned to leap right over them. I allus figured they must be crossbred with jackrabbits."

They tried outtalking him but this only increased his intensity. They tried ignoring him but he paid them no mind and continued his tall stories as they rode along. If an errant steer interrupted the story and it took a couple of hours to bring calm, he was able to pick up the tale as though there had been no delay. They conspired to keep him riding drag, hoping the billowing dust would give him a sore throat and choke him down for a while. It didn't work.

The moment he made evening camp he began a tale about seeing sand storms in New Mexico so thick you had to dismount and cut through the air with a shovel. Men groaned and hastened to their bedrolls since the rule of the trail was never to talk loud while men were bedded down.

Tiny Barton was helping Pancake set the wagon tongue of the chuckwagon pointing to the North Star so that when Seth arose in the morning he would have a quick compass bearing. Kid Bozal grabbed a last biscuit and cup of coffee. Tiny casually mentioned he had seen this part of the country during a cold snap. Kid Bozal swallowed the remainder of his biscuit.

"Why boys, I'll tell you for a fact about cold. Back in the winter of 'seventy-three I was riding the grub line up in Wyoming. I barely made it to this log cabin owned by old man McDevlin. Now, I've seen cows freeze in their tracks, but it was so cold that I actually saw one froze solid with her feet still in the air.

"McDevlin threw a bucket of water out the window. The water froze into a solid block in midair and hit his favorite hound. Killed it on the spot. Old McDevlin swore it was so cold you could talk into a bucket and come the spring thaw the words would pop right out, clear and sharp."

Kid Bozal had a story for any subject, but his all-time favorites dealt with his prowess as a fighter. Several hands were of a mind to test his ability in fisticuffs, but Seth would have fired them on the spot. No one was absolutely sure just how much truth lay behind all the tall brags. A bobcat isn't very big but he's a little tornado of a scrapper.

"We got to figure a way to tone the kid down," Jessie Eldon remarked to Llano Perkins as they rode along.

"You got that right. But how? We've tried just about everything short of hog-tying him and threatening his life and limbs."

"I know, and Seth agrees, but he says we can't do anything drastic. The kid is a good hand and Seth doesn't want to lose him."

Llano nodded. "I'm thinking these cows are hurrying to Dodge just to get away from hearing Kid Bozal."

Jessie Eldon and Llano debated on how to accomplish the matter but neither came up with a solution. For a while they were too busy guiding the herd in the direction the scout had laid out to be concerned with Kid Bozal.

After their shift was over, Jessie Eldon helped himself to a generous plate of Sonofabitch Stew, then squatted on the ground beside Curly Jake.

Curly Jake wiped his plate clean with the remains of a biscuit. "Jessie Eldon, how long you figure 'fore we reach Dodge City?"

Jessie Eldon dipped his spoon into the stew, spoke with his mouth full as he squinted at the terrain. "About a week. More or less."

"I hear it's a real up-coming town, full of wild women and strong drink. You been there before?"

"A couple of times. It's a fair ripsnorter, all right.'

Kid Bozal squatted beside them, balancing his tin plate filled with stew and biscuits. "I never been to Dodge City," he said, matter-of-factly.

There was a strained moment of silence around the chuck wagon. "But," Kid Bozal added, slurping a spoonful of hot stew, "it's about time I tipped my hat to the Dodge City ladies and indulged in a little free-for-all. It can't be no worse than the time I got into a bare-knuckle brawl with a blacksmith in New Orleans.

"I remember I had tipped my hat to this cute little Cajun gal in one of the Quarter honky-tonks. Now, I was off my feed and weak of limb and he darned near cleaned my frame. Said he was going to run me out of town. We fought in the bar and out on the street, face to face and knuckle to knuckle and doing all sorts of harmful things.

"Finally I brought up a punch from the sidewalk and snapped his nose and changed the count of his teeth. After that I stayed in town till several of the urges left, 'cause I tell you for a fact, I ain't never been run out of any place I wanted to stay in."

"Kid, what would happen if you was to get thrown out of a place?" Jessie Eldon wanted to know.

Kid Bozal lowered his plate, gazed a moment at the evening sky. He looked around at the silent, staring faces. He grinned.

"Why boys, I don't know. The thought never seriously occurred to me."

Jessie Eldon set his empty plate on the ground, rolled a Bull Durham smoke. After he lighted it, he drawled, "Kid, I'll make you a bet that you get thrown out by the bouncer of the first saloon we make in Dodge City."

Kid Bozal scratched an ear, studied Jessie Eldon for a moment. "A single, solitary bouncer? How much would you bet?"

"I figure maybe twenty dollars."

"No gun play, or anything like that?"

"No guns. Me and the boys would see to that."

Kid Bozal slapped his knees, laughed. "Why, sure. That would be like found money. I figure by the time we reach Dodge I'll have three dollars less than a hundred. I'll put up any or all."

The others, knowing Jessie Eldon was a cautious gambler, spoke up for their share and covered the kid's coming salary.

"There's one more thing," Jessie Eldon commented, marking down the bets. "If you get thrown out of the Shangri-las Saloon, which is the first place we stop, then from now on you're never to repeat a wild story about the fights you've been in. Agreed?"

Kid Bozal laughed again. "Why, I tell you for a fact, if I was to ever get thrown out by any one bouncer, I'd be too ashamed to ever call myself a scrapping man. Why, I'd feel as useless as a knot in a stake rope. I remember one time down on the Rio Grande, I met—"

Jessie Eldon interrupted. "Okay. It's a bet. Excuse me, kid, I got to clean up my gear and hit the sack."

The last week into Dodge, Kid Bozal reminded them several times of the bet. "Yes sir, I tell you for a fact, boys, I'm going to drink the best Kansas sheep-dip toddies, smoke the biggest cigars, kiss all the prettiest saloon girls. Yessir, it's a fact. They will remember Kid Bozal for a long time. Why, it reminds me of once down in Cross Cut, Texas. I had enough coin jingling in my pocket to make me feel handsome, and I—"

Jessie Eldon spurred toward an errant mossyhorn, shouted back, "Better get ready, kid. We should hit Dodge City about tomorrow."

At the sight of Dodge City the hands were anxious in the saddle, but first they had to guide the cattle into numerous corrals by the railhead. They tallied the herd amid the bellowing cows, trains clanking and hooting. The wooden chutes were drummed by the echo of hoofs and the wooden sidewalks were hammered by the staccato beat of cowboy boots and jingling spurs.

Seth bargained for a sale and by the end of the day paid off the wranglers, each having earned nearly a hundred dollars.

Pancake White held the bets, it being one of the duties of a trail cook. Kid Bozal placed his earnings in the cook's hand with a flourish.

"You hang on to my money, Pancake. I'll be collecting it right soon." He turned to the others. "Boys, now you just point out this here

Shangri-las Saloon and I'll be a richer man for it."

Curly Jake looked worried and drew Jessie Eldon to one side. "You sure about this? Is that bouncer really mean enough to do the trick?"

Jessie Eldon reassured him. "I'm as certain as I can be. I've been thrown out of a lot a places, but never as hard and swift as in the Shangri-las."

"That bouncer must be as fast as lightning and meaner than a stepped-on rattlesnake."

"Something like you've never seen."

On the main street a continual cloud of dust rose from men, horses, and wagons. Cowboys swaggered in knots along the walks. They raised their voices in greetings to old friends whom they had not seen for a year since back in Texas. They milled past bunches of Northern meat packers and Midwestern feeders making deals of thousands of dollars on handshakes alone.

In front of the Shangri-las, a black minstrel strummed on a guitar, attempting to lure the cowboys inside. From behind the swinging doors came music from a scratchy fiddle and tinny piano playing 'The Lakes of Killarney,' mingled with the hard laughter of saloon girls, the clicking of poker chips, and the shouting over faro and monte games.

Kid Bozal, with a cigar in one corner of his mouth, hat tilted to one side, stepped through the doorway. Close behind him came Jessie Eldon, Pancake, Llano, and Curly Jake, with Tiny bringing up the rear.

The Shangri-las, like its counterparts, was a huge, high-ceilinged, open-beamed room. Clouds of foul-smelling cigar smoke curled upward, along with the sharp odors of strong beer, rotgut whiskey, unbathed trail hands. A long brass-railed bar stretched across one end, crowded with dozens of cowboys raising their glasses and voices.

In the center, more cowboys hunched over crude wooden-plank tables, some drinking, some playing cards or monte, some nestling bar girls on their laps, and some engaged in all the activities at once.

"Kid," Jessie Eldon said, raising his voice above the din. "I don't think they'll pay you any attention amongst all this."

Kid Bozal grunted, drew his pistol, sent a shot through the ceiling. Instantly the music stopped. The voices stilled to a strange hush and all eyes turned on the kid. He holstered his pistol, rocked back on his boot heels, hands on his hips.

"Boys," he called out, "I'm a ripsnorter, a son of wild Texas. I tell you for a fact, there ain't a man that I can't lick nor a woman too ugly to kiss. I mean to drink all the Kansas sheep-dip toddies in the joint and maybe break a couple of jaws, 'cause I ain't never been thrown out of no place I didn't want to leave. Kid Bozal is the name and I mean to clean out the town or sell my saddle."

A murmur swept through the crowd. Jessie Eldon looked back at Llano and the others, saw a look of apprehension leap from face to face.

Then Jessie Eldon smiled as a movement came from the back of the darkened room. He figured the woman must weigh at least 350 pounds and stand near six feet tall in her high heels. She lumbered forward like a Conestoga wagon. The plank floor groaned under her massive frame. She was stuffed into a bright red dress decorated with huge white flowers, cut low in front. Two strands of fake pearls wrapped around her thick throat and several bracelets clanged on her heavy wrists.

Her eyes, behind puffed and painted lids, glared like those of a rankled red-eyed longhorn bull. Her painted lips quivered.

Kid Bozal didn't blink an eye. He tipped his hat, smiled broadly. "Howdy, ma'am. Kid Bozal is the name, up from Texas. I'm—"

She gave a disturbed mama grizzly growl, her stomach vibrating. Her ham-sized ball of knuckles struck at nose level with the weight of a new anvil.

Kid Bozal rose slightly off the floor, a cloud of trail dust puffing up from his shirt and hat. It sifted slowly back, but missed finding him since he was reeling backward.

The corpulent form shifted forward, caught him, whirled him around, grabbed the seat of his britches with one hand and the nape of his neck with the other. She easily lifted him up on his tiptoes, making his spurs jingle rapidly.

She advanced to the swinging doors and heaved the body like pitching hay to a cow. Kid Bozal flew through the low doors, taking one with him as he grabbed air. He hit the hitching rail with his stomach, let out a Comanche yell as he sailed over it, smashing the small door he grasped in his hands as he landed facedown among the horses' hoofs, splashing mud and fresh, sticky manure. The horses jerked at the lines, sidestepped.

Kid Bozal tried to roll away from the prancing hoofs, and lost his hat. His shirt was ripped almost off his back, one sleeve torn. Several splinters from the pine door stuck in his shoulder and one leg was raw meat from a hoof.

Jessie Eldon and the others stood over him.

Pancake withdrew the money and solemnly passed out the winnings.

Kid Bozal nursed his jaw, mumbled, "What happened? Was anybody else hurt in the stampede?"

"Why, son," Jessie Eldon said, counting his money, "you just got thrown out of a Dodge City saloon by a woman, and you wasn't even ready to leave."

Kid Bozal groaned and lay back, shaking his head. Jessie Eldon started to walk away, then turned back.

"One thing I forgot to mention, kid. The Shangri-las is owned by that big 'ol gal name of Toothsome Sally. If I was you, I'd stay clear of her. There's three things on this earth that she doesn't like, at all. The first is loudmouthed cowboys, the second is loudmouthed, bragging cowboys, and the third is loudmouthed, bragging cowboys from Texas."

CHORAMPIK,
by Sally Zanjani

An adjunct assistant professor of political science at the University of Nevada at Reno, Sally Zanjani has published numerous articles on Nevada history and three nonfiction books: The Unspiked Rail: Memoir of a Nevada Rebel *(1981)*; The Ignoble Conspiracy: Radicalism on Trial in Nevada, *with Guy L. Rocha (1986), which was largely responsible for posthumous pardons granted to Goldfield union radicals Morrie Preston and Joseph Smith in 1987, eighty years after their conviction; and* Jack Longstreet: Last of the Desert Frontiersmen *(1988). "Chorampik," the name of Jack Longstreet's Indian wife, is a fictionalized version of an incident recorded in the last-named book. This fine, moving story of the Southern Paiutes' view of life, love, and death is Ms. Zanjani's first published fiction.*

• CHORAMPIK •
by Sally Zanjani

The trouble was that Jack was taking so long to die.

The morning light was just sifting into the canyons when Chorampik heard him fall with the heavy suddenness of a mountain avalanche outside the cabin door. She knew he would die sooner if she let him lie where he had fallen. But some foolish weakness inside her screamed out against leaving him there in the dust, staring blindly into the sun. So, ever so slowly, groaning with the strain, she dragged him inside the cabin door. Even though the powerful hard-muscled body she knew so well had finally slackened with time, he was still stone-heavy for a man of perhaps ninety summers. Chorampik herself was nearly thirty summers younger than Jack, but the effort made her feel as old as he. She had to lean back against the rough log walls of the cabin, with her heart flailing against her chest like the sinewy meats she pounded on her working stone. Ignoring her breathless curses, the white dog followed, whining and licking at Jack's hand.

Beside her Jack neither moved nor spoke, and his eyes, still of the same strange deep blue as the waters of the great river, seemed not to see. For an instant that passed swifter than a flying swallow, the fear had seized her that Tokwar might have taken him at last, but she realized that this could not be so. When Tokwar came, it was always by night, and this was a summer morning, growing hotter every minute, as the sun climbed higher in the sky. What had befallen her husband was not Tokwar's doing. It was the frozen sickness that her mother had called "death in life," the sickness that strikes an old one where he stands as the fiery arrow of a god seeks out a lone tree in a great storm and sets it ablaze. But a man so stricken does not burn. He freezes. He stops where he is, he falls, he moves and speaks no more, or if he does make sounds, it is in the speech of an animal that none of the people can understand. Such an illness is not an evil demon that can be driven from a man's body in the usual ways, by placing hot coals upon his flesh, cutting him with an obsidian knife, or beating him with clubs. That is because the body of one stricken with the frozen sickness has died before his spirit, but very soon his spirit learns that the ashes of his campfire are cold and his body empty as an abandoned wickiup. Then his spirit departs for Naguntuweap.

But Jack's spirit was different. Jack had always been different, from the first time she saw him, so many winters past, chanting with the people at the great Ghost Dance high on the peaks of the White Mountains. She had known who he was at once, for she had long heard stories told around the campfires of a great chief, a *tavanav*, who had come out of the land beyond the great river to lead the people in their time of need. He wore a notched gun that was magic, they said, for it flew from his holster to his hand faster than eyes could see and it never missed its mark. Because it was an enchanted gun, he

kept it always by his side. It was said that he
was born a white man, with hair like pale straw,
yet he spoke their tongue like a son of the people and he knew the hidden trails of their land
as surely as the coyote. In Yuwau-uk, the hungry desert, where the poor weak white men
quickly went mad and died with black tongues
swollen by thirst, the desert where the people
say even the wise ant will starve, there in the
land of sand and black rocks where so few had
gone and lived to tell, the gods whispered to
him where the secret waters were hidden and
he passed as easily as other men rode a well-
beaten trail in the lands of rich grass and bubbling springs.

That night, before the leaping flames of the
bonfire, Chorampik had seen that all the people
said of him was true. She had stared at the big
blond *tavanav* and wondered how it felt to be
loved by such a man. Then his eyes had fallen
on her and she had not known whether it was
the leaping orange flames at the center of the
dancing that turned her skin warm or the blue
fire of his eyes.

She wished she had the medicine man squatting near to explain Jack's lingering to her, but
she thought she understood why he refused to
die in an easy way like ordinary men. He was a
tavanav, taller in body than other men, greater
in spirit, and more powerful in his medicine.
Always he had done as he chose, alone in the
mountains, far from any tribe, ignoring both the
laws of the white man and the ways of the people. She had heard tales of the great battles he
had fought and won, though Jack never spoke
of them. She knew he stood above the kind of
boasting by which small men try to make themselves appear large. Perhaps it was because he

strode from the smoke of these battles as one the people call a *punumantua*, an impenetrable man who cannot be killed by bullet or arrow, that Jack's spirit refused to leave. So often had he prevailed with his notched gun that his spirit did not understand why the frozen sickness, "death in life," could not be conquered like another gunfighter. She decided that she should try to speak to his spirit. Kneeling beside him on the earthen floor with one of his big still hands clasped in hers, she half spoke, half chanted in the tongue of the people.

"Listen, my husband, called Andrew Jackson Longstreet, even the greatest *tavanav* must die, and this day your time has come. Yes, even the greatest chiefs have died. None that I saw with these two eyes, none of whom I heard the old ones speak at the storytelling times around the campfires of my people have lived so long as you. Many, many summers have you walked upon this earth. In the long-ago time, before the white man came to destroy my people, you were born in the faraway green place of which you have spoken, where the rains come day after day and there are many tall trees with long white beards. You fought with the blue and gray soldiers in that mighty battle you call 'the great *wah*,' and also the others that came after. For years you wandered over many strange lands before the voice of a god brought you to my people.

"Now, my husband, you have been struck with 'death in life.' You must leave this body and pass into the other world, Naguntuweap, while there is still time. You know the teachings of the ancient ones, my husband. He who lingers too long in this life, a burden to his people, is denied his passage into the joyous spirit world where the game is always plentiful and the grass grows deep and sweet. Such a one is condemned to wander this earth forever. And then, every night, until the earth itself grows old and dies, you must do battle in these mountains with that evil one, Tokwar.

"Let it not be so, my husband. You have a dangerous journey before you. Your spirit must pass through the dark cavern where the monstrous creatures fly and scream. You must cross without a slip of the foot over the thin bridge that sways over the bottomless chasm from which no fallen spirit ever rises. Then you will step into the green meadows of Naguntuweap. A great *tavanav* like you, of all men, will pass the dangers the gods have placed to test the brave. This my heart knows. But, my husband, you must go quickly."

The stillness, drumming with the distant sound of bees in the wild roses by the creek outside, seemed to echo in the cabin. Chorampik realized that for some time she had not spoken the words with her voice, only said them inside her head. Perhaps Jack had heard her all the same. They had not spoken much in the years since the death of Tokwar, but they understood each other without words. Jack heard her angry silence as surely as if she had screamed her fury in a stream of black words that flew at him like bats from the mouth of a cave. And he knew her yielding silence, when the touch of his lips on her skin made her quiver as the taut bowstring seeks release, and for a while, she forgot the vows she had made to save him. They had told each other so much without words, Jack and she.

But she sensed no response in his silence now. Had his spirit left then? She slipped her hand

inside his rough blue shirt. No, his heart beat
still. His stubborn spirit had refused to listen.
With her red bandanna, she wiped the sticky
beads of sweat from his forehead, smoothing
his beard and the long white hair covering the
shame thing of which she must never speak.
Jack was looking at her now with his deep blue
eyes, and she knew he saw her. She could feel
a great effort building in him, struggling like an
earthquake to break the frozenness. His hand
twitched and half clenched. His dry cracked lips
parted. With all the strength that was in him,
he was trying to speak. At last, from deep inside, his voice came, but it was not a word, only
a hoarse croak like "waa." She knew what it
meant. He wanted water. Kneeling beside him,
she bowed her head.

"Forgive me, my husband. I cannot bring you
water. You must have none of the comforts of
this world, so that your spirit knows he must
leave quickly for Naguntuweap."

She saw wet splotches on his face and realized they were her own salt tears. Though his
tongue would not obey him, the deep blue eyes
seemed to blaze into hers. Unable to meet his
angry stare, she fled outside the cabin.

Should she ride for help after all? Slowly she
walked over to the round corral where one of
the last horses Jack had kept from his great
herd waited, a fine swift-footed sorrel sent on
the iron horse from a far land called "Ken-
tuck." The animal whickered gently and nosed
at her hand over the uneven palings of the cedar fence. It was hard sometimes being so far
from her people. If the medicine man and the
headman and her sister and family were around
her, they would have known among them what
she should do. But they were more than three

days ride to the south in Ash Meadows. Here, in these northern mountains where Jack had brought her, there were no Southern Paiutes, only the Shoshone people, and none of them camped anywhere near Jack's ranch. Somehow, she must decide, though she could feel her own will washing away like sand in the blue torrent of Jack's accusing eyes.

Of this much she was certain. If she rode over the mountains to the mine, where Jack used to visit his friend Mr. Morison nearly every day, they would bring Jack to the place of many white beds that they called "hospital" in Tonopah and the white medicine man would do charms on him. Perhaps they could make the frozen sickness go away. The white medicine man called "doctor" had some strong potions, and the white men treated him with such reverence that they did not even kill him when his patients died the way the Southern Paiutes killed a failed medicine man. Then Jack would not look on her with angry eyes.

Yet she still remembered the dance of the old ones she had seen as a small child when she fled down the trail away from her band in search of her grandmother. There in the darkness was her grandmother with the other old women circling slowly around a bonfire in the abandoned campsite and singing a strange chant that was new to Chorampik's ears. Eerily elongated shadows like skeleton dancers grew away from the old women's feet and circled with them. Over and over they repeated their death songs:

"Ai-ai Ai-ai ai-ai
ai-ai ai-ai ai-ai.
Here long enough have I walked the earth.
Here long enough have I walked the earth.

Enough! Enough!
Let me die, let me die."

Then Chorampik's mother had caught up with
her and drawn her back along the trail, explaining that when someone has lived so long upon
this earth that he knows his time has come to
die, he stays behind without food or water when
the band moves on to their next campsite, or
goes by himself into the mountains until death
takes him. It is no time for sorrow, her mother
had said, for we will be seeing Grandmother
again when we too pass into the green meadows
of the gods where none ever hunger or grieve.
We sorrow only for the old one who lingers on
beyond his time and will never know the joys
of the other world.

Chorampik turned her back on the nuzzling
horse and leaned heavily against the corral
fence. Even here at midday, with the hot July
sun beating down upon her, the black shapes of
the old women circling the fire seemed to shim-
mer before her eyes like a mirage and their
death chant sang inside her head.

"Here long enough have I walked the earth."
She knew that she herself was the one who
deserved to wander forever as a cowardly ghost.
The teachings of her people were clear as the
picture drawings the ancient ones had made on
the sides of the southern cliffs. But her love of
this man made her weak. Because she longed to
quench his thirst with water, because her heart
wanted him to live, she had allowed the secret
hope to grow inside her that a *tavanav* like Jack
was somehow outside the laws of life and death
that governed all the people. She must kill this
softness of hers as she would crush the head of

a snake with a stone. Somehow she must find the strength to let Jack die.

And then, there was the matter of Tokwar.

Feeling dizzy and ill, she walked to the creek and drank a dipper of water from the little pool. Because she had denied it to Jack, the good sweet mountain creek tasted more bitter to her mouth than the foulest alkali seep in the dessert, but she knew she must drink, and also take food, so that she would have strength for the night ahead when Tokwar would surely come. The air was so still. Not a breeze rustled the pinyons and junipers on the canyon slopes, as if the mountain itself were holding its breath, waiting for Jack's spirit to plume away like smoke into the blue distance. The hot sun seemed to pound inside her head, each pulse reminding her how the heat must feel to Jack, as he lay burning in his thirst.

Inside the cabin the dry rasp of his tortured breath told Chorampik that he still lived, but she avoided his eyes. Although her stomach churned in rebellion, she managed to choke down some bread and cold beans. How strange it seemed, after more than twenty years of cooking for Jack, gathering the wood for his fires, shoeing his horses, and cranking up the heavy windlass at the place where he dug for gold in the mountainside, to wait on him no more. How unnatural, as though the sun had rolled backward across the sky, to take food when Jack did not. This single plate, she told herself, was how she would eat all the rest of her days. It was an idea impossible to grasp. Her thoughts could no more stretch around it than her arms could circle the rocky parapets that stood guard where the mountains met the

Stone Cabin Valley. Just one plate to fill, on and on, for the rest of her life.

After she had eaten, she took a bath in the creek to purify herself before her prayers, put on her clean red calico dress, and braided her long black hair anew. When the sun at last began to sink toward the crest of the western mountains, she took her sacred things from the corner of Jack's big metal trunk, the eagle feathers, the little pouches of colored earths, the crystal rock, and the soft worked antelope skin on which the medicine man had made his designs. Calling on her memory to speak, trying to raise the ceremonies seen in her girlhood to the surface of her consciousness like water from a deep well, she drew the remembered figures in the dust in front of the door, so that Tokwar could not come in that way. Mixing a little water with her colored earths, she made markings on the window and the metal stovepipe as well, and traced her designs in a careful circle on the beaten earth of the floor all the way around Jack. Then she knelt down beside him and spread the antelope skin with the sacred pictures over his chest. His eyes were closed now, and the heart beneath her questing hand beat more faintly, with an irregular rhythm, but still it did not stop.

She waited. Darkness was falling, and there was a rustling in the trees outside. Some might mistake it for the evening wind, but Chorampik knew better. She could hear the footsteps of Tokwar and his evil followers rushing over the mountains under cover of the wind. On many nights, Tokwar did not stop at the cabin in Longstreet Canyon and ran on with the lengthening shadows into the Stone Cabin Valley. That was because the sacrifice she had made kept

him away from Jack. But she knew he would
come tonight, seeking his revenge, while Jack
lay stricken and helpless. In the shifting black
and silver of the summer night, she waited,
watching for the twisted masklike face so often
seen in dreams to peer inside the window.
Softly she chanted a prayer to Tovwots, the father of the gods. The hours passed, how many
she did not know, and the chill of midnight
seeped into her bones. Finally, the big white dog
snarled softly in his corner. Chorampik smelled
the stench of warm blood, as she always did
when Tokwar was near. She was not certain
what form he would take tonight nor what evil
he intended. No one, save the murdered men
who tell no tales, knew half the evil he had done.

Tokwar was at the window. She glimpsed his
shadow in a quiver of moonlight, but the sacred
figures she had drawn prevented him from entering. Louder she prayed, waving the eagle
feathers with one hand while she clutched the
crystal in the other. When she stopped to gather
her breath, she could hear Tokwar dashing
round and round the cabin with the night wind,
prying, probing, testing, squeezing, fingering,
searching for a way inside. She bent low over
Jack to smooth the sacred antelope skin over
his chest, to whisper again and again the words
that went with the medicine man's drawings,
and to listen to the tortured rasp of his breath.

Tokwar was inside the cabin now. Somehow,
with his evil ingenuity, he must have found a
chink between the logs of the cabin walls and
sifted through it. The blood running from the
open wound in his belly was a pool on the
earthen floor that dissolved the sacred designs
in its own blackness. That was how he undid
her defenses. Helpless and sick with horror, she

felt him sidle forward to reach out and steal Jack's spirit.

"No, get you away from my husband, Tokwar. You have no right," she cried, leaning over Jack and beating the evil one back with flailing hands. "You're the one that tried to kill Jack, and though you were killed instead, your blood has been paid for to the last drop. None of the tribes would come to your burial because of the evil you did, but we gave you a white man's funeral, the best that money could buy. And I mourned you according to the ways of our people. Did I not leave my husband and go alone into the mountains to pray for you all through the growing and waning of the moon? Is it my fault your spirit found no rest and walks the mountains by night?"

Against her knees she felt Jack make a convulsive twist and knew that Tokwar's dark bloody hand had reached inside him, trying to wrench his spirit from his frozen body. "No, you shall not have him!" she screamed and felt the weight of Tokwar pushing against her hands like a heavy wind as she thrust him away from Jack. "You have no right, I say. Did I not keep my vow? When I mourned you on the mountain, did you not come to me in a vision and tell me what I must do to atone for your blood? And did I not do it, as the gods themselves know? It is enough. You shall not have my husband's spirit too."

She called on the gods one by one, Tovwots, the father of all gods, Shinauav, the younger god, Patsuts, the bat god who lives in the craggy mountains of Naguntuweap, and all the rest, to bear witness to her sacrifice. She called on the spirits of all those Tokwar had murdered to lay their hands on him and drag him away. She repeated every prayer she could remember, over and over. And at last, she felt the weight against her outstretched hands grow lighter. A hoot and a rush of wings outside the cabin told her that Tokwar had assumed the shape of an owl and flown away.

When the sky had paled with the dawn of the second day since Jack became a frozen one, she saw that the sacred designs circled him once more, restored by the light of the sun. Jack's eyes were watching her. Though a mistiness had started to film the deep blue, there was recognition in those eyes, and no more anger. She bent to kiss Jack's forehead. How good it would be to touch neither food nor water and to lie down, nestled against him with his hand clasped in hers, until their spirits flew away like two hawks wheeling high into the clouds. But it could not be. He needed her strength to defend him against Tokwar. She sighed and rose wearily to her feet to carry on with the tedious chore of living.

The day passed, and another night, but on the third day, Jack still drew breath, though his eyes no longer seemed to know her. Chorampik wondered numbly if Tokwar had somehow pushed them through a hole between the suns where Jack must stay suspended in his frozenness, neither alive nor dead, and she must watch and wait without surcease. Two nights of doing battle with Tokwar for Jack's spirit had drained away her strength. When all her work was done and she had resumed her place beside Jack, she must have fallen into a deep and dreamless sleep. She was awakened by Morison standing in the doorway.

"My God, Jack!" he said, his gray eyes gazing around the cabin silent in the heat and gathering shadows of late afternoon. "I should've known something was wrong when you didn't come riding over the mountain like usual." Then he was beside Jack with busy attentions, feeling his forehead, chafing the unmoving hands, pressing his ear to Jack's chest. "When did this happen?" he asked Chorampik.

"Three sunups."

"Day before yesterday morning!" Morison's spurs clanged bell-like as he rocked slowly back on his heels, and he stared at her with incredulous eyes. "You mean Jack Longstreet had a stroke and you left him lay here for three days without calling the doctor or nobody? He's thirsty. Look at those cracked lips and that baked tongue. You never gave him water, did you?"

Chorampik stared at him mutely.

Morison rose to his feet, kicked the sacred crystal aside, and shoved her roughly back against the wall. "Three days!" he cried. "Three of the hottest days ever, and you left him lay without water while you drew them heathenish scrawls in the dirt. He ought to have sent you back to your tepees and your lizard soup years ago, long about the time he killed that renegade brother of yours. Filthy squaw!"

Chorampik's black eyes slid down to Jack, as though he would somehow rise from his frozenness, seize Morison with his big hands, and cast him out of the cabin. White people might have called Jack "squawman" behind his back and whispered about the thing under his long hair, but never before in Jack's presence would anyone have dared to say such words as "filthy squaw" to her. Morison caught her thought and seemed ashamed. Once more he grew busy, hurrying out to the creek, trickling water slowly down Jack's throat, bathing his face, and cranking up Jack's horseless wagon called "auto." Chorampik was surprised that the contraption started, because Jack so seldom used it, having much preferred the sorrel horse or the wagon and team. After they had carried Jack out to the auto and tied him securely in the back seat, Morison faced her stiffly,

"I'm takin' him into the hospital in Tonopah," he said. "I don't know whether the doctor can save him, far gone as he is, and if he lives, it's no thanks to you. I ain't bringin' you. After what you done, I cain't rightly stand the sight of you."

Chorampik stared silently back at him, the eyes above her jutting cheekbones dull as flint, her full lips compressed in a stubborn line, but inside her head the thoughts buzzed angrily as wasps. White men were such fools sometimes. Even ancient ones unable to rise from their beds, even maimed ones who could hardly totter down the road on sticks still clung to life like silly children who wouldn't let go a toy. Didn't they know that when a man's time has come to die, he accepts it without these senseless struggles? To do otherwise was to fight the gods themselves. Had not Shinauav, the younger god, wisely decided to replace the dead world of stone where nothing ever changed with a green living world where all things are born, grow old, and die? So too with man. So too with her Jack, though even she, who acknowledged the wisdom of Shinauav, could not hold back her tears.

In the distance she could hear the auto struggling down the rough canyon road. She walked heavily back toward the cabin. Tokwar would not be back tonight, now that Morison had taken Jack away, but she had much praying to do. The white doctor must not be allowed to delay Jack's passage into the spirit world.

In mid-afternoon of the fourth day, Chorampik heard a horseless wagon jolting noisily up the canyon road. Her heart knew that Jack still lived. Could they be bringing him home after all? Her thoughts struggled with each other like two wrestlers of matched strength; sometimes her prayer for his death was on top, but there were moments when the insane hope that he might live broke free and pinned her prayer to the ground.

The driver and sole occupant of the auto turned out to be Lee Henderson. She remembered him as a youngster, watching wide-eyed from the corral fence while Jack and his cowboys broke horses. Finally Jack, who was always kind to young ones, handed Lee a halter and taught him how to stay in the saddle of a rearing, plunging mustang. You could say that Lee had his breaking, along with the horses. Then, for a few years, all that Lee wanted in the world was to gallop over the range with Jack and his wild riders. Lee was older now, a bit stockier, and he kept a big grease-smelling barn for broken autos in Tonopah, but he still revered Jack much as he did when he was a youngster hanging on the corral fence.

"Your husband hasn't much time left," he told her when he got out of the auto. "I think you'd better come, Fannie."

She nodded. Fannie was her white name. Like all her people, she never told her Indian name to white men or spoke her thoughts.

After the auto had lurched down the rough canyon road like a bucking horse and turned south toward Tonopah, she knew that Jack had died. Just as they were passing Point of Rock

Springs, a haze spread over the sun, the color drained away from the day, the warm rose of the far mountains turned to gray, and the green-gold of the blooming rabbit brush dulled as though the winds had coated the Stone Cabin Valley with dust. Near the mesa she saw a string of mustangs, chestnut, pinto, and black, trotting in single file toward the western mountains. Never, while Jack lived, would they have dared to come here. They had learned that Jack would round them up, bridle them, break them in his round corral, and add them to his herds of horses. For all the years that she had been Jack's woman, the mustangs had ranged far away from Longstreet Canyon. Now, already, they were returning.

Having seen these signs, Chorampik was not surprised when they arrived at the hospital and the doctor in his white coat told her that Jack was dead. They led her through this place of strange whiteness to the bed where Jack lay beneath the sheet, but she could not commune with a spirit now departed on his journey, and in this alien place among these white people she could not speak to the gods. So she stood silently, waiting to see what they expected Jack's widow to do. When Morison glared at her from the other side of Jack's bed and strode angrily from the room, Lee put a comforting arm around her shoulders.

"It's all right, Fannie," he said. "Jack knew you were a good wife to him according to your ways."

Later Lee told her other things. He said that he was the executor of Jack's estate. Chorampik didn't understand, and he explained that this meant Jack had left money for her and Lee was to give her some of it every month, so that she would always have plenty to eat.

"Is the money enough to buy many horses?" she asked Lee.

"Most of the horses in Nye County, I guess," said Lee, with a puzzled look. "Jack saved up enough money in his old suitcase to leave you well provided for. What do you want with many horses, Fannie?"

"He who has just gone to the spirit world," she said carefully, for it was disrespectful to speak the name of one recently dead, "was a great *tavanav*, and he must have a funeral worthy of a *tavanav*. I wish to buy many horses for the funeral races."

Lee frowned, "You mean race the horses till they drop and shoot them on Jack's grave? That's a savage old custom, Fannie. Those things aren't done anymore, not in the year of our Lord nineteen twenty-eight. Old Jack may have been an outlaw with a cropped ear, but he was a white man and the last of the old breed, and a lot of folks around here respected him."

Chorampik stared at him with unbelieving eyes. Even Lee! He too was speaking words that would never have been said while Jack lived— "savage old custom." And he dared to talk of the shame thing under Jack's hair that even when she lay in Jack's arms she had always pretended she did not know. How differently people behaved when Jack was no longer there to keep them in their proper places.

"You say this money is mine," said Chorampik. "I wish to buy many horses. My husband's spirit will be very angry if he does not have a funeral worthy of a *tavanav*. He may have been born white, but he chose to be one of my people." Fear clawed at her heart when she remembered the anger in Jack's eyes when she refused him water. Only if many horses died on his grave could she be certain that his spirit was appeased. But Lee would not be moved.

So she went where they told her to go. She stood dumbly in the field of white men's graves beside the rocky crags on the western side of the mountains. She watched them shovel earth over the wooden box and place the carved stone slab over it. Impassively she waited while they filed past her saying soft words to which she did not listen. When they were finished, she walked away and began to climb through the pinyon and juniper toward the high places where the good spirit, the snow-white *kunishuv*, lived and she could pray. Lee hurried after her.

"Where are you going, Fannie?" he said. "I'll take you home. That's what Jack would have wanted."

Chorampik stared back at him contemptuously. How wrong she had been to have credited him with understanding. Didn't he know that Jack's spirit might return to the cabin in anger? Of course the cabin must be burned. Once more she plodded forward.

"Fannie, come back," Lee insisted. "You don't have any food or blankets. You can't just walk away into the mountains. How will you live?"

Did he suppose she would starve like the foolish whites? She who had known how to survive in the mountains since she was a *nuint* no taller than the sagebrush? Chorampik climbed the steepening slope without another backward glance, and eventually Lee stopped following.

When she reached the heights many hours later, Chorampik chose a spot that felt like the crest of the world. The mountains fell away to both the east and the west, tumbling downward, fold on fold, blue range on shadowed range, into the wide valleys. She thought the earth must have looked like this to Nagah, the mountain sheep, when he climbed the high peak of no return, and she felt the dizziness and despair that seized the lonely Nagah before the god who was his father reached down to turn him into the North Star. Here she knelt, facing toward the sun, and tried to explain to Jack about the horses. But she felt no answering in the pine-scented silence and knew he had not heard. She told herself that this was as it should be, because his spirit had gone to Naguntuweap where she could no longer speak with him. Still, she would have given much to know that Jack was not displeased with her over the paltry white man's box and the absence of horses.

Instead of reaching toward his silence, she tried to picture Jack in the green meadows of Naguntuweap. One day she would join him there. She thought of how he would lift her up and carry her into his wickiup. Once again she would wrap her arms joyously around him, as she had done in their sweet early time together before the death of Tokwar. Jack would understand that she had done only what she had to do to save him from Tokwar's evil ghost, and all the years when she had turned away from him in cold silence would burn away like morning mists in the golden rays of the sun.

Sun, yet more than sun. She could feel the glow already of something hotter than sun, something that hissed and darted and danced. It was fire. All around her the flames licked and crackled, orange, gold, red, and blue, higher and higher in brilliant quivering curtains. The acrid taste of smoke stung her throat. It was by fire she would go to him. When the flames had consumed her body, her spirit would fly free like a small orange spark whirled away on the wind. Sometimes, moved by the grief of those who called their names, the gods sent these visions of a time to come. Fire would carry her to Jack, so bright a fire that in the night-time darkness it would illuminate a mountain from afar. She saw the lake of flame spurting in front of her eyes, felt its heat burning away her flesh. And this fire would come soon, in two, maybe three, winters' time.

"Uwa, kumaruweav," she whispered. Yes, husband. I follow.

HISTORICAL NOVELS
OF THE AMERICAN FRONTIERS